Let everybody know what you thought of this book!

It was great!	It was okay.	It was awful.

D1226821

Go to http://waynebookdiscussion.blogspot.com/ to tell us more about this book, or any others you may be reading!

OCT 27 2011

THE DRAGON WITH
THE GIRL TATTOO

The Dragon with the Girl Tattoo

ADAM ROBERTS

GOLLANCZ

LONDON

Copyright © Adam Roberts 2010
All rights reserved

The right of Adam Roberts to be identified as the author of this
work has been asserted by him in accordance with the
Copyright, Designs and Patents Act 1988.

First published in Great Britain in 2010 by
Gollancz
An imprint of the Orion Publishing Group
Orion House, 5 Upper St Martin's Lane,
London WC2H 9EA
An Hachette UK Company

A CIP catalogue record for this book
is available from the British Library

ISBN 978 0 575 10091 6

3 5 7 9 10 8 6 4 2

Typeset at The Spartan Press Ltd,
Lymington, Hants

Printed in Great Britain by
CPI Mackays, Chatham ME5 8TD

The Orion Publishing Group's policy is to use papers that
are natural, renewable and recyclable products and made
from wood grown in sustainable forests. The logging and
manufacturing processes are expected to conform to the
environmental regulations of the country of origin.

www.adamroberts.com
www.orionbooks.co.uk

'Never laugh at live dragons . . .' *This later became a proverb.*

Antique Ape Saga

PROLOGUE

It happened every year and had done so without fail for three centuries. The parcel arrived, as it always did, and the elderly dragon regarded it with a more than usually grim expression. Believe me, you've never seen a face with a grim expression until you've seen a dragon face with a grim expression.

The parcel lay on his desk. He already knew what it contained, and knew the debilitating heart-sinking he would feel when he unwrapped it; but it couldn't be avoided. First things first. He called a firedrake into his study. 'Where are we over?'

'Limbchopping,' the servant replied.

'Of course. Be so good as to leave the island. Fly down to the city, and ask Detective Superintendent Smaug to pay me a visit.'

The firedrake glanced at the desk, and saw the package. He knew what it contained, just as well as his master, and understood the gravity of his commission. He curled around in mid-air, wings beating a humming-bird rhythm, and flew straight through the main window.

'You'll find him in the main Police Castle,' the old dragon called after him, although the firedrake didn't need telling. It would not be the first time he had summoned the Detective Superintendent to attend the opening of one of these parcels. In mid-air the drake ducked and was gone.

Leaving the parcel on the desk, Helltrik Vagner went to the window to wait with the sort of patience that comes easy to a being half a millennium old. It was a pleasant afternoon in late summer. Light was slanting in from the empty west, as the sun – that great sphere of whitegold fire – bestowed its superb treasure upon the world with its habitual carelessness. To look down was to observe a great many white bobbly clouds, like Moomins, overlaying the distant landscape. But to look up and west was to see a great stretch of high cirrus, tinted pale tangerine, stretched like a wing of fire around the horizon.

Shortly, Helltrik watched in silence. He was, as you might expect with a dragon his age, large and gnarly, his once golden scales now going cream-coloured at the edges. Immediately below his window lay the western gardens of the Vagner floating island, Doorbraak. To say that the garden was well-manicured was both true and false. It was true in the sense that every hedge and flowerbed was perfectly trimmed and maintained; but false in the sense that 'manicure' is something one does to a hand. This garden was not a hand. It had no fingernails. It was, as I think I have mentioned, a garden. Broad lawns of blond, bristly grass were mowed to a perfect flatness. Ash, willow, elm were planted in rows, and small-leaved limes grew at the edge, overlooking the small wall and the mile-long drop. The trees cast fishnet shadow in the summer light. Smoke from a dozing dragon – another member of the large Vagner clan – spilled over the hedge like poured pollen. And as Helltrik watched this peaceful world, the unwrapped parcel sat on his desk, mutely accusing.

Soon enough there came the sound of something large in flight, and up over the edge of the island a very large-bellied, impressive-looking dragon appeared. Helltrik's firedrake was flying by his side, although he hardly needed guiding. He flew straight over the garden, broad wings forcefully massaging the air, and alighted a little heavily on the stone of Helltrik's personal balcony.

'Sammy,' said Helltrik. 'Thanks for coming.'

Detective Superintendent Smaug came through the balcony door and settled his prodigious rump into an easy chair. He was no longer young, and the exertion of the flight had roughened the edge of his breathing a little. 'Another one?' he wheezed.

'I'm afraid so.'

'Same time of year, same thing,' said Smaug, peering at the parcel. 'Well – are you going to open it?'

'I suppose I must,' said Helltrik, heavily. 'I dread doing so, even though I know what is inside – of course, *because* I know what is inside.'

'Come on, Trikky,' said the Detective Superintendent. 'Let's get it over with.'

Vagner took the parcel and, in a few easy gestures, tore its wrapping away. Inside was a narrow strip of leather, a spotted dark purple in colour, more than a metre long and shaped into a chevron at one end.

The two elderly dragons looked eagerly at it, as if

3

hoping to *read* its pattern of pale purple mottles. But if such was their intention, they were frustrated. They both sat back, Vagner holding the limp strip in his right foreclaw.

'There's nothing very distinctive about it, this year,' said Detective Superintendent Smaug. 'It's clearly from a mature beast, though.'

'I'm never quite sure what we're looking for,' Vagner admitted, in a weary voice. 'I mean, when we *peruse* them like this.'

'Well – distinguishing marks, I suppose,' said the policedragon. They sat in silence for a while. 'I almost feel,' the Detective Superintendent added, 'as if we should open a bottle of firewater. Drink to it.'

'*Drink* to it?'

'Oh it's poor taste, I daresay. But – well, it's the *three hundredth*, after all! That's quite a remarkable statistic: every single year without fail for three entire centuries. You don't think we should mark the significance of that fact?'

'I've never understood the hobgoblin hold *whole numbers* have over the minds of otherwise sane dragons,' said Vagner. 'My father wanted to host the largest party Scandragonia had ever seen when I reached a hundred. But why? It's no different to reaching the age of ninety-nine, or a hundred and one.'

'Come, come, Trikky,' said Smaug, indulgently. 'You don't mean that. Three hundred *is* significant.'

'Its significance,' said Vagner, a little stiffly, 'lies only in telling me one thing. That this has been going on for far too long. I have become complacent. It's time to act.

4

Time to call in outside help, to get to the bottom of this once and for all.'

Detective Superintendent Smaug shook his equine head briskly. 'There's really nothing more the police can do, my friend. We've investigated as thoroughly as any police force can. We've in-*and*-outvestigated it. We've been all over it. It's been all over us.'

'I meant, somebody exterior to the police, Sammy.'

'Oh!' said Smaug. 'A *private* investigator? Well, good luck with that.'

Helltrik sensed his friend's grumpiness. 'I'm not saying we can't share a dram, old boy. What'll it be? Firewater? Or shall we burn some sack?

'The former, for preference. And I suppose you'd better hand that . . . that thing over to me. I'll take it into official police custody, and lay it in the vault with the other two hundred and ninety-nine tongues.'

Vagner passed the item across. 'Three hundred dragon tongues,' he mused, as he busied himself at the drink's cabinet. 'All laid out together in a police vault. If only they could talk, eh? Three hundred tongues, and none of them capable of saying a single word.'

'Being ripped from the mouth does tend to diminish the loquacious potential of the tongue,' said the Detective Superintendent. He took his drink from Vagner's outstretched claw.

'But who is *sending* them, eh, Sammy?' Vagner asked, sitting himself down. 'Always the same thing, every year without fail. Such a grisly, horrible thing! *Why* are they sending them? To me?'

'Where are they getting them *from*, is the question

uppermost on my police mind,' said Smaug. 'Ripping them out of some poor anonymous dragon's –*bottoms*' he lifted his glass '*up* – mouth. Think of the draconic suffering! Three hundred tongues!' He drained the fire-water, and blew a sharp little red-orange flame.

'I'm still stuck on why,' said Vagner. 'Ever since . . .'

'Now, Trikky, I know what you're going to say. It's never been *conclusively* proved that these tongues have anything to do with . . . your poor grandniece's lament-able and mysterious fate.'

'Not conclusively proved?' Vagner repeated. He drained his own glass, and belched a shining violet-coloured flame. 'Come come, Sammy. Who can doubt it? Whoever it was murdered my grandniece – and is the same dragon who's sending me these horrible . . . tokens. They're mocking me. Mocking me with their continuing impunity. And, as you say, continuing with their horrible crimes! Mutilating and killing a dragon every year!'

'We've no evidence of the killing part.'

'You think there are three hundred *live* dragons flying about with no tongues in their heads? You don't think that would be noticed? No, no, he tortures them, kills them, and disposes of their bodies – sinks them in the seas, or something like that. All the loved ones know is that a dragon has vanished. He must be caught, Sammy. We must catch him.'

'Well,' said Detective Superintendent Smaug, getting up on his hindlegs and tucking the severed dragon tongue away in a pouch slung from a golden belt. 'Of course the police would like nothing better than to apprehend him. And, as with the others, I'll make enquiries. But, as with all the others, I'd be amazed if anything comes of it. And as for your grandniece . . . I'm afraid that case was closed long ago.'

'We'll see,' said Vagner. 'I have somebody in mind. Apparently he's a genius at the new arts of *finding stuff out.*'

'Here's hoping,' said the Detective Superintendent, stepping from the balcony and into the air. 'Here's hoping!'

1

Käal Morekill Brimstön was widely known as a genius at 'finding stuff out'. In fact, he was rubbish at finding stuff out. But reputation trumps reality in the card game of life. Provided the card game is one that uses trumps. Like bridge. Or canasta. The two of clubs of Käal's fame laid on top of the King of Diamonds of his true incompetence. If we have previously agreed that clubs are trumps. If you see what I mean.

Käal worked for a small but influential Saga, whose central Starkhelm office was kitted out with only the very trendiest Drakea furniture. Come to think of it, I'm not sure canasta uses a trump system. It doesn't matter. Anyway, the Saga – *Köschfagold Saga* – specialized in financial news, on the understanding that the proportion of dragonkind interested in money (which is: *all of it*, give or take) would ensure it a steady readership. It hadn't worked out that way. But although it was not widely read, the Saga was widely respected. There were Sagas that sold more copies, of course: the celebrity news-based *Sptöüägbble Saga*, for instance, the literary review *Flblloljalblblkklbl Saga,* or the cookery-themed *Pütunth-lobstrëënthpotborkborkbork Saga*. But few had the extra-ordinary reputation for finding things out of *Köschfagold*.

And even fewer had the top-range swivel chairs. And Käal was the star reporter. There were other dragons on staff: the editor, Beargrr, a forceful female with lapis-lazuli coloured spines running down her ample back; and Fyrstarter the deputy editor. But neither of them quite looked the part the way Käal did.

His scales overlapped as neatly as roof-tiles, and were of a similar brick red and orange-rind colour. He was not young, exactly – his size alone told you that – yet he still had the glamour of youth. His wings, when he stretched them to full length, were entirely free of gaps, holes or tatters. His eyes were so pale they looked almost a white; but a gleaming, handsome sort of white. All these things counted for a good deal in Scandragonia.

For years he had coasted on these splendid looks, and on the work done by minimum-wage researchers. But then, *Köschfagold Saga* had run a story on a senior dragon businessman called Wintermute. Wintermute had sued.

When the raven first arrived at the Saga with the news that they were going to have to defend the story in court, Beargrr had an editorial conversation with Käal. 'I'll need to see your notes, records, and all your sources.'

'Right,' said Käal. 'What?'

'All your notes,' she said. 'So we can ready the court-room defence.'

Käal shrugged his wings. It took Beargrr several repetitions of her request for her to comprehend that he knew nothing at all about the story that he himself had written.

'But you researched it!' she kept saying. 'You must

have sources – you must have notes, files, unpublished material.'

'I can barely remember it,' he said. 'Was that the one with the red-and-yellow border on the front page?'

'But *how* can you not know?' she berated him. 'You *wrote* the story!'

'I wrote it,' said Käal, ingenuously. 'But that doesn't mean I researched it. It's the same as all my stuff. I sent a raven down to the researchers, and they sent all the facts up. I just arranged them in Saga form, putting in all the necessary alliteration and so on.'

'That,' said Beargrr, 'is not what a journalist *does!*'

At this Käal had looked slightly confused. 'Are you sure?' he said. 'Because I was working on the assumption that it, well, *was*.'

'Are you kidding me?'

'No.' He thought about it. 'Kid as in goat, do you mean? Are you hungry?'

'Kid,' said Beargrr, in a dull voice, 'as in: setting up my Saga for financial ruin in an unwinnable court case.'

Now, the situation between these two dragons was complicated. Beargrr was hamfast with another dragon, a well-respected Swedragenish medical man. But despite that, she had started a relationship with Käal. She had done so because she had found him attractive, but a large part of that attraction had to do with his reputation as a Super Journalist. This, it now seemed, was an unfounded reputation.

'Look,' he said. 'Putting raw data into Saga form is not easy. And we've always employed researchers – haven't we? I mean, isn't that the point of employing researchers? That they do the research and I write it up?'

'No,' said Beargrr, looking at her lover with cold eyes. 'The point of researchers is that they relieve the journalists of tedious or repetitive tasks. But the journalists are still supposed to go out and actually find stuff out.'

'Oh,' said Käal, looking interested. 'I did not know that.'

'What do you mean you didn't know that!' Beargrr yelled. 'You're my *star reporter*! How can you be a star reporter and not know what a star reporter even *does*?'

'Well,' said Käal, mildly. 'It's never seemed to be a problem before. You liked the Quetzoacoatlofmanycolours story I filed? That won an award!' Quetzoacoatlofmanycolours had been a soap merchant. *Köschfagold Saga* had run a story exposing that his company stock had been involved in a Bubble.

'I assumed you'd gone out and interviewed Quetzoacoatlofmanycolours yourself. I assumed you'd asked about, looking in dustbins, checked the archives of local Sagas, and slowly pieced together the story of the cover-up. *Please tell me* that you interviewed Quetzoacoatlofmanycolours yourself, asked about, looked in dustbins, checked the archives of local Sagas, and slowly pieced together the story of the cover-up?'

'Nope, I didn't do any of that.'

'What *did* you do?'

'Well, I sent a raven down to the researcher's office, like I always do. There's a young researcher who's usually pretty good: still a Salamander, I think. I asked her: what's up with this Quetzoacoatlofmanycolours geezer? You'd told me to look into him, you see. After a few days she sent all the data back – by raven – and I wrote it up.'

'But you were away for a week!'

'I was in the sauna, mostly.'

'I thought you were doing star reporter investigative stuff!'

'No. Just sauna stuff.'

'I can't *believe* this!' Beargrr howled, blowing a bright spire of orange flame straight from the back of her throat. Fire licked and blazed across the office filing cabinet.

'You're angry!' said Käal, laughing. Then, the gravity of the situation striking him for the first time, he said it again, without the laugh. 'You're angry.' Then, very sombrely: 'You're going to sack me, aren't you.'

'How can I *sack* you?' Beargrr roared, leaping into the air and hurtling round the room, near the ceiling. 'You're my star reporter! What would that say about the credibility of the Saga? We're just about to go to court! I can't afford to admit that our star report was a grade 1 gumbo.'

'Plus,' said Käal, with a hopeful inflection, turning his head to try and follow her, and wringing his own neck like a wet rag, 'not forgetting that we're lovers – ack!' He uncoiled his neck.

'Don't remind me,' snapped Beargrr, coming down to the floor again. 'What about the Firegate story? The political corruption one?'

'Well, you asked me to investigate it. So I sent a raven down to the researcher's office, and when the raven came back with all the facts I wrote it out in Saga form, making sure that the alliteration . . .'

'Aaarh!' said Beargrr, with some force.

Everything was quiet in the office for a bit.

'I blame myself,' said Beargrr, in a calmer voice. 'I should have realized that you are not star-reporter material. In retrospect, I've been foolish. I thought your twittish, louche, bumbling manner was a clever persona that you could use to coax information out of people. Looking back I can see that you just are a twittish, louche, bumbling dragon.'

'Maybe a little louche,' Käal conceded.

'But you reflected glory upon *Köschfagold Saga*. Dragons all over Scandragonia think that you – and therefore *we* – have a genius for "finding stuff out". And it turns out, in the end, that we are nothing of the sort . . . that there's some researcher in the bowels of the building who is the real genius.'

'Maybe we should give her a staff job?'

'Right now,' snapped Beargrr, 'we have to handle this Wintermute *disaster*. This could bankrupt the whole Saga, you know! We can't go into the court case admitting, in effect, that we are incompetent. No, we're going to present a confident, unified front, whilst I try and figure out how to handle this.'

'I could go back to the sauna,' Käal offered. When Beargrr gave him a hard stare, he added: 'You could come too, of course. If you wanted to.'

'You don't seem to understand,' she said. 'The entire future of *Köschfagold Saga* hangs in the balance. Wintermute is an extremely powerful and influential dragon. If

I send you into court to substantiate your own article, his lawyers will rip you to pieces. In fact,' she said, her face registering that she had had a good idea, 'I think you had better make yourself scarce.'

'I *am* quite scared, actually,' Käal agreed, nodding. 'You're so cross! Plus, all this talk of courtrooms is quite putting the willies up me.'

'Scarce, not scared,' said Beargrr. She flew-leapt to her desk, and rummaged through the pile of scrolls littering its surface. 'There was something . . .'

'Scarce!' said Käal. 'Yes, I *knew* you meant that. Obviously I'm not *scared*. That would be pitiable! I'm a dragon, aren't I?'

'A request for your services . . .' Beargrr said.

'And making myself scarce is a good idea,' said Käal. 'I could go to a really big sauna and just spend a couple of weeks . . .'

'Here!' Beargrr held up a gold-trimmed scroll. 'You've heard of the mystery of the Vagner clan?'

'Vagner – ah yes, Vagner,' said Käal, nodding sagely and scratching his underchin with one talon. 'No, never heard of them.'

'I asked if you'd heard of the mystery of the Vagner clan, and you reply that you've not even heard of the Vagner clan?'

'No!'

'Joking aside, Käal,' said Beargrr. 'You have heard of them.'

'Nope.'

'How can you *not* have heard of them?' she bellowed.

'They're one of the wealthiest nests in the whole of Scandragonia!'

'Are they really?'

'They keep putting out fantastically advanced consumer durables. Everything they market turns to gold. Nobody knows where they get all their new ideas.'

'Interesting.'

'They're behind the flashfire drive – the supersonic Skylligator – the computer.'

'No. Not ringing any bells.'

Beargrr sighed. 'The head of the clan, Helltrik Vagner, is five hundred years old. He's personal friends with several Dragonlords.'

'That's nice.'

'You *must* have heard of Doorbraak?'

'Door—? No.'

'The floating island?'

'Nope.'

'You're my *star reporter*! How can you *not know* of the famous Vagner floating island? It floats through the sky, north across Swedragenia, south over Fangland, and round over the mainland.'

'Golly,' said Käal.

Beargrr contemplated her (mentally she inserted 'former') lover and star reporter with disdain. Then she put her head on one side and looked at him with datdain. Eventually she said: 'I don't care. I need you out of the way, such that I can plausibly tell the court you're unavailable. Vagner has asked for your help – specifically for you. He believes that you have a genius for finding stuff out. Apparently some terrible thing happened in the family three centuries ago, and nobody has ever got to the bottom of it.'

'And you'd like me to solve the mystery?'

'Old *Vagner* wants you to do that. All I care about it that you'll be out of sight for a couple of months, whilst I try and clear up this Wintermute mess. So, you will accept Vagner's generous invitation, and go to Door-braak.'

'Um,' said Käal.

'No ums,' said Beargrr, forcefully.

'Right. Do I go straight off . . . ?'

'Go buy a Skylligator ticket for Limbchopping. That's where the floating island is, now. I'll send a raven telling Vagner that you've accepted his invitation.'

'I haven't had breakfast, yet . . .' Käal said.

'Oh for crying out loud. Go grab a sheep, and *then* take the Skylligator to the Vagner estate.'

'Right!' said Käal, brightly.

Before he quit the office, he sent a raven down to the Saga's researchers. '*Lizbreath? I'm off to Doorbraak, which apparently is a floating island. I'm supposed to solve a mystery concerning the Vagners. Anything you can give me?*'

Then he went outside and grabbed a sheep from a roadside booth. *Then* he flew off to the Skylligator terminal.

The raven croaked and flew off, carrying its charge. It circled down the gleaming flame-shaped tower, passed the busy thoroughfare and its thronging crowds of dragons, workwyrms and firedrakes. The bird ducked through a vent, and flew down into a poorly lit room beneath the main office.

A slender young dragon called Lizbreath Salamander listened to the raven's message. 'The Vagner clan, eh?' she mused. 'Doorbraak, no less. This could be interesting.'

Salamander was taupe, which is a colour, actually; a dark gleaming shade with a fine sheen in the light. She was not large, her shoulders no wider than her pelvis, and her wings were a little undersized. But there was something strangely attractive about her. And up by the shoulder of her right wing she carried the picture of a young female human being. Very few dragons had seen anything like it.

She knew about the Vagners, of course; and about their fabulously expensive floating island Doorbraak – borne aloft in the sky by some strange magic (for it did not fly with wings) that most of dragonkind wot not of. Indeed, what they wot of was beyond the wit of many dragons to, er, woot.

What?

At any rate, Lizbreath had a personal interest in the Vagners. They were a mysterious, reclusive, fabulously wealthy family; and she knew all about the rumours of a dark secret at the heart of the clan. Lizbreath liked dark secrets, the darker the better.

And she had her own reasons for wanting to get closer to Doorbraak.

There was no question but that this was a project that interested her. But to pursue it properly, she would need more money for essential equipment. And that, unfortunately, meant begging her new Guardian for some cash.

It was not a pleasant prospect. But it had to be done.

2

The Skylligator set down at Limbchopping, and Käal disembarked, tripping over a tooth as he did so. It was exciting. The Vagners' floating island – Doorbraak – was unmistakably there in the sky, a vast hanging planet half a mile over the city, a rough egg shape. Rough, there, being understood to modify *shape* rather than *egg*. Clouds drifted beneath it. What I meant, with the 'rough egg shape' line, was that Doorbraak, being an elongated oblate sphere, approximated the *shape*, though not the *texture*, of an egg. I wasn't trying to imply that it was *exactly* shaped like a *rough egg*.

Just so as we're clear.

Käal was standing with his long neck curled back on itself, like a C, so as to be able to gawp at the enormousness of the suspended object above him, when a scrawny and indeed scraw-entireleg firedrake coughed at his right wing. 'Käal Brimstön?'

'Yes.'

'Mon. Vagner sent me to meet you. Come with me, please.'

'How does it – how does it stay up there?' Käal asked, wonderingly.

'Magic,' replied the firedrake, in a *what-else?* tone

of voice. Then he added: 'Please come along,' in an *I-haven't-got-all-day* tone of voice.

Without more ado this firedrake clambered up into the sky on slowly flexing wings, with Käal following. From below, Doorbraak was a convex mass of crusted mud and rock, from which occasional roots poked, white as exposed nerves. But pulling himself, with hauling wingstrokes, up through the clouds, brought the island's upper portions into view: a rim of superbly maintained gardens and parks arranged around a large central castle, whose many tapering towers and spires reached above like the antennae of a prawn. Or, now that I come to think of it, perhaps like something a little more romantic and evocative.

The firedrake alit on a pink marble balcony about halfway up the towering central structure. Käal followed suit. 'Mon. Vagner will see you straight away,' the firedrake told him. He indicated the direction with a toss of his firedrakey head.

Käal went inside.

'Ah! Brimstön. Come in,' said Old Vagner. 'Sit down, please. Take the weight off.'

Käal found himself in a superbly appointed sitting room. A vaulted granite ceiling and polished marble floor defined a huge space. Exquisite wall-mosaics displayed scenes of dragon heroics, or 'draconoics' as they are sometimes called. An exquisite scent of sulphur wafted from an incense burner.

Two sofas faced one another. Vagner made his way towards one, so Käal went to the other. The couch in question was ancient, and very expensive-looking. That might even have been real apeskin covering it. But it was not very big. Dragons had *been* smaller, of course, in the old days, before prosperity and adequate nutrition added length to the long bones and bulk to the body. But that meant that the honour of being offered an antique sofa as a seat was undermined by the titchiness of the artefact itself. Käal looked at the sofa, and then back at his host. Old Vagner had settled himself on the opposite couch and was now tilted into an upright posture, with his fat hindlimbs akimbo and his forelimbs hunched before him like two letters 'r'.

'Please,' he said again. 'Sit down.'

Käal took a deep breath, and tackled the business of sitting. Lifting his tail, he tried to fit its fat diamond-shaped tip through the slot at the back. The slot was narrow, and his angle of approach was not quite right, so instead of slipping neatly through – thereby permitting the rest of his tail to follow so that Käal could seat his rump upon the upholstery – it got stuck. Käal pushed, but it wouldn't go through. He tried to pull it back, but it wouldn't come out either. He tugged the tail, and the couch shifted a yard across the marble with a friction squeal like a monkey in pain. Käal looked round at Old Vagner, who was watching him with placid patience.

Käal smiled. Old Vagner smiled back.

Making the decision, Käal turned his whole body to face his host, and curled up his tail as best he could, coiling it over the cushionry of the sofa, before seating himself upon it. This was not a very comfortable arrangement, and the added bulk of his own tailflesh lifted him comically and pushed him rather precariously forward on the seat. But at least he was sitting. He cleared his throat.

'Thank you for coming to see me,' said Old Vagner. 'I have long been an admirer of your Saga work.'

'You have?'

'Certainly I have. You have a talent for – *discovering* things. It's not common, among dragons, of course. Most of us disdain the implicit *novelty* in discovery. But you're different.'

'More different than you imagine,' Käal said proudly.

'I want to put that talent to good use here on Door-braak. You see, there's something I want you to *find out*.'

Käal cleared his throat again. 'What do you want me to find out?'

'There is a tragedy at the heart of this family,' said Old Vagner.

Attempting, covertly, to adjust his awkwardly coiled tail beneath him, Käal stretched his rump muscles min-utely, hoping with a delicately handled squeeze to *pop* his tail through the slot. He felt the end of his tail shift an inch deeper into the slot. In his mind a beguiling image presented itself, perfectly and fully formed: he pictured the tail-end plopping through, and the rest of the clumped-up tail following smoothly and easily after. He could almost *feel* the relief of settling his bum properly on the sofa cushions. He gave another discreet rumpward heave. One more would do it.

'My grandniece,' said Old Vagner, his voice breaking with emotion. 'My beautiful, innocent, young grand-niece was . . . horribly murdered.'

Käal pushed. The couch lurched under Käal's bulk, with a high-pitched whistle-scraping sound. Käal tumbled backwards. The sofa karoomed off the granite wall and, still tethered to the younger dragon by his tail, twanged straight back at Käal's head. There was a muffled wham, and Käal's head was punched forward by the impact of the hurtling furniture. When he lifted his face again, he was sat on his broad buttocks on the cold marble. He was wearing the sofa as a hat.

Old Vagner was looking at him.

'Murdered, you say?' Käal said. Then, because his voice seemed to have been rather squeakily sopranoized by events, he cleared his throat and repeated with more bass-toned gravity of expression: 'Murdered you say?'

'*Horribly* murdered,' said old Vagner.

'Horribly, mm,' said Käal. Very slowly – so as not to puncture the serious mood – he lifted the sofa off his head with his tail. '*Horrible.* Yes.'

'Slain in the fullness of her youth.'

With hardly a wobble, Käal lowered the item of furniture to the floor beside him. Trying, again, to be discreet, he lifted his hefty right hand-leg and placed its foot on the sofa. Pushing out with his thigh and simultaneously pulling with his tail, he tried to extract himself from the sofa slot. There was a sound of rending, and fabric and stuffing flew up. But at least the tail came free. Käal hazarded a smile; then, thinking of the grave situation he was in, he snapped the smile down into a frown. Then, worried that he looked merely grumpy, or perhaps ungrateful, he tried the smile again. That wasn't right. Finally he settled his mouth into a neutral expression.

'It,' Old Vagner said, shortly, regarding Käal with a slightly puzzled expression in his eyes, 'it – happened here.'

Käal was surprised. 'In this room?'

'No, no, I mean on this island. I mean: on Door-braak.'

The magnitude of what Old Vagner was saying began to dawn on Käal. 'Wait – you say she was *murdered*?'

'That's right.'

'As in – killed.'

'Murdered as in killed, yes,' said Old Vagner, drily.

'But that's horrible!'

'I couldn't agree more. It evokes horror, yes.'

'It evokes more than horror,' said Käal, the full force of the situation finally coming home to him. 'It is *horrible*! It is both *horror* and – er,' he said, looked about the echoey chamber rather at a loss for words, 'and *ible*, hence, hence.' His voice trailed away. 'Horrible,' he concluded. The silence gaped. 'Ibble, ibble, wibble,' he added, a minute later, although he wasn't exactly sure why.

Old Vagner was looking intently at him. 'Are you *mocking* me?' he asked, softly.

'Good grief! Not at all!' said Käal, genuinely.

'Only there are those who think,' Vagner went on, 'that I have lost my *mind*. They say the grief at my loss has driven me out of my mind. That, and the torment-ing knowledge that the crime is unsolved, and the

24

murderer unpunished. Do *you* think I have lost my mind?'

'Oh, no, er, ah,' said Käal, startled by this direct question. 'No! And even if you have, I'm sure I don't mind.'

'Don't *mind*?' asked Old Vagner, sharply.

'Don't mind!' said Käal, panicking a little. 'Don't mind *your* mind. That you've lost your mind. Or not. Would *you* mind if I were unmanned in my mind? Or, er, was,' he added, losing the thread again, 'what were you saying?'

'I was saying,' said Vagner, severely, 'that I have *not* lost my mind. Though I have brooded over my poor innocent girl's death – brooded for three hundred years – it has *not* driven me mad. Brooded.'

'Brooded,' repeated Käal.

'Brooded,' said Old Vagner again, his countenance falling as the memories of those three long centuries came back to him. 'Three centuries of brooding!'

'Brooded,' noted Käal.

'Broo—' said Old Vagner. His eyes defocused, lost in thought, or memory. There was a long silence. 'Dead!' he said, abruptly, sitting up straight again.

'What was she called?'

'Hellfire,' said the old dragon.

'A very sweet and charming name,' said Käal, with feeling.

'Oh, she was, she was *very* sweet and charming. She was an innocent young fledgling.'

'And you are certain she was murdered?'

'Certain.'

25

'Then why not approach the authorities?'

'The police have looked into it. But there's not a great deal they can do. You see, I do not have her body.'

'Oh! There's no carcass?'

'No. I have spoken to the Dragonlords, of course. I am friendly with them all –a dragon of my seniority, lineage and wealth could hardly be otherwise. But without a carcass there is nothing than can be done, legally.'

'I suppose they think she might still be alive,' said Käal.

'Perhaps they do,' agreed Old Vagner. 'But I know better.'

'You're convinced it *is* murder?'

'I am.'

'So – let me see if I understand you: you want me to use my talents to find the body. Because, once we have that . . .'

'Käal,' said Old Vagner. 'I want you to do more than that. I want you to discover *that* she was murdered, yes, so that the world can finally acknowledge the fact. But I also want you to discover *how* she was murdered – and *who did it*!'

Käal let out a long whistle, and a plume of steam, from both nostrils. 'You're asking for a great deal.'

'I know I am. But I am prepared to *pay* a great deal.'

Käal's ears twitched. 'Really?'

'I want you to compose a Saga for me. I want you to compose the Vagner Saga. In return I will gift you a magic hoard.'

Käal couldn't believe his ears. 'A magic one?'

'If you succeed in unmasking my grandniece's murderer – you shall have the Siegfried treasure.'

This was something so staggering, so enormous, that Käal could produce no smoke at all for almost a minute. 'The Siegfried treasure?' he rasped, when he got his throat burning again. 'For real?'

'Yes.'

'You're kidding though – yes?' Of all the treasures from the mythic age, the Siegfried treasure was one of the most famous: a magic hoard, including a huge helm of terror and the magic 'Niebelung' ring. The thought that it could be *his* amazed Käal.

'I'm not kidding,' said Helltrik. 'That's how much getting Hellfire back means to me.'

'You would give *me* the Siegfried treasure?'

'If you can solve the mystery, yes.'

'Ah!' said Käal, pointing with one claw. 'So there *is* a catch.'

'I wouldn't call it a catch, exactly,' said old Vagner. 'It is, after all, why I have invited you to be here.'

'Still,' said Käal, stars in his eyes. 'If I had the Siegfried treasure—'

'I'm sure it would be very useful. I *have* heard, for instance,' said Old Vagner, 'that *Köschfagold Saga* is undergoing financial difficulties. You could support the Saga through several large court cases with such funds.'

'Yes,' said Käal. 'I could – do that. It's certainly a very tempting prize,' he added. 'But I can't help feeling that you only offer it to me because you know the task to be impossible.'

'I offer it to you because the task has defeated me for

centuries now, and because I'm at the end of my tether. I offer it to you because I think you *can* do it, if you have the proper incentive.'

'The whole Siegfried treasure?' said Käal.

'All except one trivial item, something that contributes very little to its worth. But the treasure I am offering you will, overnight, make you one of the wealthiest dragons in the whole of Scandragonia. It will be more than enough to raise capital and keep your Financial Saga running. All you need do is compose the Saga of my family. Hellfire's murder is an integral part of that story, so by composing the Saga you will be addressing the mystery that has tormented me. Perhaps your young eyes will spot clues that have eluded me; perhaps your – by all accounts (and I mean no disrespect when I say so) – *unusual* mind might escape the rut of conventional thinking that has failed to produce a result.'

'I'm boggled,' said Käal. 'Nobody has ever propositioned me like this before.'

To Käal's astonishment, he saw the old dragon's eyes filling with tears. He was actually crying! 'I miss her so desperately!' he sobbed.

'There, there,' said Käal, vaguely, looking panicked.

'My darling girl! Without her my life is so bare!' said Old Vagner. Tears ran over the scales of his snout and dripped to the granite, where they hissed and sputtered, burning shallow holes in the marble. 'Bare!' he said. 'Bare! Bare!'

Käal stared in frank astonishment at Vagner's display of naked emotional pain. He sounded like a sheep!

It was actively embarrassing. Käal thought for a

moment if he should tell the senior dragon that he sounded like a sheep. He decided not to. 'All right, Mon. Vagner – please, don't cry!'

'You'll,' said Vagner, reining in his tears, 'you'll help me?'

'I'll certainly have a go,' said Käal, shifting uncomfortably on the floor. The acid stench of Vagner's tears was pungent in his nostrils. 'Although I can't promise anything.'

'Thank you,' said Vagner, in a small voice. 'In that case,' he went on, pushing a tear back up his snout with one gnarled old talon, 'permit me to have the servants bring in a larger couch.'

'A larger . . . ?'

'You'll need to seat yourself more comfortably. I will need to tell you the story of my grandniece's murder, and it is not a brief tale.'

'Ah,' said Käal, experiencing that sinking feeling you get when somebody you thought was coming to the end of what they were saying reveals that they have only just begun. 'Excellent!'

3

Lizbreath Salamander flew down the broad Starkhelm mainstreet, dodging the omnibus kites and the lances of pedestrians, and alighted gently on the marble platform of her lawyer's office. A plate on the double door read: BURNBLAST, ATTORNEY-AT-LAW. Underneath smaller letters spelled out the directions: 'Down The Stairs, Cavern On Left'. Finally a handwritten parchment, pinned with a bone pin, specified hours of business: 'Burnblast will be on his hoard to receive clients from Wodensday to Fireday.'

Lizbreath had an appointment. She was expected. Burnblast was her Guardian, and under Dragon Law she had to consult with him and receive his permission before undertaking any move. She hated this arrangement, and chafed against it; for although technically a Salamander still, by weight, she was – in terms of chronological years – old enough to be accounted a dragon. She knew herself to be adult, and was perfectly capable of looking after herself. But for various reasons, the law did not see it like that. Even that transition, from youngling to oldling, depended upon the permission of her Guardian. And it was clear that he agreed with everyone else – that there was something *not quite right* about Lizbreath Salamander.

Though small, she was a sleek, rather beautiful young dragon. Her hindlegs could have done with more meat on them, and her torso was thin. But she moved with sinuous grace, and she possessed a beautiful face – her tapering snout was a glistening taupe, which *is* a colour, look it up if you don't believe me, and her teeth were white and sharp as icicles. Her snout ended in two perfectly formed large, round nostrils, like binoculars. If you see what I mean. Only, you know: nasal, not ocular. 'Binasalars', I suppose you could call them. Although, no, that looks stupid. Anyway, not to get, uh, bogged down. She folded away her wings and looked over her shoulder, surveying the street, sniffing suspiciously. It was thronged with ordinary dragons going about their ordinary business. She didn't know any of them, but that didn't stop her disliking them. She disliked them on principle.

With a clack of her claws upon the mahogany she pushed open one flap of the double door and darted down the carved granite stairs. Oh, she was *slinky*: in the rather specialized sense that she was *shiny, springlike* and seemed to *pour herself down the stairs*. With one flowing motion Lizbreath emerged from the bottom into the secretarial antechamber. The Secretary, a short, fat male Dragonet, snorted black smoke from his nose as she approached. His name was Galgewater.

'You want to see Burnblast, I suppose?' he said.

'I have no desire to see him, or you, ever again in my life,' said Lizbreath.

'You don't do yourself any favours,' Galgewater said, making a revoltingly fluid snuffling sound in his throat as he spoke. 'With your attitude, you know.'

'Favours is just another word for bribes,' Lizbreath said. 'Do *myself* a favour? Since I consider the whole hierarchy of patronage, favour-giving and *sucking-up* corrupt, why would I want to practise it upon myself?'

This was too subtle a point for Galgewater to absorb. He shuffled uneasily, perched on a compact hoard of gold behind his desk. Lizbreath, who had been to this office many time, and had had occasion to observe it fairly closely, suspected that some of the items were polished brass. He looked severely at her, snorted some brown smoke, and could think of nothing more effective to do than repeat himself. 'That's what I'm talking about. When I say "you don't do yourself any favours with your attitude", that's precisely the sort of non-favour-doing attitude I'm talking about.'

'If Burnblast doesn't want to see me,' Lizbreath said, letting the green smoke of boredom seep out of both sides of her mouth, 'then I'll be happy to go away.'

'Oh no,' said Galgewater, in a snide voice. 'He's ready for you. Go on through.'

Lizbreath wrinkled her snout and darted rapidly left, under the carved granite arch and along the connecting corridor. She could hear the Secretary tutting behind her.

You may be asking yourself; what, precisely, was the problem with Lizbreath Salamander? In a phrase it was that she *refused to conform*. In the social organization of most creatures this would be awkward; but in a world of dragons, where status, hierarchy and conformity were enormously, even overwhelmingly potent, shaping forces, it was like a deformity. Lizbreath just wouldn't behave herself.

The odd thing was that, everybody agreed, she had been a remarkably conventional egg: pliant and agreeable, exactly the right plump oval shape. She had sat perfectly still for the three years of her incubation. Of course, eggs always do, being eggs. But the point is: nothing in her eggishness suggested her future rebellious manner. Nobody at the hatchery could recall a better-behaved egg. As Burnblast was in the habit of saying to his colleagues: from being an immaculately behaved egg Lizbreath had changed almost immediately upon hatching. From the very beginning she had declined to show proper deference to older dragons; had disobeyed, or displayed dumb-insolence. She had shown almost no interest in learning the codes of politeness, and often absented herself to fly solo.

Most shocking of all was her complete indifference to gold. She had not worked, like the other hatchlings, to acquire the beginnings of her own hoard. On the contrary she had vocally disdained gold as a useless, lumpish, urinously-coloured substance varying in density from cheese to dried chewing gum. Such blasphemy did not endear her to anybody.

Of course she was taken away from her family and into care – her mother was so shocked by her daughter-dragon's words that she had retreated to a mountain-top rest-cure facility, ringed with fire. It might not have mattered if Lizbreath had been some form of lower wyrm. But she was, by blood and lineage, related to the highest, driest and fieriest dragons in the northern hemisphere: lineally a descendant of Regin the Regal, no less. She could not simply be shuffled off into a menial job and ignored.

A series of Legal Guardians had attempted, by the powers of persuasion, or by more forceful interventions, to bring her back to the proper path. All had failed. By the time the Dragon Authorities hired Burnblast, Lizbreath Salamander was a notorious tearaway and rebel. She associated with lowly wyrms, refused all invitations to Official Flypasts, Fire-balls or At-Hoards, and did worse. When word got out that she was assembling a hoard after all, some dragons breathed rose-red smoky sighs of relief. But then, one day, a Court Officer came to visit to get her to sign a legal parchment, and discovered the appalling truth: her hoard was not gold at all. It was silver!

The shock ran about Dragondom in a day. The perversity! A silver hoard? Who ever *heard* of such a thing! It could only be one thing: a calculated insult to the millennia-hallowed customs and traditions of dragonkind. What made it worse was that Lizbreath had gone *to some lengths* to assemble all the tatty, tinsel-shiny silver items upon which she now coiled herself. It was no mere whim, no passing smart-mouth quip. It was the deliberately and carefully assembled mark of deep-rooted disrespect. It meant that something was deeply awry inside Lizbreath Salamander's dragon mind.

A job was found for her in the Saga office. It was hoped that daily exposure to the great Sagas of dragon-kind might, perhaps, instil in her some respect for the magnitude and dignity of draconic history. But it had no such effect. At first she absented herself from work, until it was made plain to her that if she continued doing so then she would be confined in a Womental Institution. After that she turned up for work at the hours specified, but she disappeared into the bowels of the Saga office, the lowest, dampest caves, and devoted her time to the most bizarre and unusual draconic Sagas.

And then there was the question of body ornamentation. Naturally, pressure was applied to get her to paint her scales. Without tint, her body was a sheeny taupe, varying in depth from supertaupe on her tail, through earthy shades of midtaupe on her midriff up to paler iridescent lowtaupe on her neck and head, all of which are colours, no really. Taupe is all very well, as a colour; and several very well regarded dragons have been taupe. But nobody could claim it is a very *flaming* colour. Painting was always an option. As people kept pointing out: all the colours of fire and jewellery were available to her. She could have glorified herself with phoenix hues and blazed through the sky. But she did none of those things. Instead she bought herself a silver collar, with puny little spikes on the outside. There were rumours that she was hanging out with 'democrats', and petty undesirables of that ilk.

And then one weekend she disappeared. When she returned on Mournday with one small painting, just under her left wingjoint. It was not of a mighty dragon

35

hero of the past, or of abstract patterns of bright jeweller; it was not even of the representation of flames painted down her sides, as was popular with some of the younger fast-flying dragons. It was of a fantastical creature.

Even that might have been OK. Some fantastical creatures are hot: unicorns, say; or mighty tusked elephants; or Sirian StarBeasts. But what Lizbreath Salamander carried upon her body was the pale outline representation of a *girl* – one of those slug-soft ape creatures that had once infested the forests, and who still sometimes haunted younglings' nightmares, or appeared in such Horror Vidisagas as could afford the special effects budgets to represent them.

Was she trying, people asked, to be hot? This painting on Lizbreath's back was *not* hot. It was revolting. One small mercy was that it was quite hard to see when her wings were out; but when she tucked them away to (for instance) come inside, it was only too obviously on display.

By this stage the other Guardians had more or less given up on the job of attending to her. She was old enough, in terms of years, to be accounted an adult; but her behaviour was still that of an erratic hatchling with water on the brain. Somewhat at a loss, the Authorities had approached Burnblast.

For Burnblast was one of the most respected and impeccable senior dragons in Scandragonia. Old, traditional and immensely fat, with an impressively large hoard of ancient gold, there was nothing funny or unusual about him whatsoever.

At their first meeting, the old Attorney had drawn attention to the image of the girl on Lizbreath's shoulder. 'What's that?' he asked, although of course he knew the answer already.

'A girl,' Lizbreath had answered.

'I can see that,' boomed Burnblast. 'Why would you paint something so horrid on yourself?'

'It's not paint,' said Lizbreath.

'*Not* paint?' rumbled Burnblast.

'I mean it is not paint. It is ink.'

'Ink?' he repeated, ponderously.

'It is a tattoo.'

'A what?'

'That's what it is called. It is a tattoo.'

'Well. Ink will just rub off, soon enough, when you flap your wings.' Yet, somehow, the image of the girl did not get rubbed away; whenever Burnblast saw Lizbreath it was still there – still as revolting, and as mysterious, as the first encounter.

Burnblast had, as he told people, 'done his best' with Lizbreath Salamander. 'But though it pains me to admit it,' he would add, spitting chunks of brimstone and picking a sheep rib from his teeth with one delicately jabbing talon, 'success has been limited. What can I do? I only have one point of influence over her, really. Because of this affectation of hers, sitting as she does on her ridiculous hoard of silver – obviously that's useless for the purposes of actually *buying* things, and so on. She is legally my ward. That means that she must come to me for money. If it weren't for that, she might fly completely off the handle.'

And money was the purpose of this morning's appointment. That was the only reason Lizbreath had steeled herself to scuttle along the echoey granite corridor. Sucking in a deep breath, she emerged into Burnblast's huge cavern.

It was old-school: rough-hewn rock, illuminated by a ring of torches embedded in the granite in a vast circle. Between the torches, a circle of pennants hung limply, carrying the design of Burnblast's coat of limbs.

Burnblast himself sat on an immense golden hoard that dominated the space. It was, if nothing else, a testament to his great age and skill in accumulating gold: it embodied in concrete material form the respect with which he was regarded by dragondom. Since his business involved meeting other dragons, Burnblast kept his hoard broad and low, arranged around a rising granite spur that enabled clients to climb and be on a level with him without committing the faux pas of treading upon his gold. Lizbreath though, loitered sulkily at the bottom, and Burnblast had to summon her specifically. 'Come up,' he said.

Reluctantly, Lizbreath clambered up. Burnblast was a huge, gnarled figure. When he shifted his weight and settled down he *spread*, the way a toad does. But there was nothing *soft* about him. His scales, though they jagged and snaggled in all sorts of directions, were nonetheless thick and tough. They presented no gaps or bald patches. Indeed, rather to the contrary they bristled with a more intimidating, stalagmitish or porcupiney force precisely because they were not being regularly tiled like other dragons. His coloration was black, except for his fanta-coloured eyes, bright and fizzing with cunning. His incidental fire, when it flickered from the sides of his mouth in myriad little almond-shaped flames, was the pale purple of methylated spirits.

'So,' he boomed. 'Lizbreath Salamander. What brings you to my lair this fine, fiery day?'

Lizbreath did not meet his eyes. 'You know why I'm here,' she said. 'Money.'

'Of course, money. I could hardly expect that you would wish to come to see your Legal Guardian for any other reason! Not, for example, to pay your respects.'

'Pay,' said Lizbreath. 'That's an apt way of putting it.'

Burnblast ignored this. 'For what do you need this money, exactly?'

'Living,' said Lizbreath, in a surly tone, 'expenses.'

'I see. And you find your famous hoard of silver is of no use to you, I suppose.' When Lizbreath didn't answer this, he went on: 'You understand, my dear, how foolish this rebellious gesture was? All that effort assembling a perfectly *useless* hoard – all the work you did, and now it's no use to you at all! Cutting off your snout to spite your face. So instead of standing on your own four feet, you must keep crawling back to me!'

Lizbreath growled low, but said nothing.

'Oh don't worry, my dear,' said Burnblast. 'I shall give you some money. But I would be failing in my duty to you as Guardian if I didn't ask you a few questions first. To discover the sort of life my ward is living. Are you still working with Sagas?'

When Lizbreath grunted, Burnblast prompted her: 'I'm afraid you really must answer me with words, my dear, or this conversation will be elongated unconscionably, and you'll never get your funds.'

'Yes,' she said.

'Which department?'

'I work in the archives of a Starkhelm Saga company.'

'Very good. And how is your private life?'

'My *what*?'

'Your private life! Don't be shocked, my dear. I'm hardly a stranger, after all. It is my duty, as your Guardian, to ensure that you are keeping respectable company. I'm as aware of the rumours as everybody – loitering in damp buildings with lower-class wyrms, associating with known democratic dragons.' Burnblast shook his head. 'All very bad.'

'My private life,' said Lizbreath, 'is very unexceptional.'

'Do you have a boyfriend?'

'As you know, legally I cannot become hamfasted without your permission.'

'That's true. But I'm not talking about anything so official. I'm sure you have boydragons interested in you. Come, you can tell me.'

'There's nobody in particular,' said Lizbreath, reluctantly.

'And sex?'

'I *beg* your pardon?'

'Come, my dear, don't be coy. You're hardly a virgin, now, are you.'

'Why is this relevant to me getting my allowance?'

'You must permit *me* to be the judge of what is relevant, my dear. The Dragonlords have placed me in authority over you. Accepting that authority is a necessary part of your larger integration into dragon society.'

Lizbreath lowered her head.

'So,' said Burnblast, scratching his snout with one curved talon big as a hippo's ribbone. 'You do have a sex life?'

Lizbreath held a pause just long enough for it to register as insolent. Then she answered in a surly voice: 'From time to time. I assume it's the same for you—'

Burnblast wagged a talon back and forth. 'Now, now, my dear. Do not get above yourself. What I do with respect to sex is not your business. But what you do *is* mine. You like it?'

'I guess.'

'I bet you do! Are you – adventurous?'

'*What?*'

'I think you heard me.'

'I don't understand what you mean by adventurous.'

'Come, now. Use your imagination. For instance: How do you feel about,' he dropped his voice, conspiratorially, 'oral sex?'

Lizbreath blinked. 'About what?'

'Oral sex. How do you *feel* about it?'

She looked at him, twitched her nostrils, and asked: 'What kind of ore? Precious metals? Iron?'

'No, no. The word is *oral* as in: relating to the mouth.'

She wasn't sure she'd heard him correctly. 'Relating what to the mouth?'

'Relating a dragon's – intimate organ. To the mouth.'

She was silent for a long minute, regarding him closely with her golden eyes. Then she said: 'You're asking me about having . . . sex in the mouth?'

'Precisely!'

'So, let me get this clear in my head. "Oral" sex: a male dragon unsheathes his delicate member from its protective bony covering, and puts it – in all its tender vulnerability – into the *mouth* of a female dragon?'

'Or male dragon – but, yes, you describe it perfectly.'

'That same mouth,' Lizbreath went on, 'from which fire blasts out on a regular basis? Flames hot enough to turn steel into soup, to blast solid lead into hot black *oil*? That mouth?'

'Indeed.'

'The mouth that can generate temperatures of up to 600 degrees Centigrade?'

'Yes,' he said.

'How do I *feel* about that?'

'Yes.'

'I feel sorry for any male dragon foolish enough to try it. Is how I feel.'

'So, would you say that the idea disgusts you?' There was a weird gurgle in his voice as he asked this. 'That it makes your scales rattle and your flesh creep? It repels you?'

'I'd say it repels sanity. It sounds crazy. What male dragon would risk it?'

Burnblast squirmed, and tapped the tips of his

slippery wings against his flanks – with, Lizbreath could see, a strange kind of *delight*. The thought of incinerating his member filled him not with a healthy aversion, but with whatever the opposite of *aversion* is. With zversion. What a creepy old dragon he was!

'Ah!,' he said, 'but the risk is what makes it exciting! Or,' he added, twisting his tentacular neck to look over his wing, as if making sure nobody was eavesdropping. 'Or so I have heard, at any rate. Rumour says that some male dragons prefer it to regular sex.'

'Some male dragons could do with a few sessions with a Fireudian analyst, it seems to me,' noted Lizbreath, sardonically. 'Either that, or Aversion Therapy. With icicles.'

'So,' said Burnblast, lifting his huge phoenix-feather pen in his right claw, and writing something on the scroll in front of him. 'You'd say that you find the idea of *oral sex* repellent.'

'You do realize,' Lizbreath pointed out, as if explaining to an idiot, 'that if a female dragon becomes sexually aroused, she can't *help* but spew fire from her mouth? That's not something we have any control over, you know.'

'Ah!' said Burnblast, 'now, yes, you raise a very interesting question. Female sexual arousal. How do you feel about *that*?'

'You're an extraordinarily creepy old dragon,' said Lizbreath, snapping her wings out briskly enough to make the pennants flutter fifty feet away. 'And I have no intention of answering any more of your disgusting, prurient questions.'

43

'Oh, but my dear young Lizbreath,' smarmed Burnblast. 'You must answer them! You are my ward, after all.'

'I could be your entire *hospital*, I still wouldn't answer your questions.' She leapt up and trod the air, moving backwards away from him. 'Whatever the laws says, I'm a mature dragon,' she called to him. 'Leave me alone.'

In an instant he was up beside her, his vast wings spread out so as to half-enclose her, and blotting out the red torchlight in the process. She could hear his huge wings slap against the vaulted stone ceiling of his cavern.

It was undeniably the case that he was much larger than her. His hind claws grabbed her about her slender waist, and she was borne downward onto the granite floor. She landed with a thumpingly solid impact. It hurt. His huge, elongated head swung from side to side, and little spurts of iridescent purple flame darted from his mouth and slid over the scales of her snout. They weren't hot enough to warm her face, but she could *smell* him in them and it wasn't a pleasant smell. 'Going somewhere?' he sneered. 'Without my permission? How *rude* you are!' Burnblast drew his huge bellying wings round and lashed out with both his hindlegs at once, driving her hard against the floor so that her ribs creaked and her breath left her in dribbles of smoke. With one of his sinewy foreclaws, he grabbed Lizbreath's left wing-joint, right in there by the tender shoulder, near her tattoo. Lizbreath couldn't stop herself wailing with the pain. She struggled, but he was simply

44

too powerful for her. 'You haven't washed off this odd little painting, then?' he hissed.

'It won't,' Lizbreath gasped, '*wash* off.'

'I suggest you scrub harder, my dear,' he said, breathing the words hotly right into her ear.

'Let me go,' she complained, trying to twist her head away from his breath.

'You go,' said Burnblast, 'when I say you *may* go, and not before.' He thrust his wing-elbows forward, together, to squash her head down against the stone floor, and prevent her from looking behind.

'You are hurting me,' she complained, hating herself for her weakness in speaking at all. But her shoulders rasped with the pain, and she intensely disliked being forced down like this.

'Whatever notions you have in your head, Lizbreath, you are *not* a mature dragon. You are a Salamander still, and subject to the dominion of the Dragonlords. In your case, and because you are so insignificant and puny a wyrm, they have delegated that dominion to *me*. Do you understand?'

She closed her teeth together, tight as the seal of a zip, and resolved not to say anything. But he pressed her snout onto the rock of the platform, and wrenched her wings painfully upon their sockets, so she was compelled to bark: 'Yes!'

'Good,' he said, relaxing his pressure a little. 'You had better remember that. Dragons are an ancient and a noble species, little Lizbreath. We have rituals and traditions stretching back hundreds of thousands of years. We don't look kindly upon little wyrms, barely out of the egg, *disrespecting* our authority, and *painting* horrible-looking creatures upon their backs.'

'It's *not* painted,' she said, through gritted teeth. 'I told you – it's a tattoo.'

'I don't care if it's a ta-*twenty*two, you contemptible Sillymander,' he snarled. 'I would advise you to try to put me in a *good mood*. Because if you don't, I shall make your life very unpleasant indeed.'

Lizbreath ducked her head with a low snarl, a sign of defeat.

She could feel his hind claws moving up and down her lower back, searching and groping. It was intensely unpleasant, not least because she had no idea how it would end, or what his intentions were. But then he seemed, suddenly, to grow bored. 'You have taken up enough of my time,' he said, releasing her. He leapt up in the air, swivelled himself about and settled back on his gold hoard. 'I have other business to attend to. Off you go.'

'But,' said Lizbreath, quailing back and trying to suppress her tremors. 'I need money.'

'Not today,' said Burnblast, imperiously.

'I need it!'

'If you need it then you will need to find a way of convincing me to give you some,' he said.

Scared and trembling as she was, this was so outrageous that Lizbreath could not let it pass. 'I'm entitled!' she said.

'Oh, you won't *starve*,' said the old dragon, sneeringly. 'You get a salary from your archive work, I suppose.

46

Spend it on mutton, rather than on adding to your crazy hoard of silver.'

'That's not the point,' Lizbreath pressed. 'You are literally sitting on my ancestral hoard – some of this gold is mine. You have no right to deny it to me!'

'Oh, but I *do* have the right, in Law, and in the eyes of the Dragonlords – of all dragon society. They know that I am a respectable old dragon who has never put a talon out of place. And they know you are a tearaway young fool, probably wrong-in-the-head, anti-establishment, drawn to ideas of democracy and certainly *not* to be trusted. Try raising the matter with the authorities and see who they believe.'

'This isn't fair!'

'Fair?' bellowed Burnblast, with sudden and genuine-seeming rage. 'You'll not speak the polluted vocabulary of democracy in *this* cave! Fair? Being a dragon is about *force*, not *fair*! You may relish squirming in the mud like a tadpole, my dear, but the rest of us rejoice in the majesty and dignity of Draconus Sapiens.' He blew a great horizontal oak-tree of flame and smoke out of his mouth. Lizbreath barely had time to clamp her eyes shut and close her nostrils before the wavefront of scalding, choking heat washed over her. When the heat passed, and she opened her eyes again, Burnblast seemed to have calmed. 'Come back, my dear, on Cinderday, and we'll see about loaning you a little money.'

Lizbreath crept backwards, towards the exit. 'You're not open on Cinderdays,' she pointed out.

'Oh, I'll *be* in the office next Cinderday. I have some scrollwork to do. Off you go now.'

With a deep sense of the humiliation she had endured – the intrusive questions, the physical bullying – and a deeper sense of her own shameful subordination, Lizbreath Salamander backed down the corridor and rushed past sneering Galgewater up the stairs and into the sunlight.

4

'There is a great shame at the heart of the Vagner clan,' old Vagner told Käal. 'It is so shameful, that we never speak of it. You see, the family is deeply implicated in—' He lowered his voice. 'I can hardly bring myself to say it to an outsider – implicated in *liberal democracy*.'

The words were like ice-water splashed in Käal's face.

'I can see that you are shocked,' said Vagner, in a grim voice. 'And I don't blame you. It's only my familiarity with this hideous blot upon the honour of our nest that prevents *me* from being shocked.' He shook his long head, slowly. From the corners of his mouth threads of sad, grey smoke trailed into the air, braiding and blurring over his head in the draught created from this motion.

'Old "Roarer" Gutfire, my grandfather, was one of the fattest and most important dragons in all Scandragonia. I'm talking a dozen centuries ago, or more – during the Scorch Wars.'

'Your grandfather fought in the Scorch Wars?'

'Oh he was a *leading* figure, a mighty dragon warrior. That fact makes his shameful secret all the more shocking, of course.'

'Where did he fight?'

'He led the squadrons that took Emberland. It wasn't *Emberland* back then, of course. In those days it was still clogged and contaminated with myriad varieties of wetlife: slime moulds such as *grasses* and *bushes* and *trees*, bags-of-mostly-water like slugs and apes. In fact it used to be called "Angerland" because it was infested with a particularly virulent and aggressive species of *hömös apes*. Infested! Really swarming with them. In Scandragonia things weren't so bad; the *hömös* infestations were much thinner here. But over *there*, the apes were virulent. They got into everything: valleys, hills, forests, underground, overground, rambling free. There was no choice. Purging them meant wrecking the land – desertifying it completely. I suspect my grandfather, Gutfire, went into battle a proud and noble dragon. But he came out of it twisted by what he had seen and done. He came out having lost his inherent faith in the cleanness of dragonkind.'

'What a terrible story,' said Käal, with feeling.

'Is it? I suppose it is. To me, the Scorch Wars are ancient history. Emberland, Scorchland, the whole desolation – it has no power to move me, because for my life it's always been that way. To me, Gutfire's fall from grace is nothing more than an occasion for shame and grief amongst those I love.' He paused. 'No, I suppose it is more than that. It is a curse that has ruined the Vagners, and dampened and drowned every spirit it has touched.'

'You think it has something to do with Hellfire's death – her disappearance, I should say?'

'Be patient, Käal,' said the old dragon. 'It is a long

and involved story, the background to the family. But you need to understand it if you are to understand what happened to Hellfire.'

'Fair enough.'

'After the war, Gutfire received the Gold Star and the Order of the Purple Heat from the grateful Dragon-lords, for his part in the Emberland campaign. If he had only bided his time, and carried on living a virtuous and regular dragon life, he would in all probability have *become* a Dragonlord, in good time. But he could not. The war had altered him. He saw the Truth and he loathed it: its brightness hurt his eye, its heat repelled him, its violence intimidated him . . . I'm guessing, because I don't really know what happened. I *do* know that he became fascinated with the Lie, as all Lie-berals are, of course. But Lie-beralism, or "Liberalism" as it is now called, was not the worst of it. More than that, he became convinced that the nobility and dignity of dragon society should be humbled. He became demo-cratic.'

Käal gulped. It seemed wrong, somehow, even to *utter* that word: it was so completely at odds with everything Scandragonia stood for. 'It's strange,' he said. 'to think that actual people living their lives by that offensive doctrine . . .'

'And yet many dragons believe in it! It is rarely talked about, but all over Scandragonia – and especially in Swedragen – there are many sly, secretive *democrats*.' He articulated the word, with, as it were, tongs; as if it were made of ice. 'And many of them are members of my family. Not me, thank Woden – I have never understood the appeal. But several of my uncles and aunts, and even my brothers and sisters.'

For a long time he stared gloomily into the middle distance. Käal removed his attention from his host, and took a proper look at the frieze that ran around the rim of the circular room. What Käal had assumed was a conventional representation of dragons in poses of triumph, was actually a stranger, more fiddly ribbon of moulded stone. Those little asterisks in various positions all along its length were, Käal could now see, apes – thousands of apes, in all their strange little jackets and leg-tubes: apes running, lying tangled in heaps. Those few dragons on the frieze were represented as treading down upon the writhing mass of hömös, but instead of glory their expressions looked oddly sorrowful. It was, on reflection, a very disagreeable piece of interior decoration.

'Not many dragons know,' said Old Vagner, after a long pause, 'that the-mockery was actually invented by the hömöses. Oh, you can call it *democracy* if you like, but I'm an old-fashioned dragon, and I like the old-fashioned ways of pronouncing words. Modern pronunciation seems so mumbly, somehow.'

'Invented by the hömöses?'

'Indeed. Interesting, no?'

'I suppose it makes a kind of sick sense,' said Käal. 'It's the kind of thing one would associate with . . . their sort.'

'The notion originally occurred to a hömös tribe in the country we now call Grits. Before that, hömös society was more like dragon society – was more elevated, I mean, more authoritarian and therefore authoritative. But then this new idea came into being. It set itself implacably against absolute leadership by the fattest and oldest dragons – that ancient, noble and dignified system, founded upon respect and reticence. That wasn't the hömöses' way. Instead, they would gather together a crowd of possible leaders, usually senior apes, every five years or so. And then they organized giant national circuses, in which the leaders were *mocked*. Mocked mercilessly and repeatedly, over and over again . . . sometimes for as long as a year, or a year and a half. It was a fantastically, destructively but worst of all *deliberately* destructive procedure. The ape who best endured "the mockery" would win, and become leader. But he or she was of course fatally diminished by the ordeal. They had no dignity left at all by the end, and a leader without dignity cannot effectively lead others. The process of "the-mockery" rendered them, in the fullest sense imaginable, *laughing-stocks*.'

'But how could society function under such conditions?'

'Well, the short answer is: badly. We can see that from hömöses. The apes did organize against us, of course, during the war – but their organization was a muddle, a mob. Some areas held out for longer than others, naturally. The apes in Dustland showed a fair bit of discipline and determination, for instance. And before being blasted, Emberland was known as "Angerland" because the apes who lived there were distinctive in the sheer *fury* with which they attacked us. But by and large ape society lacked the necessary solidity and resilience to oppose us. We were able to burn them out. To eradicate them. They're a legend now; a bugaboo to frighten hatchlings. Horrible tiny scuttling creatures, incapable of flight but full of malice and cruel quick-witted ingenuity.'

Käal knew all the folkstories, of course. 'So what you're saying is that this crazy apean political philosophy was entirely discredited during the Scorch Wars. I can see that. What I don't understand is why any sane dragon would think it was a good idea to resurrect it.'

Old Vagner nodded. 'Of course you're right. You know Scandragonia as it is often represented in the Tourist Sagas: noble, fiery, hierarchical, martial – a place of savage grandeur, a place anathema to everything petty. But there's another Scandragonia that co-exists with that fire-tinted vision – however shameful it may be to admit it, however much we want to close our eyes to it. This is the subaerial world of *democratic* Scandragonia: a world of . . .' He steeled himself to go on. 'A world of egalitarianism, of social responsibility and,' his voice fell to a whisper, 'taxes. A world of welfare extended to the weak and helpless . . .'

'As if the helpless want their misery prolonged!' Käal expostulated. 'As if the weak want anything at all except the one crucial thing – *not to be weak*! To be strong!'

'I couldn't have put it better myself,' agreed Vagner. 'Taxes! The very *idea* of taxes is emasculating! To have somebody rob me of a portion of my gold – right in front of my snout? – to expect me to smile and nod? Never! Robbery is one thing; it has its noble pedigree. But to be robbed and expected *not* to come out flaming with death-hatred? And why – to give my gold to some disease- or age-raddled dragon too weak to steal his own? Where's the honour *for him* in that?'

Old Vagner paused for a moment. 'Yet,' he went on, shortly, 'key members of my family thinks this system should be instituted throughout dragondom! They want to see the Dragonlords swept away, and all the old solidity overturned.'

'It would be chaos!' Käal cried.

'Oh you don't have to persuade *me* that it is madness,' said Vagner. 'But it was the peculiar madness of my grandfather. He passed it down to his descendants. His eldest son, Joblair, had gone blithely to war with his father – by all accounts he was a smirking and insignific- ant figure, easily influenced and pathetically eager to waste the lands of others. But Joblair was killed in the Scorch Wars, struck down and drowned in the Enough Sea, so Gutfire's wealth eventually came to his other son, Firedrake.'

'Firedrake,' said Käal, trying to hold these names in mind.

'My father. Firedrake was a secretive though dedi- cated supporter of the-mockeries. Immediately after the war, times were hard for such people. Pretty much all the great dragon families had lost members in the fighting, and much of the world had been ruined and wasted. By eliminating the apes, we had also destroyed much of the farmland necessary to grow

55

our food. Several decades passed before proper intensive factory farming of goats, sheeps and pigs was established – they were, by all accounts, hungry times for many dragons.'

Käal, nodding, didn't want to interrupt the old man's flow, not least because he wanted to get to the end of this story before Dragontterdammerung rolled up the scroll of the world. But he couldn't help himself. He was not the biggest, bravest or fieriest dragon in Scandragonia, but he was certainly the most *pedantic*.

'Sheep,' he said.

Helltrik stopped. 'What?'

'Sheep. Just, sheep.'

'Yes indeed, sheeps.'

'The plural of sheep is sheep.'

'What?' Old Vagner looked confused.

'I'm sorry,' said Käal. 'I didn't mean to break up your flow. You said that, after the war, dragons developed the factory-farming of goats, pigs and "sheeps". That was all.'

'What's your point?'

'Only that – forgive me – I thought I ought to point out: the plural of sheep is sheep.'

'What's that about plural?' Vagner looked bleary-eyed. 'Did I get it wrong?'

'I'm afraid you did. It hardly matters – only, I have an eye for details like that.'

'I see. So the plural is?'

'Sheep,' said Käal.

'Yes, the plural of sheep.' He waited expectantly. 'Is . . . ?'

'Sheep.'

'Yes. And the *plural* is?'

'Sheep,' said Käal. 'It's sheep.'

'Really, Mon. Brimstön, *you're* the one who interrupted *me* on this matter. The least you can do is tell me what the plural *is*.'

'You don't understand what I'm saying, Monster Vagner. The plural of sheep is – sheep.'

Vagner's brow folded, the scales on his head snapping as he frowned. 'You've lost me.'

'The singular is sheep, one sheep, a sheep. But the plural is also sheep. It's not sheeps, which is what you said. You don't add the s. That's all.'

The creased-up brow did not uncrease. 'Are you sure?'

'Yes – but, look, ignore me, it doesn't matter. Which is to say: perhaps it *matters*, a little, but it's not relevant, not exactly relevant to what you were saying. Go on with your story.'

'Is it – then, pig the plural of pig, goat the plural of goat?'

'No, no,' said Käal, shifting uncomfortably on the floor. 'Pigs, goats, that's fine. You can say *sheeps*, too if you like. Why not? Nobody cares, really.'

'No, no, I want to get it right. Sheep. But why should it be different to the other barnyard animal names? That's what I don't understand. Do *you* know, why, Monster Brimstön?'

'No,' said Käal. 'No, I don't. It's one of the mysteries of language. Can we go on with your narrative, please,

Monster Vagner? You were telling me of the devotion of your father to democracy . . . ?'

'Was I? Oh, yes, Firedrake. Well, the political climate after the war was not conducive to those who thought that democracy might benefit dra— Sheep? Are you sure that it's not one of those words that shifts its medial *vowel* in the plural? Like *drink* becomes *drank*, you know?'

'Um,' said Käal. 'Look—'

'It could be shap, say? One *sheep*, several *shap* – doesn't that sound right?'

'I really don't think—'

'Yes,' said Old Vagner, ruminatively. 'That must be it. After all, there must be something to differentiate singular and plural, don't you think?'

'I rather regret raising the matter, to be honest.'

'Well, otherwise a trader could come along, and you might ask him: "What have you got for sale today, Mon. Trader?" and he – or *she*, of course – could answer "sheep" and you wouldn't know if they were trying to sell you one sheep or twenty, uh, shap.'

'I suppose,' said Käal, in a strangled voice, 'I suppose you could work it out from context? Could you maybe do that? Or else just ask him: "Mon. Trader, do you mean a single sheep or more than one?" Wouldn't that be a . . . thing you could do?'

'But that would surely be wasteful, and inefficient. I mean, communication-wise.'

Käal thought about this. 'Mon. Vagner, perhaps you could go on with your backstory . . . ? We don't have all the time in the world, after all.'

'What? Yes. Well I was telling you about my father, Firedrake. He'd been as brave and noble a dragon as you might hope for, during the war, though he'd been too young to more than fight in the last stages, when we had the apes on the run and were just mopping up. But somehow, after the war ended, he became – *persuaded* by Old Gutfire's the-mockery arguments. I don't know how it happened, or how a noble, honest dragon was converted to a . . . democrat. Perhaps it was a kind of nihilism – a desire to bring dragon society crashing into chaos out of existential despair?'

'Logically, though,' Käal said, 'I suppose it's unlikely he would have a single sheep to sell.'

'What?'

'The sheep trader. In your example. If he, or she, came up and said "wanna buy sheep?" you wouldn't automatically think he, or she, was offering you a single sheep.' Käal spread his lips in an unconvincing smile. 'I mean, who sells individual sheep, in this day and age? I heard a Financial Saga that said the sheep factory outside Limbchopping handles forty thousand head of livestock every day. Every day!'

Vagner was looking coolly at him.

'I'm sorry,' Käal said. 'Do go on.'

'As I *say*,' the old dragon resumed. 'At first Firedrake was bitterly disappointed to have missed the glory days of war. He wanted nothing more than to train in the arts of the warrior. Then something happened, and all that changed. He began attending secret the-mockery cabals, and he lost his desire to fight completely. He made hamfast with a female dragon – Ulrikaka – and in quick succession my mother laid five eggs, one after the other, with no more than a year between them. Five! It must have set a record for fecundity! At least for the high-born families of Regin-bloodline dragons. It was as if my mother and father were trying, single-handedly, to boost the general dragon population! First my oldest brother Reekhard, then Hydra, my older sister, and Greendragon, and my other brother Ghastly – he lives here on Doorbraak. You'll meet him, I daresay. And finally me.'

'Five!' said Käal, admiringly.

'Indeed. But the shame of it is: *four* of those five were inducted into the ways of the-mockery. Luckily for her, Hydra never *really* believed all that, I think. But Reekhard believed it with *fanatical* single-mindedness, and Ghastly is quite open about his repellent views. Now Reekhard made hamfast with a fierce young dragon called Thatcheretta; they had a son whom, in grandfilial duty, Reekhard named Gutfire, and whom the family tends to call "Gutfire II" so as not to get confused, or else, "Young Gutfire", except that he's not young any more – he's only a hundred years younger than me. He was a tearaway, dedicated mostly to party-ing, drinking fire-water and driving in Dragon-car Races. But he married eventually, under pressure from his father, my brother, a beautiful young dragon from the Necesseriona family – Isabella, her name. Hydra married after the Prodigy Scandal and the Dencrash: a decent, rather dull dragon called Igniter. Greendragon married Girder, of whom perhaps you have heard . . . if you follow contemporary music at all.'

Käal shook his head, self-deprecatingly. 'I'm afraid not.'

'No? He's quite famous. Now, anyway . . .'

'Er,' said Käal. 'Could I just . . .'

'And Ghastly never married. Who'd have him? Despite his wealth, he's ugly, his breath smells of watercress and he holds objectionable democratic views to which he gives voice night and day. Anyway, Gutfire and Isabella *were* married.'

'Stop a moment,' said Käal, grinning awkwardly. 'Could I just ask you to stop? I'm finding it hard to, er, visualize all these family interrelations.'

'Really?' said Vagner, haughtily. 'What do you want? Should I *draw it all out*, like a hatchling's primer? Come along, it's perfectly straightforward. Gutfire and Isabella were the parents of Marrer and Hellfire.'

'. . . who died in the war?'

'No! No! They were born long *after* the war, of course. It was *Joblair* died in the war. But that was a different Gutfire. Hydra and Igniter had three children. I sometimes wonder if they set out trying to emulate my parents for fecundity but were forced to give up. Now it's important to remember that Bürner, their oldest son, was younger than the younger child of Gutfire.'

'Ghastly?' Käal hazarded.

'No, no,' snapped Vagner, growing irritated. 'Are you an idiot? The younger child of Gutfire Vagner was Hellfire Vagner. Her brother—'

'Bürner,' said Käal, to show he had been paying attention,

'No! No! *Bürner?*' The incredulity with which he repeated the name was a mixture of disbelief and ferocity. 'No! Of *course* not Bürner! Her brother wasn't *Bürner.*'

'Azazel?' Käal tried.

'Azazel's a *girl!*' Old Vagner's face was assuming a look almost of disgust. 'Were you even *listening* when I explained it all before? Is it so hard to get the relationships of the various members of my family clear in your head?'

'I'm sorry,' said Käal, becoming flustered and starting to leak mahogany-coloured smoke. 'It's just that there are quite a few individuals, and . . .'

'It's disrespectful, is what it is!' thundered the senior dragon. 'It's the symptom of a degenerate age!'

'I think,' said Käal, 'with just one more explanation of the various relations . . .'

Vagner gave him a hard stare. 'My *grandfather* was called Gutfire,' he said, shortly.

'And so was your . . . uncle?'

'So was my *nephew*. Honestly! I'm starting to have my doubts about you, Mon. Brimstön.'

'Your nephew! Yes, of course. I think I've got it clear in my head now.'

'Do you, Käal? Do you *really?*' Helltrik looked witheringly doubtful. 'In that case, you'll be able to tell me what relationship *I* have to Alexandragon?'

Käal was pretty sure that old Vagner had never mentioned an Alexandragon. 'Uncle?' he guessed.

Old Helltrik looked at him closely. 'That's right,' he said eventually. 'Assuming you meant to say that *I* am *his* uncle – not that *he* is *my* uncle – which would be ridiculous!'

'Ridiculous,' agreed Käal.

'Well. All right. Do you think you have a sense of it, now?'

'Absolutely,' Käal lied.

'Good. Because you'll need to get a good sense of the family interrelations if you are going to write our Saga. Won't you!' Suddenly Old Vagner began chuckling, a resonant repeating sound like a goose tut-tutting the sloppy workmanship of another goose. 'How comical it would be, if you attempted to write our Saga, and you didn't even know that Isabel and Azazel were second cousins once removed!'

'That *would* be insane,' Käal agreed, tight-voiced. 'So, you were—'

'Richly comical!' laughed Old Vagner.

'—you were telling me about the secret shame of the Vagners?'

'Only imagine, thinking Bürner was Hellfire's *brother*!' Old Vagner's laughter deepened and stretched out. The more he thought about this the funnier it seemed to become to him. 'What a crazy thought! Just fancy! It's funny! To imagine those two brother and sister! Oh, that *would* have been a bizarreness!'

Käal waited until the old dragon's laughter slowed and settled, before prompting him again. 'The secret shame of the Vagners? Democracy?'

'Oh – yes. Well, there have been, and there still are, a lot of the-mockeryites in my family. We have paid a considerable amount of money to keep the news out of the Gossip Sagas, I can tell you.'

'And you think this has something to do with the disappearance of, er, ah,' but the name was simply not in Käal's short-term memory. 'Your grandniece?' he concluded.

'I think so. You need to understand how poisonous this pervasive ideological commitment to mockery is. A family is like a society in miniature: it *needs* a degree of respect, of solidity, to function. What has happened with the Vagners is that this toxin has worked itself into all our relationships. None of us *respect* one another. According to the beliefs of democracy everybody is on a level with everybody else, everyone is competing with and trying to put everybody else down. Mockery, sniping, ridicule, nastiness – this is the currency of inter-personal relationships under such a regime. You'll be able to see for yourself, Mon. Brimstön, if you stay on Doorbraak – as I hope you will.'

'You want me to stay here?'

'Oh, you'll need to, if you're going to write our Saga. Don't worry, it needn't be for very long – a year at most. And you will be *very* well rewarded, after all.'

'Hmmm,' said Käal.

'You have other plans, perhaps?'

'It's just that – well, frankly, Doorbraak seems a little *grand* for a modern dragon like me.'

'You must help me, Käal,' said Old Vagner. 'I'm elderly, frail – my time is almost up. I cannot go into the shadow without discovering the truth of what happened to my beautiful grandniece! I must know the truth, and you can uncover it for me.'

How could Käal refuse? Well, he could either have said 'I refuse', or else, 'no thank you', or some variant of that. But he didn't. He said: 'I'll do it!'

5

'So,' said Käal, settling himself. 'Tell me how it happened – Hellfire's murder, I mean.'

'Ah!' said old Vagner. 'You see that it must *be* murder?'

'To be honest,' said Käal, 'I don't. It *may* have been, I concede that. But why do you say, *must?*'

'First of all, you have to understand that Doorbraak is an island, here in the sky.'

'Of course.'

'Well, we are well separated from the mainland. I keep an eye above and an eye below. Our privacy is important to us, you see, and we like to keep comings and goings in view. But the crucial thing is that neither eye saw Hellfire leave. Had she flown above, or ducked below, then she would have been observed.'

'Did *nobody* leave?'

'Not a person. For the whole of that last day, the day of her disappearance, we were surrounded by drizzle.'

'Woden!' Käal swore. 'For a *whole day?*'

Old Vagner nodded.

'What kind of drizzle?'

The old dragon looked straight at him. 'The thin sort that really sticks to you – the worst kind. Cold, moist, invasive.' He shuddered, his scales rattling as he did so like a beggar's tin.

'But—' said Käal, finding it hard to believe: 'all *day*? Where did this rain come from?'

'That's a very good question. We maintain this flying island at this altitude for a reason, Mon. Brimstön, as I'm sure you can imagine. We exist above most of the low-lying weather fronts, all those seed clouds that rain to keep grass green for our mutton to graze. Up here, you see, the sky is gloriously dry and windy. Every now and again we get a freak shower, of course, but never for more than a half-hour. But that day – the day Hellfire was murdered – it rained *all day*. It is too much of a coincidence.'

'You think it might have been – arranged?'

'Over the centuries I have become more and more convinced that it must have been. You see, the day in question the whole nest had gathered. It is something we do every decade. But, because so many *members* of the family are so hostile to one another – so mocking, so snide – these get-togethers are never very comfortable. There were several flaming rows.'

'Hmm?'

'. . . which is what you'd expect in any family, of course. And not all the disagreements were as healthy as that. Some of the arguments were positively *icy*.'

'No!'

'I'm afraid so. Some really chilly, slushy, *cold* argu-ments. The last I saw of Hellfire, she flew from the main dining hall, after Reekhard and Isabella had an icy clash. I think that seeing her mother and her grandfather behaving so abominably to one another drove her to genuine grief.'

'And that's the last you saw of her?'

'Yes. Asheila saw her about fifteen minutes afterwards, heading down to the main hall. But I myself went into that hall five minutes after this sighting, and she wasn't there.'

'Maybe she went into the hall and came out again?'

Old Vagner shook his head. 'It is where the main hoard is kept. There is only one entrance, and it can only be approached by a long winding corridor. I came down that corridor looking for her – I wasn't unobservant. If Hellfire had left, she would have come straight past me. She didn't: I didn't see anything. So I don't believe she went into the great hall at all.'

'So she went another way. What else is down in that direction?'

'The great hall is right at the heart of Doorbraak. If, instead of heading down the approach tunnel, a dragon decided to take a different corridor – well you could go pretty much anywhere in the complex.'

'So that doesn't help narrow it down. What other clues are there?'

'Well, Hellfire's room was untouched. If she had somehow decided to leave home – to become a flyaway, as the authorities suggest she did – then she would have taken some items with her. Her diary scroll, for instance. Her lucky elephant foot. Her favourite clawboots. She would not have left without these things.'

'How can you be so sure?'

'Because she and I were very close. These things had

immense sentimental value to her. You know how young dragons are. Now, I have given this a lot of thought, over the years. Of course it's possible to imagine circumstances in which she was forced to leave them – if she were kidnapped, say – or in which she might deliberately leave them, to create a false trail. Both things are possible. But after centuries of reflection I am convinced that neither is likely. The probability is massively on the other side: that she is dead.'

Käal coughed up a piece of sticky brimstone, and spat it discreetly into the spittoon. It landed in the copper concavity with a sonorous chime, like a bell. 'Forgive me Mr Vagner. I need to get this clear in my head before I can begin trying to solve it. You are convinced that Hellfire was murdered?'

'I am.'

'That is, in part at least, because you're convinced she couldn't have sneaked off the island?'

'Absolutely not.'

'She couldn't be hiding on Doorbraak somewhere? It's quite an extensive place.'

'For three hundred years? Come, Käal, show some dragonsense.'

'What you're saying is: you have had the place searched?'

'Over and over again. Now, there are two halves to this floating paradise, the top part, and the bottom. The top half, as you saw when you flew in, is spacious gardens, animal pens, large marble halls – the main hoardroom, of course, from where we run Vagner

Industries, and smaller hoardrooms for the junior executives to practise sitting on their hoards. All of this has been searched. Every room, every open space. I personally sifted through every item in the main Vagner hoard. Can you imagine it? I was so tortured by not knowing what had happened to my grandniece that I wondered if she had burrowed into the family hoard, and was lying doggo underneath all that gold.'

'She wasn't there?'

'No.'

'And was anything missing?'

Old Vagner looked up abruptly, his yellow eyeslit narrowing even further, like the last moment before a total solar eclipse. 'One trivial item. Nothing important.'

Käal was instantly struck by this reply. For the first time in his dealings with the old snake, he felt the whiff of cold and rainy *distrust*. No dragon would blithely talk about losing 'one trivial item' from his or her hoard – for no part of a hoard was trivial, from the biggest helmet, nugget and ingot right down to that last extracted gold hömös tooth, or those microscopic lower-case letter 't's so many of the apes had liked wearing, for unfathomable reasons, about their necks. To search one's entire hoard (and the Vagner hoard, accumulated over millennia and rarely spent from) must have been an immense undertaking. But once it *was* searched, any dragon discovering that he had been robbed of even the smallest piece would fly into a blasting, fiery rage. And not rest until he got it back. 'Did you look for these missing items?' Käal asked.

'I can see you're surprised,' said old Vagner, in a

weary voice. 'I understand why, too. I comprehend the vigour of youth, when your energies are dedicated to assembling your hoard. And don't make the mistake of thinking I don't prize it. In the normal course of things, if I had missed a golden cup or a golden candlestick, something of that nature, then of course I would have raged about searching for it and scorching everything to cinders. But try to understand: I have lost something far more precious than gold. I have lost my grandniece. That was all I could think about.'

Käal supposed he could believe this. 'OK,' he said. 'So you've searched the upper part of Doorbraak. What about the lower?'

'Indeed,' said Old Vagner, nodding ponderously. 'Hellfire was never much of a digging dragon. Her blood was too *aristocratic*, you understand – too aetherial. She yearned for the high, empty spaces where the fire of the sunlight is purest. True to her lineage, you see. But – naturally I considered the possibility that, to escape some unknown threat, she might have tossed her dignity to the rain and burrowed underground like a common *Möle*. It's unlikely, but I had to consider it.'

'Would she have to dig?' asked Käal. 'Aren't there tunnels?'

'Naturally there are. And naturally we searched them – I myself squeezed myself through them, though their soil was crumbly and smelt horribly of moisture. But I searched them anyway – many times, so desperate was I to glean any facts that might uncover my grandniece's fate. When that proved bootless I searched into the great mass of soil itself.'

'What? You did what?'

'Yes, into the very soil itself.'

'No – not that. What did you say, just before that?'

This wrongfooted Vagner slightly. 'What?'

'Just before the stuff about the soil?'

'So desperate was I to glean . . .' the old dragon offered.

'No – no – after that.'

'Erm . . . to glean any facts that might uncover my . . .'

'No,' said Käal. 'I said *after* that.'

'That bit *came* after that! I mean, that was the bit that came after the other bit.'

'In that case, what did you say *after* the bit that came after the other bit?'

'Wait,' said Vagner. 'I'm confused. What do you want me to do?'

'If you'll be so kind, I'd like you to repeat the, eh, the,' said Käal, losing the thread himself a little. 'The bit you said immediately before the last bit you said, but after all the other stuff you said previously, that you've just repeated to me, and which you described as the bit after the came after that other bit.'

Vagner stared gloomily at him for a long time. 'My brain is not,' he said, 'as lively as once it was. Perhaps if I repeated the whole thing?'

'OK,' said Käal.

'I searched them anyway,' old Vagner said, in a beaten-down voice. 'Many times so desperate was I to glean any facts that might uncover my grandniece's fate and when that proved bootless I . . .'

'There!' said Käal. 'That's it! That's the bit I wanted you to repeat before, er, the last bit but after the bit that you initially repeated with the, er . . .'

'What?'

'The boot bit.'

' "Bootless"? said Vagner. 'That?'

'Yes.'

'Why? Is it important?' He stuck his long neck out and brought his big snout nearer Käal's. 'Is it *a clue*?'

'No. I just don't know what it means.'

Old Vagner surveyed him, and very slowly drew his neck back in. Speaking slowly, he said: 'You don't know what—'

'I don't know what it means. No.'

'It means *fruitless*. It means that *nothing came of it.*'

'Oh!' said Käal. 'Ah. Good. I understand now. Please, continue.'

'You'd never heard that word before?'

'No.'

'It's a very,' said Helltrik, 'common word.'

'I'm sure it is. Please, go on with your story.'

'Well,' said Vagner, collecting himself. 'I was telling you how I had the soil searched, very thoroughly, by . . .'

'Why *boot*, though?' Käal interrupted.

'What?'

'I understand *fruitless*, because a tree comes into fruit, and if that isn't, er, fulfilled then the tree is fruitless. But why boot?'

'It's just a—'

'Is it a cobbling metaphor?'

73

'It's just a word! It's just a turn of phrase! Can we please leave it?'

Käal opened his eyes very wide. 'I'm curious,' he said, in a hurt voice, his nostril smoke turning sepia. 'That's all. It's why you want to hire me, isn't it? My curiosity?'

'Yes, my dear Käal, of course,' said old Vagner. 'I only meant that it does not seem to me relevant to . . .'

'No-no,' said Käal, waving his right forearm, 'please, go on. Please carry on. Don't mind me.'

Vagner harrumphed a little. 'I was only going to explain how I searched the soil.'

'How?'

'I hired earthwyrms.'

'Oh!' Käal was surprised.

'Perhaps you are prejudiced against them?'

'Prejudiced?' said Käal. 'Not, not at all. I knew several earthwyrms when I was at universerpenty. But they are a little . . . oh I don't know . . .'

'Slimy?'

'Well – yes.'

'I agree.'

'I mean, that's a neutral observation. It's empirically the case. Earthwyrms are a little . . .'

'Slimy yes. But who better to search the great mass of soil upon which Doorbraak is built? I hired half a dozen, the younger no bigger than a Salamander, the oldest longer and more muscled than I am myself. They spent a year and a half going through the soil. Nothing.'

'Nothing at all?'

'Earthwyrms can tell when soil has previously been disturbed, and when it is virgin and undug. It's a sort of sonar they possess. Hellfire was not in any of the old tunnels, and nobody had dug any new tunnels.'

'So, she's not in the top half and not in the bottom half,' said Käal, ruminatively. 'So she must be off Doorbraak.'

Old Vagner looked at him.

'That's logical!' he said.

'So if she's not on Doorbraak – then where is she?'

'I believe her body was smuggled off the island at a later stage,' said Helltrik. 'That afternoon, when we realized Hellfire was missing, we did look through the castle – although the *extensive* searches I talked about, they didn't happen until many days later. So, conceivably, it would have been possible for somebody to murder Hellfire, hide her body somewhere – in the subterranean tunnels, maybe – and then, when the drizzle had stopped, to smuggle the corpse off the island.'

'Smuggle how? The eyes above and below were still functioning, weren't they?'

'Indeed. But there are two ways. One would be to smuggle the body inside a cargo transport. We have deliveries by Skylligator, for instance, once a week. The top eye might see the Beast fly in, and fly away again, without seeing what was *inside* it.'

'And the other way?'

'One of the first things the authorities did, when we notified them of Hellfire's disappearance, was to consult the eyes. A police dragon flew up to check the top eye. That took, I suppose, an hour or so. It's not possible to go through all that visual data in an instant. Plop out your own eye, stick in the surveillance eye . . .

depending on how rapidly your brain works, it would probably be closer to two hours. Obviously, the eye can't record any new data when it's being checked like that. Maybe the murderer flew off with Hellfire's body whilst that procedure was under way.'

'Right under the noses of the police? I mean – literally under their noses.'

'Literally under their entire bodies.'

'Yes. Sounds risky to me.'

'I agree,' said Helltrik. 'But when you have eliminated the improbable, whatever remains, however impossible, must be the truth.' A look of uncertainty flickered across Old Vagner's face. 'I think I've got that right.'

Käal thought about this. 'So, this beautiful young dragon was murdered here – by one of her own family.'

'It must be. The only dragons here were her own family!'

'What about servants?'

'Well, none of them are dragons, of course,' said Vagner. 'Most are lowly wyrms. I don't see how a fire-drake, say, *could* murder a dragon. I don't see how they'd even go about it.'

'Well that's an issue, isn't it?' said Käal. 'How *was* she murdered? Even if she was young, it's not easy to imagine how it could have happened. I agree: no lowly wyrm would be able to penetrate her scales. So what does that leave? Poison? Drowning?'

'The last is out of the question,' said Vagner, firmly. 'There's no open water on Doorbraak at all. There's hardly enough water to moisten a Dry-Wipe.'

'So, poison? Why would Hellfire be so foolish as to

ingest anything? And wouldn't her death cries have resonated throughout the whole island?'

'You would think so. Yet I know she is dead.'

'How?'

'Because the killer sent me her tongue.'

'Ugh! Her *tongue*?'

'Cut from her mouth.'

'How do you know it was hers?'

'When she was a little Salamander she did something foolish. She played a dare with some girlfriends. They urged her to lick an ice cream. You know the sorts of foolish things kids get up to. So she licked the ice cream, and of course her tongue was scarred by the substance. It was unmistakable: a blotchy discoloration on the right fork of the tongue's end. That's how I know the tongue was hers.'

'Why would the killer send you her severed tongue?'

'I assume he was gloating.'

' "He"?'

'Or she. But there's more.'

'What?'

'Every year, on the anniversary of Hellfire's death I have received a new tongue.'

'You have received a *new tongue*?'

'In the post.'

'A new *severed* tongue?'

'Well, yes. How could I receive a tongue through the post, if it were still attached to a dragon?'

'I suppose: somebody would have to mail you the entire dragon.'

'That's,' said Helltrik, 'not what has been happening.

Just severed tongues, one a year, every year, since her disappearance.'

'Every year? That must be – what, three hundred tongues?'

'That's right.'

'Good Woden, that's horrific! What have you done with them all?'

'I've sewed them together to make a waistcoat,' snapped Vagner. 'Idiot! I've given them all to the authorities, of course. What did you think?'

'I'm sorry, I'm just a little startled by all this,' said Käal. 'Why cut out her tongue? Why send it to you? And then – three hundred other tongues! It's positively apean in its cruelty! None of it makes any sense.'

'It *is* a great mystery,' said Vagner. 'It has dominated my life for centuries. That's why I've approached you.'

Käal made up his mind. Rising from the couch, and pulling his tail from the (comfortably larger) slot at the back. 'I'll solve it, Monster Vagner. I'll write your Saga, and get to the bottom of your mystery. It *is* intriguing. We have a murder victim: but we don't know why she was murdered, or how, or by whom, or even *if*. An enterprising dragon could write a Whodunnit, a Howdunnit, a Whomdunnit or an Ifdunnit! I don't believe anyone's ever written an Ifdunnit before! It's a real three-smoke problem.'

'I'm delighted you feel you can agree to take the case!' said Vagner, rising similarly. 'I'll have a servant show you to your room in the castle. In due course you'll meet those members of the family who live here. You'll begin to understand the sorts of pressures under which poor

Hellfire lived – the moral contagion that has polluted the entire clan.'

Käal made his way towards the exit. He stopped at the threshold. 'There's one other thing.'

'Yes?'

'Your theory is that Hellfire was murdered here on the island that day, three centuries ago; and then her body was smuggled out some days or perhaps even weeks later. Yes?'

'Yes.'

'And I've agreed to investigate her murder.'

'Yes.'

'Well – what if it turns out that she's not dead after all? That there is no murder to investigate, that Hellfire simply hid for a day and then smuggled herself, alone or with an accomplice, off the island? If the tongue was a red herring, to throw you off the scent?'

'What are you saying?' Vagner asked.

'Well – you're offering a fabulous treasure for me to solve a murder. But what if there *isn't* a murder? What if she's been living a new life, under a pseudonym, in some faraway place like Brazenilia, or Hostileia?'

'Well,' said Vagner, scratching in between his front teeth with his talons. 'That would be . . . what's the word?'

'Anticlimactic?'

'Yes, exactly. That's the word. That would be a big anticlimax.'

'It *would* be rather disappointing,' said Käal, 'wouldn't it, though?'

'It would. Disappointing is exactly the *mot juste*. I might even feel . . . *cheated* . . .'

'Cheated, exactly,' Käal agreed.

'. . . by such a resolution to my lifelong, centuries-old mystery. For that reason, if for none others, I find it hard to believe that such a . . . how could we call it? *Facile* solution?'

'Facile, yes,' said Käal.

'Nothing so crude or, yes, so facile would deserve the reputation of a great mystery,' said Vagner, in a decisive voice. 'Do not fear, young Mon. Brimstön. The mystery will be a good deal more convoluted and surprising than just that she is living in Hostileia under an assumed name.'

Käal, nodding, left the room.

6

The fact that Lizbreath Salamander needed money meant that having access to her inheritance would have been very useful for her. But more than that: the fact that Burnblast had access to her hoard – her rightful hoard! – and she did not filled her with the resentment that attends injustice. Chronologically old enough to be counted a dragon, the frustratingness of the situation rankled. She felt the rankle from nostril to ankle: that was how wide-ranging a rankle it was. Frustration, I meant. Not 'frustratingness'. That's not even a word.

Anyway.

There is an old dragon proverb: 'Don't get mad – get even *more mad than your enemy.'* It's one of many dragon proverbs that imply that the true route to satisfaction lies in giving oneself over wholly to a towering, flaming rage.

That worked for Lizbreath.

Not that she was skint, exactly. She worked for a number of Financial and News Sagas, who made use of her extraordinary talent for *finding things out* – a talent that very few dragons could match. She found stuff *out*; the Sagas stuffed her finds *in*; their circulation rose and everybody was happy. But it was pin money – gold pins, naturally, but small ones. It would take many hundreds of thousands of them to even begin to resemble a reasonable-sized hoard. Plus, a hoard made entirely of gold pins would not be terribly comfortable to lie upon, even for a dragon. Lizbreath didn't try. She kept the pins in a lockable silver-coloured box, in her chichi Starkhelm apartment. They might have paid her mortifyingage, and kept her in fresh mutton (she really didn't eat very much), but it wasn't enough to buy the various gadgets and tech-toys that filled her home. She had a great many of these, but she still needed more. And that meant crawling on her belly and abasing herself before horrible Burnblast.

The situation was so intolerable that she brooded over what to do. A different sort of dragon might have contemplated approaching the authorities – perhaps even petitioning the Dragonlords themselves – and complaining about her Guardian's behaviour, demanding legal recognition as a dragon and access to her inheritance. And although every dragon regarded Lizbreath as fruityloops and *non-combust-mentis*, nobody could deny that she was high-born, and that meant that approaching the Dragonlords was within her rights. But that was not Lizbreath's way.

The truth was she despised almost all older male dragons. Since dragon society was a rigid hierarchy, in which political, social and cultural power was in the talons of a group of absolutist elderly dragons – almost all of them male – that fact meant that she was bound to be a misfit. She didn't lose any sleep over this. If the older male dragons who ran so much of society just left her alone, she would have been perfectly content. But her experience was that they didn't. Take Burnblast, as an example. It was hard to imagine a more senior, respectable and widely respected fellow. To all intents and purposes he was the very model of draconic rectitude and elevation. But the truth was that not only did he withhold Lizbreath's money from her, he used his power over her to force her to listen to his talk of the most disgusting and foul sexual perversions! If respectable dragon society found out about that side of his personality, he would be shamed – perhaps even chased from his position of legal responsibility.

Lizbreath liked the sound of *that*.

She hatched an idea. Ideas, you see, are hatched – like dragons. And like dragons, ideas can *burn*. But unlike dragons, ideas are not four-legged scaled creatures that weigh anything from one to forty tonnes. The analogy is not precise in every particular.

She had a commission from the *Hrothfjngleraxlotls Saga* to supply data concerning the seasonal alterations in polar ice – one of their senior Saga writers was composing a piece of speculative Saga Fiction, a world in which all the oceans were covered in ice, drowning was a thing of the past and Dragontopia a possibility. But that wasn't going to take her very long. In point of fact, she could do it without leaving her apartment, thanks to her collection of high-tech devices. By lunchtime she had completed it, scrolled the results, and sent it by raven to the *Hrothfjngleraxlotls* office. That left the rest of the day free to plan her revenge.

She flew to the fashionable Lundalligatar district, to a discreet cave where one of her friends ran a shop.

'Fang,' she said. 'I need to buy an ear. But a really *small* one.'

Fang was a stout, black-green dragon, not much older than Lizbreath herself. His snout was short and almost retroussé, his two front teeth unusually long, sharp and a creamy yellow (hence his nickname), but the thing that struck you most forcefully upon meeting him for the first time were his piercings. He appeared to have had half a dozen or more metal bolts inserted *through* his scales: three in his right ear, one through each nostril and another in at the corner of his mouth. It had to be an illusion, of course, for after all, there is literally nothing in the world that can pierce dragon scales. But it was a very *convincing* illusion. Visitors would peer closely at them, and try to work out how it was done. The most popular theory was that Fang had fashioned a series of elaborate clip-on bolts, and then applied them to areas on his body where he happened to have naturally occurring little indentations in his scales, such that they really looked like they went all the way through. A sizeable minority believed that magic was involved. If asked, Fang would snort grey-smoke and evade the question.

Lizbreath knew how it was done, of course. She just wasn't telling anybody.

'A small one?' Fang repeated.

'I need to eavesdrop on somebody. I don't want them to know that I'm carrying an ear.'

Fang knew better than to pry into Lizbreath's affairs. 'I can do that,' he said. 'Though, obviously, a smaller ear is less good at, you know, hearing stuff than a proper-sized one.'

'Just so long as it can record what an elderly dragon says, so that others can hear it at a later date.'

'Oho!' said Fang. 'I see. In that case, I shall make a suggestion. Take an eye too.'

'Do I need an eye?'

'With just an ear,' said Fang, 'it can be difficult pinning the words on a particular individual. They can deny that it was them speaking; or say that it's a vocal impersonator. But if you have both the words in the ear, *and* the sight in the eye – well, even the most sceptical policedragon is liable to be convinced.'

'I shan't be going to any policedragons,' said Lizbreath.

'Of course you won't,' said Fang. 'But you see what I mean.' He went to the back of his cave, where a huge pile of metal items, of all sizes and shapes, was heaped in seeming abandon. 'Here,' he said, throwing a small item to Lizbreath. 'There's your miniature ear. I've got a miniature eye back here somewhere too. You going to pay me in pins again?'

'Pins are legal tender,' she noted, turning over the tiny ear in her hands. It was a weirdly rounded shape, flesh set in a silver-coloured metal rim. 'It doesn't look like an ear.'

'It's not dragon,' said Fang. 'Ah – here's the eye.'

'What's this metal it's set in?'

'Chrome.'

'Is it what I *think* it is?' Lizbreath asked, holding it close against her eye. There was a funny little whorl, or curling ridge, in the middle of it. 'That shape?'

'Sure. Pins may be legal tender, but they're fiddly.'

'They're gold. Stop complaining.'

'Here's the eye,' said Fang, coming to the front again. He handed it over: it was tiny. It was, at least, eye-shaped; properly globular, although it was a bleached white colour, and the pupil was oddly squashed top and bottom; almost a circle. 'How do they work?'

'There's no need to sound so suspicious,' said Fang. 'You're the one who came to *me* demanding miniaturized technology.'

'They're perfect,' Lizbreath clarified. 'I was just asking from a practical perspective.'

'The ear records when you twist the metal rim. Then when you want to listen to what's been overheard, you just twist the rim the other way, and pop it inside your ear –like this.' Fang demonstrated, and the little device went into the gaping flap of his ear. 'You need to be sure you don't lose it, is all.'

'And the eye?'

'That's a little trickier. With a regular eye, you pop your own eyeball out and replace it with the device, yeah? Well, with this one you don't need to have your own eyeball dangling on your cheek like a conker on a string. You just fit this miniature eye into your tear duct . . . like . . . this.' He balanced the little globe on the top of his talon, brought it gingerly up towards his own eye, and, grimacing, slid it into the duct. Then he made a series of bizarre faces: opening his mouth very wide, blinking like an epileptic, shutting his mouth, and going 'uurrrghh!'

'You all right?'

'It takes a little getting used to, that's all. But once it's in you'd hardly know it was there.'

'Your eyes are watering.'

'Oh, hardly at all.'

Fat drops of hot fluid were banging noisily onto the granite floor of the cave, burning craters in the solid rock and sending up reeky clouds of acid-smoke. 'I'll just,' said Fang, 'get it out of there.'

Lizbreath sat back on her hindlegs and folded her forearms as Fang rummaged around in the corner of his eye with his talons. 'Nearly,' he said, several time. 'Oh! Ah! Uh!'

'Do you want me to have a look?' she offered.

'No! It's OK! I've nearly got it, with a . . . uh! Oh! *There* it is! Easy – see?' Fang held the object he had retrieved from his eye in front of his other eye. 'No,' he said, matter of factly. 'That's not it. That's a ripped out portion of my cornea. Try again!' Back in went the talon, and after a five-minute rummage, he finally brought out the miniaturized eye.

'Easy,' said Lizbreath, dubiously.

'You might need to practise it a little,' looking pained and blinking rapidly. 'But you did ask for miniature!'

'Thanks.'

As she flew away from Fang's cave she went through it in her head. Her plan was, she hoped, straightforward. The sunlight was hard as chalk; the air as hot and blue as smoke. At the very top of the sky, a passing Skyl-ligator on its way to some far-distant destination drew a white vapour trail after it. It looked as though it was cutting a white slit in the sky. Closer to the horizon, the sky was cluttered with pellet-hard white clouds. As she flew east, the cellophane shimmer of the ocean came more and more into view. The flexing and warping of light into life, the poisonous cold of the sea somehow, magically, transformed into brightness and flame.

Burnblast had told her to come to his office on Cinderday, to collect her money. That in itself was suspicious. Nobody conducted business on Cinderday, the dead ashes of the week. But Lizbreath had an inkling of why Burnblast had specified that day. Or if not quite an inkling, then certainly a pencilling. She figured he wanted to *talk dirty* to her again, the way he had done before. Him on his huge pile of gold (a good chunk of which was rightfully *her* gold!), her on the ground below him, and nobody else about in the office – the ideal environment to indulge his disgusting peccadillo. Lizbreath did not relish having to sit and listen once again to him going on and on about *oral sex*, and who-knows-what other repellent sexual perversions. But, she told herself, she could endure it one more time.

Plan: go to Burnblast's cavern, and act the meek little Salamander whilst he slobbered over her with his bizarre fantasies. But record everything in the miniature ear she had just bought! At a later date, compel his obedience to her with the threat of blackmail. After that things would change: after that the tables would be turned. Burnblast would no longer have the power over Lizbreath Salamander.

She wouldn't torment him *too* much, she decided, alighting outside her apartment. She wasn't a sadist. And blackmail wasn't the right word either, not exactly.

A blackmailer extorts what doesn't belong to him; uses his or her leverage to *steal* from their victim. Lizbreath had no intention of stealing anything. She wanted two things only, and they both – really – belonged to her already. She wanted her gold. And she wanted to be *left alone*.

Cinderday came round, and she flew over to Burnblast's office with a certain sense of trepidation. It was more than trepidation, in fact. What she felt was more like quadripidation, perhaps even quintipidation. But one thing that Lizbreath's life on the margins of dragon society had taught her was how to hide her inner uncertainty. She had the miniaturized eye and ear wedged unobtrusively in at the cracks between two of the scales on her rump. Only the most minute exam-ination would have discovered them there, and Liz-breath had no intention of letting Burnblast undertake any such exam.

She took one last look about the street – almost entirely deserted, of course – took a deep breath, and blew out a blast of scorching, white-flickering flame. Then she ducked in at the door and slunk down the stairway.

As she turned left at the bottom, through the empty reception and unmanned desk, she had a sudden access of doubt. What if Burnblast *did* want to inspect her rump? What if he wanted to do more than just talk dirty to her? What if he wanted to have sexual relations with her?

That made her stop.

Knowing the filthy old brute, it was certainly possible. She rebuked herself, inwardly, for not considering the idea earlier.

Lizbreath was no virgin-dragon, of course; and the thought of having sex with Burnblast – whilst certainly not a *pleasant* one – was not entirely intolerable to her. She could just turn around and fly away, of course; but that would leave her stuck in the same horrid situation as before. Maybe he'd want to talk dirty, or maybe he'd want to climb on her back. If he did either thing, she could bear it, and she would come away with the incident recorded by both eye and ear. Indeed, if Burnblast took advantage of his legal status as her protector to shag her, she would have much better material with which to blackmail him.

She decided to risk it.

Her only residual worry was that she had placed the eye and the ear in the wrong place about her body. If the old boy was going to mount her, then he might conceivably dislodge or perhaps even crush the technology. She paused by the cavern entrance just long enough to pick the two tiny items from her rump and fit them in between two neck-scales. She was ready.

In she went.

As soon as she entered Burnblast's cavern, though, she could tell something was wrong. For one thing, Burnblast was not alone. As she came through, the granite door to the chamber was slammed behind her by a fat, brutish-looking male with deep purple scales and eyes of piercing, malicious redness.

Burnblast himself was not lying on his hoard. Instead he was on the far side of his cavern, standing on his hind legs and holding in his forehands a large, angular piece of ironmongery. 'Lizbreath, my dear,' he boomed. 'Delightful to see you again.'

'Who's this?' Lizbreath demanded, spinning about to face the nasty-looking male.

'This? This is Human, my dear.'

' "Human"?'

'An associate of mine. Not his actual name, of course; a nickname. And you can be assured he didn't acquire a nickname like *that* by behaving with *honour*, *restraint* or *kindness*.' Burnblast chuckled, a hideous cooing-clucking sound, like waves in Satan's lake of liquid ice lapping at the pier-legs of Hell itself.

Lizbreath's heart started galloping in her breast. This was not what she had anticipated. It required a conscious act of will to keep her outward composure.

Human approached her, and spread his ugly face in a wide grin. 'Guardian,' Lizbreath said, over her shoulder. 'I've only come for my allowance – that's all.'

'In good time, my dear,' said Burnblast, walking over towards her awkwardly on his hind legs. As he approached, she got a better view of what he was holding in his forehands: a pair of large metal pincers linked by an iron chain to a large, half-folded oval of iron. It looked rather like a mantrap. 'In good time. First you and I will work on our *friendship*.'

There's a dragon expression: *too close to the water*. That was, metaphorically speaking, where Lizbreath found herself now. Her whole blackmail plan was starting to look laughably naive. She scuttled round to face the massive bulk of her Legal Guardian, and then, hearing Human moving behind her, leapt about again to face him.

'Oh, *she's* a fidget,' said Human. His voice was low and gravelly even for a dragon.

'*Full* of energy, my lovely Lizbreath,' said Burnblast. 'It's a mistake to judge by appearances, don't you think?'

'Oh!' said Human, his voice rumbling and rolling about the roof. '*Very* true.'

'If you judged little Lizbreath by appearances,' said Burnblast, tapping the two weighty iron clamps against one another to make a dull, clunking sound, 'then you'd think she was a simple-minded, immature little Salamander. You'd think lead wouldn't melt in her mouth. But that's not the truth.'

'No?' grinned Human.

'Stop this charade,' said Lizbreath, swinging her head from the one male to the other. But there was no force in her words; it trembled – she was deeply afraid, and it showed in her voice.

'For example, you'd never guess what she and I discussed the last time she was here,' said Burnblast.

'Go on,' said Human.

'Oral sex!' said her Guardian.

'No! Shock-*ing*! Dirty girl!' Human's voice was deadpan. It was beyond deadpan. It was zombiepan.

'Perverted, no?' chucked Burnblast. 'You'd never guess it – to look at her. She looks so innocent, on the outside. Although she has painted the picture of a human girl on her back.'

'It's not *painted*,' snapped Lizbreath.

'Such a pretty dragon,' drawled Human. 'To have such a creepy thing painted on her!'

'Stop,' said Lizbreath backing away. Human moved easily to get behind her again. 'I don't want my gold,' she said, unable to keep the desperation out of her voice. 'I just want to go – I'll leave and not bother you again.'

'Not until we have repaired our friendship, my dear,' said Burnblast. 'I feel – I have been remiss. You are my ward, after all. But our relationship has become chillier, of late.'

Lizbreath felt a spurt of warmth in her breast. Cowering wasn't going to do her any good, after all. 'That's because you've stolen my rightful gold, you hideous old sack of damp!'

The two male dragons laughed throatily at this. 'Oho,' said Human. 'Do you bite your mother with that mouth, little girl?'

'A little *fire* in her breast,' said Burnblast. 'I *like* that. And now, my dear, it's time for us to become better acquainted. The last time we spoke, you seemed very interested in oral sex. Let me show you how that is done.'

'No!' she cried.

But Human had already pounced, and landed on her back. He was stocky and heavy, and squashed her easily against the floor. Both his hind- and forelegs were immensely muscled. His back legs grabbed *her* back legs, strong claws clamping her left and right thigh. His forelegs seized her wings, and pulled them hard backwards, to stop her spreading them. It was a very painful heave, wrenching the socket and scraping the leathern membrane hard.

But that wasn't the worst. Burnblast, with a foul smirk upon his face, approached with his strange equipment. He danced ponderously to the right of her head, and pressed down with one hindleg, putting pressure exactly between her eyes. Then he heaved her mouth open with his right forearm, and rammed the odd-shaped iron ring in behind her teeth with his left. It forced her mouth open: with it digging painfully into the tissue of her gums she couldn't bite down or close. She was as surprised as she was physically hurt by this, but there was nothing she could do. She tried shaking her head from side to side, but Burnblast's foot was too strong to dislodge. Then, the worst got even worse. He reached down *inside* her mouth with his right forearm. She got one quick blast of white fire out, and he grimaced briefly, but then she felt something unyielding clamp round the flesh of first one and then the other fire duct.

It was deeply horrible: a combination of intense physical discomfort and a kind of existential horror. Burnblast pulled his arm out of her mouth, and came round to the front. He was gloating. 'There you are, my dear,' he said. 'Not so bad, when they're in, I daresay.'

Lizbreath couldn't speak. She drew a breath and tried to send a wave of incandescent fire straight in his face. His scales were so thick, and old, he would probably have barely even felt it. But it would at least have melted this ridiculous ironwork clamping her mouth open. But, push with her flame-diaphragm hard as she could, no fire came out. The ducts were completely closed off.

Behind her, she heard Human's grumbly laugh. 'She's trying to puff the clamps off, boss.'

'I'm sure she is,' said Burnblast, settling back on his hindlegs. 'It'll do no good.' From the hard exterior sheath under his belly he brought out the pinky-purple exposed flesh of male member. 'Now, my dear,' he said. 'The last time we spoke you raised a number of perfectly valid objections to the very idea of oral sex. And now I find myself in the position where I can demonstrate how it is possible to use the mouth as a copulatory site *without* getting anything more than a pleasant tingling in my tender member. How widely you have opened your eyes, my dear! All the better, I suppose, to . . . *see* . . . this . . . with . . .'

And so he advanced upon her, his swag-belly wobbling and his organ coming, horribly, closer and closer to her face.

The ordeal lasted an hour. On more than one occasion during it, Lizbreath really thought she was going to suffocate to death. The gagging was profoundly horrible. When Burnblast had finally finished, and removed himself, she gasped and sputtered, sucking air in her lungs and feeling her oesophagus pulse as if her whole stomach, lining and all, were about to come splurging out. Burnblast chuckled to himself, padded about his cavern.

'I think she liked it, boss,' said Human.

'I think she did,' mewed Burnblast. 'Oh I think she did.'

Then the weight on her back was released, as Human jumped through the air with a brief thresh of wings, the sound of a flag fluttering in a strong breeze. He was directly in front of her. Lizbreath felt the appalling, plunging fear that Burnblast's henchdragon was now about to enact the same violation upon her as his boss. But, for whatever reason (either because it wouldn't have been appropriate to trespass upon the senior dragon's object of pleasure, or perhaps simply because he didn't like the thought of it) he didn't. Instead he reached into her mouth, released the clamps, and pulled them out. The iron brace followed, and Lizbreath was able to close her traumatized mouth.

She coughed, gagged, coughed, and drew a long painful trail of hot phlegm out of her throat. But she couldn't flame: the fire ducts had swollen agonizingly under their brutal treatment. They had effectively sealed themselves.

She quailed, and backed against the wall: completely cowed. Burnblast had climbed up upon his hoard. 'I'm going to give you a banker's scroll, my dear,' he said, 'for your allowance. Drawn on my personal hoard. You'll find no difficulty in cashing it. *My* name is good for it.'

'I'd say she's earned her money, boss,' chuckled Human, his wicked tongue slopping wetly over the fence of his lower teeth.

'Oh, indeed,' said Burnblast. 'Here.' The scroll fluttered down through the air, and – despising herself –

Lizbreath reached out and seized it. She couldn't say anything; her mouth was too raw and painful to make any articulate sound at all.

Human went over to the granite door and swung it open. Seeing the exit clear, Lizbreath scuttled towards it. But before she got to it, Burnblast leapt into the air and swooped down upon her, pinning her under his weight.

'I think we have gone *some* way,' he whispered, directly into her ear, 'to repairing the breach in our relationship, my dear. You will come back here the same time next week. Don't say anything – I'd be surprised if you *could* say anything! Just nod your head.'

Feeling abject, in great pain, and brimming with self-loathing at her cravenness, Lizbreath nodded.

'You *will* come next week. We won't need Human. I think we'd both welcome a little privacy. Of course, if you make trouble I'll call him through. But I don't think you will make trouble, will you. Because I think you have learned your lesson – *haven't* you?'

Again: a shallow nod.

'Very good. If you apply the clamps yourself, the flesh of the fire duct is less . . . inflamed afterwards.'

The shudder went through Lizbreath's soul. Horror, and despair, and rage, and impotence – a hideous emulsion of feelings – filled her so completely that she couldn't even manage a nod.

'If you continue to please me, my dear,' said Burnblast, stepping off Lizbreath's back, 'you'll discover I'm a very useful ally. *Personally* friendly with two of the

Dragonlords. With my help, you should have no difficulty in reintegrating yourself into dragon society.'

But Lizbreath had seized the moment. She scuttled through the open door and rushed up the stairs to the bright light outside.

7

Käal was shown to his chambers by a slender firedrake of indeterminate age. 'Anything you need,' croaked the creature. 'Let me know.'

'I'd like to take a look around,' he said.

'Go anywhere you like,' said the firedrake, fluttering around Käal's head in a tight circle. 'Though I'd advise against poking around the chamber with my master's hoard in. Without his express permission, that is. It's right at the centre of the castle.'

'Naturally!' The idea of *poking around* another dragon's hoard was anathema to Käal. He wasn't a thief!

'And below that,' the firedrake said, 'is the Vagner vault. Millennia of old Vagners are interred there, Nobody's allowed inside. Apart from that, you can look anywhere you like.'

Käal flew out and made a general circuit of the whole island. He had to admit that Doorbraak was a beautiful place. The central castle sent graceful spires high into the sky, like tapering flames gorgonized into solidity. The high sunlight drew gleaming vertical bars of light along the pink and white stone towers. Indeed, the quality of light at this altitude was something special. Käal wandered through the impeccably kept gardens to the rim of the island and looked down. Clouds below, like bolts of close-packed cloth, reflected the sunlight up to meet the fall of natural light from above. It gave the air an unusual vividness, like a heightened reality.

He landed by the perimeter wall, and had a look down.

'Referendum,' said somebody, unpleasantly, right into Käal's ear.

Käal leapt up onto his back limbs in fright. 'Aargh!' he squealed.

Standing beside him was a very broken-down, disreputable-looking elderly dragon. He was old: that much was obvious from the length of his talons and teeth, and the tatterdemalion nature of his half-folded wings. But he was neither broad nor tall, and looked, if anything, rather shrivelled. Käal felt an instinctive, gut-level revulsion.

'Sometimes,' this newcomer said, in a voice so grating it could have turned a hundredweight of cheese into shards merely by singing at it, 'sometimes the thing yer looking for is right in front of ye. No?'

'You startled me,' said Käal, with rather undraconic wimpishness. Then, as anger flowed in to fill the space hollowed out in his mind by fear, he added: 'I might have jumped right off the edge! What do you think you're playing at?'

'You're the Saga writer?' the newcomer snarled. 'I heard about you. BALLOT!'

'Käal Brimstön,' said Käal, ignoring this last incomprehensible disyllable. 'And your name is . . . ?'

'Ghastly,' snarled the dragon.

'Oh! I've heard about you. You're Helltrik's older brother.'

'So you heard about me, eh? I'll wager they told you I was re-turn-ING OFF-*CER* mad, did they?'

Käal looked down at this withered relic of a powerful nest, and made a conscious attempt to temper his revulsion with pity. 'Not mad, no. I did hear that,' he said, 'I did hear that you harboured political opinions considered by most right-thinking dragons to be . . .'

'Democracy,' said Ghastly, in a low voice.

'Well, not to put too fine a point on it, yes.'

'You don't know nothing *abaaahht* it!' Ghastly wailed, in evident distress, the hot phlegm in his throat thrumming and bubbling. He writhed like a streamer in the wind, curling and uncurling his long scrawny body upon the lawn. 'Electoral COLLEGE!' he yelled. 'I got a recognized medical *condition* checks-and-balances.'

'A recognized medical . . . what, a sickness?'

'I suffer from Democratourette's. Can't help myself. Can't stop myself shouting out offensive single trans FUR!' he wailed, 'ABLE! VOTE! *words* all hours of the day and night constituency party selection parameters.'

'Gosh,' said Käal. 'How extraordinary! And embarrassing – for you!'

Ghastly did not reply, as he was trying to stop himself from saying anything further by pressing his forelimbs down over the top of his snout.

'Am I to understand,' said Käal, with that sense of slow-dawning realization filtering through him. 'That you do not *actually* endorse the politics of democracy?'

Ghastly mumbled something inaudible, rocking from flank to flank upon the ground in front of him.

'That your condition has led people to the conclusion that . . .'

'Mmm!'

'I see.'

'Oh there's other reasons people don't like me,' said Ghastly, unclamping his mouth. 'There's some residual family prejudice grounded in the fact that I separate! *shun*! *of*! *church*! *and*! *state*! hate everybody and everybody hates me. They're all bastards. But that has nothing to do with political opinion. I have no political opinions. I hate everyone. I hate you, and I've only just met you. BICAMERALISM!'

'Oh,' said Käal. 'But why do you hate me? Why hate everyone?'

'Why? Oh, because they're all ba-*bundesrat*-ba-BASTards!' stuttered the withered old dragon. 'But don't fret. It's nothing personal. I know why you're here, at any rate.'

'You do?'

'My bastard brother. He wants you to solve Hellfire's disappearance.'

'Officially I'm here to write a Saga of the Vagner family.'

'Oh yers, oh *yes*! oh yerrrrs,' said Ghastly, with perhaps over-telegraphed sarcasm. 'I'm sure you *are*. Helltrik isn't the only member of our family obsessed with the poor girl's death, you know! We all are, in our way! We've all obsessed over it.'

'Including you, Mon. Ghastly?' Käal asked.

'Mr Speaker!' Ghastly yelped, in apparent assent.

'And does that mean you have a theory as to what happened?'

Instead of answering immediately, Ghastly wriggled over to the low wall at the garden's extreme edge. 'Long way down, ain't it?' he said.

'You think she went over the edge? You mean – she just flew away?'

'No, I think she was gerrymandering *killed*,' Ghastly barked. 'I think she had her wings nobbled, and then she was pushed over the edge.'

'There's an eye directly underneath the island,' Käal pointed out.

'OH!' exclaimed Ghastly, with enormous if murky significance.

'If she fell, then the lower eye would have seen and recorded the fact. Surely!'

'OH!' exclaimed Ghastly again, with even greater vehemence.

'Are you saying that the lower eye might have been . . . tampered with?' asked Käal. But the disgusting old dragon was already writhing his way over the blond grass, towards the castle. 'Wait,' Käal cried. But the dragon hissed nastily, and vanished into a thicket of rattling bushes with an insolent wiggle of his withered hind hips. Looking down, Käal noted with some distaste that the old fellow had left a trail of slime behind him.

8

Käal looked around some more, trying to make it look as though he were deploying his famous skills for *finding stuff out*. But since he had no idea how anybody actually found stuff out, this wasn't easy. To be truthful he quickly grew bored, and was happy for the distraction when he chanced upon an attractive female dragon of mature years.

He had half-leapt, half-flown up from the garden to the castle's main terrace – a beautiful expanse of dark pink marble, mottled with folds and curls of white like the best butchers' meat. From there, the view over the early evening sky was breathtaking, or flametaking: the clouds, crusted with gold and pearl, blushing deeper by the minute; the sun settling over the dusty deserts of the long-dead western realms – Emberland, Scorched-land – and acquiring a deep cough-sweet-coloured ruby redness.

It took Käal a little while to realize that he was wasn't alone. Another dragon was also admiring the view.

'Hello,' he said, twisting his head right around over his right wing. 'How do you do?'

'You're Käal,' said the female dragon, stalking seductively over. 'My uncle Helltrik told me about you.'

'I am indeed. And you are?'

'I'm Asheila.'

'So you're Helltrik's, um, sister's cousin's niece?'

'Helltrik is my uncle,' she said. 'Are the rumours true? Has Helltrik hired you to write a Saga chronicling our family?'

'That's right.'

'Hel-*lo* Saga,' she said, flirtatiously. 'So you'll be staying in the castle?'

'That's right.'

'I have an apartment in the castle myself – top floor, of course. In fact, I have the feeling that your rooms are just down the corridor from mine.'

'Really? I thought I was in the middle of the castle somewhere.'

'You were. But I've just had a word with my uncle,' said Asheila, with a little squeal. 'Aren't I naughty?'

'Naughty dragon!' said Käal.

The two dragons circled one another in what might – just – have passed for the polite pas-de-deux of well-bred beasts meeting for the first time. But no experienced dragon watcher would have been fooled. This was something more atavistic. This was a male and a female attempting simultaneously to sniff each other's rumps.

Käal could see straight away that Asheila was no spring chicken. Nor was she a summer chicken, nor even an autumn one. Indeed, there's no need to prolong this, she wasn't a chicken at all. She was a dragon. Let there be no mistake on that count. Nevertheless her non-chickenness was of an attractive, dragonly sort. But she had clearly *looked after* herself, that's my point. A regimen of continual smoking and lots of harsh ultra-violet light had hardened and firmed up her scales, and brought out a beguiling greeny-yellow sheen in their predominantly pale purple coloration. Her eyes were a witty bright pink, and her tongue, as it lolled lasciviously between her two main fangs, was an attractive liver colour.

'Is that *really* why you're here though?' Asheila said. 'Is it truly to write a Saga?'

'You think I have an ulterior motive?'

'Ulterior!' she said. 'That means *behind*, doesn't it? Get you! Oh, you're *saucy*, Mon. Brimstön, with your talk of *behinds*. And me an unattached, alluring dragon whom age cannot wither nor custom stale? Bottoms!'

'Well, ' said Käal. 'Um.'

'You are naughty but I lick you. With flames, I mean. Flames licking over you.'

'How naughty *you* are, Mis Vagner!' Käal countered. He flicked his tail over his head, tapping her lightly on the small of her back, with the sound of a motor vehicle falling thirty feet onto a courtyard entirely coated in shellac.

'*You're* naughty, you mean,' she returned.

'Not as naughty as you!' he countered, getting into the swing of things.

She simpered at him. 'How *old* are you, Mon. Brimstön?'

'I shall only answer,' giggled Käal, 'if you call me Käal.'

'Very well, Käal. How old are you?'

'I'm eleventy one.'

'A mere pup! So, Käal. And how old do you think – I – am?'

Käal made a rapid calculation. His memory of the maze of Vagner family relations was not very clear, but he figured that Asheila must be the daughter of Hydra, Helltrick's older sister. So: probably old enough to be Helltrik's daughter, plus a few years. He calculated: two hundred and ninety. Then, for the sake of sparing a lady's feelings, and, more to the point, of maximizing the possibility of him getting his end away, he said: 'I'm going to stick my neck out and suggest – one ninety?'

Asheila's eyes bugged, momently, and Käal realized that he had miscalculated the depth of her vanity. One fifty would have been a safer guess. But it was clear from her expression that wounded vanity was battling with randy enforced celibacy in her heart, and the latter won. 'Spot on!' she said.

'I prefer a more mature dragon,' said Käal, in a confidential tone of voice. 'Those rope-thin Salamanders do nothing for me. You're—' They made another revolution around one another. 'You're a *very* attractive dragon, if you don't mind me saying so.'

'Oh!' exclaimed Asheila. 'You're just saying that!'

'I *am* saying that,' replied Käal, mishearing slightly.

'You're *just* saying that,' Asheila repeated, with an edge to her voice. That time, Käal heard her properly.

'Not at all, not at all! Not *just* saying that. I really mean it. You're a very beautiful dragon.' He smiled at her. 'I'm not blowing smoke up your arse, you know.'

'Oh!' said Asheila. 'Would you like to?'

'Well – obviously.'

'Then what are we waiting for?'

She scuttled rapidly through the doorway and into the castle. Käal's out-of-shape draconic heart was pumping vigorously at the prospect of coitus. Asheila slithered very attractively up the wide curving stairway, and Käal followed. The stairs hugged the walls of the vaulted hallway before leading the two of them up through a dagger-shaped gap in the ceiling and into the upper floors of the castle.

'My apartment is – through here,' Asheila breathed.

Käal had not had sex for almost a month. For Asheila, the period of enforced unwilling abstinence had been considerably longer. Each found the other attractive; and neither was hamfast with any third party. Accordingly, they retired to Asheila's apartment and engaged in sexual activity.

Asheila, in bed, was wholly conventional, even unadventurous. But Käal didn't mind that. She liked having smoke blown up her arse, obviously. For, after all, who doesn't? And, like everybody else, she enjoyed having a yard-long, scaly *membrum virilis* inserted enthusiastically and repeatedly into her back-passage, like the drive-shaft of some kind of meat traction engine. There was nothing more exotic about her sexual tastes than this, but Käal actually preferred his sex vanilla. He was secretly relieved that he wasn't expected to do anything too weird.

The mating concluded with Käal thrusting into Asheila's draginal canal, whilst biting down so hard upon the back of her armoured neck that he scratched his own dentine. At her climax she blasted a great plume of fire from deep in her throat, so extensive and so heated that the flame-proofed tapestry in her room showed, after the event, distinctive scorch-marks.

Afterwards they lay, side by side, on the asbestos mattress, their eight legs waggling slowly and contentedly in the air. 'Smoke?' Asheila asked.

'Naturally,' replied Käal.

Together, they opened their mouths and puffed great billows of contented white smoke at the ceiling.

They chatted, easily and fluently, as if they'd known each other for a long time. Käal opened up. Helltrik had told him to be discreet, but he hadn't exactly sworn him to secrecy. And besides, Asheila was family. 'My cover story is that I'm here to write the Family Saga. But in fact that story is actually covering up my real reason for being here. Your uncle Helltrik wants me to uncover the mystery of young Hellfire's disappearance. Her murder, he says.'

Asheila murmured understandingly. 'It's driven him mad, really,' she said. 'I love my uncle, but he has become increasingly obsessed with what happened to Hellfire. Erratic.'

'A what?'

'Erratic.'

'What's a *rat-tick*?'

'Erratic. Up-and-down. It's sad. And now he thinks *you* can solve the mystery?'

'The way I see it: we need to think logically about things,' said Käal. 'The undisputable fact is that, three hundred years ago, young Hellfire disappeared. Either she was murdered, as Helltrik thinks; or else she was not. If she was murdered, it would explain her absence, although it raises a series of other problems. How was she killed? By whom and why? How was her body smuggled off Doorbraak? And so on. But if she *wasn't* killed then there are just as many questions. Was she kidnapped, or did she herself steal away secretly? And in either case, how could she possibly have left the island? And why? And how has she kept out of the public eye for such a long time? A few years, maybe; but a fully grown, high-blood dragon? How could she possibly keep herself secret all this time in Scandragonia? So she must be in some other country, probably far away. And there's the tongues . . .'

'Ugh,' said Asheila, shuddering with the sound of a mah-jong set being shaken in its box. 'The tongues are so horrible! One a year for three centuries – imagine it! It almost makes me want to run away . . . all the way to Hostileia'

'It *is* horrible.'

'I don't know what happened to my little niece,' said Asheila. 'But for all the reasons you mention, I believe that she *is* dead. Either she was murdered here, on the island; or else smuggled off and killed later. For if she were alive, why has she not been found? Helltrik has searched the whole island, and sent agents throughout Scandragonia – all over the world, in fact. He has offered rewards for information, fabulous rewards. He's scattered eyes in myriad places. Nothing!'

'If she is dead, then where do you think her body is?'

'I can't be sure. But I can imagine. I fear her stomach was filled with concrete and her body plunged in the deep blue sea. Quite apart from anything else . . .'

'Yes?'

'Don't think me odd,' said Asheila. 'But after all this time, with the whole family turned upside down, all this grief and mystery and misery . . . if it turned out that she was *alive all this time* . . .'

'Yes?' prompted Käal.

'Well it would be such an anticlimax.'

Käal nodded. 'I see what you mean.'

'It would feel like a let-down.'

'It *would* be a sort of cop-out,' agreed Käal.

'Wouldn't it, though? I have no idea what the solution to this mystery is, but I feel certain that it must be something better than that she's been alive all this time and, oh I don't know, living in Hostileia running a sheep factory. Or something.'

'Oh that would be lame.'

'There *must* be more to it that!'

'It would be . . . like a slap in the face, really,' said Käal.

'So. Given that the solution to the mystery, whatever it is, won't be as facile and, uh, disappointing as *that*,' said Asheila. 'Do you have any theories of your own?'

'Ah!' said Käal. 'That would be telling!'

'I see,' said Asheila. 'And what would it be telling?'

'It would be telling you: no,' said Käal. 'No, I haven't got any theories.'

Later that evening, Käal returned to his chambers.

The fact that he had no theories embarrassed him. He took a raven out of its cage, dictated a message to his chief researcher, and sent it off. Then he fell into a deep sleep.

9

Lizbreath Salamander went back to her apartment in a state of almost complete collapse. Her throat was horribly sore, throbbing with a raw pain. A watery, faintly acid discharge leaked from her fire ducts, which she was forced to spit into a ceramic bowl by her bedside. This substance didn't scald her black horny-sheathed tongue, or the front of her mouth of course; but it dribbled back down her throat where it reacted hissingly with the lining of her oesophagus. From time to time she would breathe in a tartly alkaline coughy-provoking steam. Quite apart from anything else, it was worrying symptom. She had no idea whether it meant that some permanent damage had been inflicted upon her ability to generate fire.

Even worse than the physical misery, though, was Lizbreath's sense of self rebuke. She had been stupid. She had misread the situation, and idiotically put herself in great danger. She should have been better prepared, she should have done more research. Wasn't research her forte, after all?

For the first day Lizbreath did nothing but lie on her hoard feeling sorry for herself, coughing and spitting out her foul discharge. On the second day her physical circumstances improved a little: the left fire duct, though still painful, was now capable of generating little knife-shaped bursts of fire. But Lizbreath's depression did not lift.

She was *cowed*. The experience had cowed her. And this, in the idiom of dragons, is one of the worse things that can happen: to be turned, metaphorically speaking, into a placid, cud-chewing milk-teater.

Her left fire duct recovered quickly, though. By the third day her right fire duct had recovered as well, and she was able to blast a few purifying thrusts of flame. That helped clear the generalized throat infection, and made her feel a *little* better. But the watery mood in her mind didn't dissipate. She turned on her computer and made some desultory searches. Some notions circulated in her thoughts. But then she turned off her equipment and returned to her hoard. It seemed as though there was an obstacle for her to overcome that was beyond her.

On the fourth day a raven arrived from the north of the country. It was another message from Brimstön, asking if she had 'found stuff out' about the Vagners. But she could not focus her thoughts on that topic. On the other hand, she did find herself growing bored of her depression. It seems a strange thing to say, for as everybody knows *depression* and *boredom* are really two words that mean the same thing; but perhaps, as fire fights fire, the two things can cancel one another out.

The raven's message annoyed her. Then she brooded about it. Then her brain started working.

She sent a message to Fang, asking him to contact a

mutual friend called Mon. Maker with certain requests. Fang replied with a terse raven. The bird barely stayed five seconds to deliver its message: 'OK, but it will cost.'

And that, of course, was the problem. She could think of various ways of proceeding, but all of them needed a good deal of money. And for that she would have to go back to Burnblast, beg him for funds. Which would mean putting up with his . . . attentions.

Another dragon might have thought of going straight to the authorities. But Lizbreath was not another dragon. From her point of view, Burnblast *was* the authorities. If she went to the Pride services, to the police, even to the Dragonlords themselves, she would find herself face to face with elderly, large, sly-eyed male dragons, just like him. Why, the supreme Firehrer himself (though of course considerably larger) had scales the same colour as her Guardian.

She was used to sorting out her own problems. But the problem with sorting this problem was that it was too large a problem for her to deproblematize. And that made it problematic.

She needed money. There was no alternative. Although every fiery fibre in her being rebelled against the thought, she would have to go back to Burnblast's office.

Cinderday came round, and Lizbreath again descended her Guardian's stairway to emerge, reluctantly, into his cavern. He was sprawled lazily on the top of his hoard, casually reading a Saga – *Hötwyrmlövin Saga* – that contained sexually explicit dragon material. Seeing him openly indulging in Pernography like that was bad enough; worse was the cruel indulgence with which he greeted her. 'How charming to see you again, my dear,' he drawled, little bundles of smoke skittering from the corners of his wide grin. 'Perhaps you are I are going to be friends, after all. That will make things so much easier – for us both.'

'I need money,' said Lizbreath, loitering by the entrance, and not meeting his gaze. She was carrying a small satchel.

'Of course you do, my dear!' Burnblast rose slowly into the air, with languorous wingbeats. 'Everybody needs money. But before we get to that part of proceedings, there are several things I want to . . . try.' He drifted down the flank of his hoard, his big head coming closer – four times her size, much stronger and hotter-breathed. It was an intimidating approach, and he knew it. 'Just the two of us today,' he said, trailing a back foot in his treasure as he descended, and setting a scree clatter of small golden objects sliding down the larger heap. 'I don't think we need Human any more. *Do* we, my dear. I think we understand one another.'

'Yes,' said Lizbreath.

She brought out the Fire Extinguisher. It was a red cylinder, about as long as Lizbreath's own head, but chunky and weighty and topped with a Medusa-tangle of cords, tubes and metal levers. Burnblast, to judge by his expression, had never seen one before. But before he could ask what it was, Lizbreath angled one of its tubes straight in his face and fired.

A megaphone-shaped splurt of white foam shot out. The stuff went straight into his eyes.

Burnblast made a resonant throaty deep squeal, and tried to twist his neck. But Lizbreath was too quick. She leapt, spinning in mid-air to seize the back of his head with her hindlimbs. With her forelimbs she angled the Fire Extinguisher down and sprayed long sloppy blasts first in one nostril, then the other, and finally – as the old dragon opened his mouth to howl in pain – straight down his throat.

Burnblast rolled and twisted in blind agony. Lizbreath was ready: she brought out the titanium hook and fixed it, and therefore its pendant chain, around one of the old dragon's spine frills. He himself did the rest, writhing and spinning, as Lizbreath jumped into the air overhead, making sure to play out enough chain to allow Burnblast to truss himself up comprehensively.

The tantrum of his agony spent itself soon enough, and he lay there on the floor, at the foot of his own hoard, chained and restrained. His fat flanks heaved against the ties, but there was nothing he could do.

From this point on, Lizbreath worked smoothly and quickly. Out of her satchel she brought out two stainless steel clamps: not unlike the ones Burnblast had used on her, though newer and a little smaller. Burnblast was opening and shutting his mouth in a cycle of gasping agony, blinded by the Fire Extinguisher foam. Lizbreath waited for the right moment, then thrust her forearm into his open maw and clamped the foam-sodden fire ducts closed.

The feel of this Extinguisher gunk on her scales was

horrible – wet and slippery and slimy. Reaching into Burnblast's mouth was the only point in the whole proceedings when she felt as if she might lose it: but bringing out her arms she held them in front of her mouth and washed them with purifying fire, which evaporated most of the moisture and turned the residue to a black tar that wasn't half so noisome.

She took a breath. The trickiest part was over.

Burnblast was making a strangulated trumpeting sound, half choking and half outrage. Lizbreath leant forward and blew hot, pale-orange fire right in his eyes. This was a kindness, although she had her reasons for it. Burnblast blinked, and blinked, and was able, finally, to see again. 'Lizbreath,' he croaked. 'Lizbreath! What have you done? This is not – wise.'

'Shut up,' said Liz, in a level voice.

Bleared and scummed as they were, there was no mistaking the way Burnblast opened his eyes wider in astonishment. He was not used to being talked at in such terms. 'Lizbreath,' he said again. 'Stop and think! What are you doing?'

'I'm using a Fire Extinguisher.'

'A Fire – what?' Burnblast's croak was incredulous. '*Extinguisher*? What are you talking about?'

'It's exactly what it sounds like. It extinguishes fire.'

'Who would want to extinguish fire?' he said.

'The thing has its uses,' said Lizbreath.

'Where did you find such a strange device?'

'Enough of your talking now,' said Lizbreath; and when Burnblast opened his mouth to retort she pushed the metal body of the Fire Extinguisher hard into the open cavity. It went down the foam-slick throat with gratifying ease. Burnblast's eyes went very wide.

'Uncomfortable, eh?' said Lizbreath. 'Still, you don't need to *speak* to communicate, do you? You are, for instance, communicating very effectively now with your whole expression. You are saying: *I shall revenge myself upon you, Salamander.* You are thinking: *When I get out of this I shall visit ruin and devastation upon you.*'

Burnblast struggled, wriggled, pushed his wings and hindlegs against the wrapped-about chain. But there was nothing he could do.

'But, you see,' Lizbreath went on. 'You won't. You will leave me in peace. In fact, you will do more than that. You will give me back my hoard, and use your influence to have my legal status altered to full dragon.'

Burnblast glowered.

'Let me explain why you will do these things.' Lizbreath held up the miniature eye and ear. 'When I was last here I had these ingenious things secreted about my body. Everything you and your henchdragon *said* and *did* is recorded in them. I've made copies. If anything happens to me – more, if you displease me in any way at all – then the Sagas are going to be full of your perverted sexual tastes. That would be a damaging blow to your credibility as a senior dragon, don't you think?'

Burnblast was very still now, fixing his malevolent eyes upon her.

'What I want, fundamentally,' said Lizbreath, 'is: *to be left alone.* So I shall take my gold, and not bother you any more. And more importantly you will not bother *me* any more.'

She unpacked the final items from her satchel.

'But there's one more thing, before I go. I told you several times that the image of the human girl on my shoulder was not painted on, but you didn't listen. So I shall show you the difference between a tattoo and a body-painting.' She held up the equipment she had brought with her. 'One difference, you see, is that you can wash a painting off. Still – it's a very rare thing among dragons, a tattoo. So you can console yourself with the exclusivity.'

She jumped and landed on Burnblast's chest. It took her quite a long time, and some of the letters came out a little wonky, what with Burnblast's wriggling and groaning, and the general unevenness of his scales. But eventually she had finished. Across the old dragon's underbelly, in clearly legible writing, it now said: I A FOUL OLD DRAGON WHO ENDULGES IN ORAL SEX PERVERSION.

'Hmm,' said Lizbreath, standing back to survey her handiwork. 'Now that I've done it, I'm not sure that is how "indulges" is spelled. Ah well. Can't be helped.'

10

The last thing Asheila said to Käal, before he left her apartment, was: 'You should have a word with my cousin Marrer.'

'I should?'

'He's been chosen by Helltrik to succeed him as the head of the clan. Plus, he's the nicest member of the family by far. I'm sure he'll be able to help you.'

Käal liked this sort of thing best of all: doing what other people told him to. 'Thanks for the suggestion!' he said brightly.

Käal left Asheila napping, and took a look around the Vagner island. The garden was maintained by a crew of Moomins. He saw them at work, but when he came over to talk to them they scattered. Shy buggers, Moomins. Although, to be fair, most non-draconic forms of life are pretty shy around dragons.

He went right round the central castle: manicured gardens on three sides, and a Chilean Flame tree orchard on the fourth. It was very pleasant and tasteful, but most of all it was evidently very expensive. Then Käal jumped up the side of the building to the main entrance balcony. He bumped into a firedrake. Käal recognized him as the creature who had met him when he first arrived. 'Hello!' Käal said. 'I didn't catch your name before . . .'

'It not being a *fish*,' was the reply; and the firedrake flew off.

'I'm looking for Marrer!' he yelled after the servant's retreating form. There was no reply.

'Charming,' said Käal, to himself. 'How on earth am I going to find Marrer now?'

'Did I hear you call my name?' said a well-modulated voice. A handsome dragon of early middle age came out of the main castle entrance.

'Are you Marrer?'

'I am. And you must be Käal. Your arrival has sent a buzz through the little world of Doorbraak.' He flashed a smile, a long mouth of neatly polished and cleaned teeth like open-and-closed brackets. 'It is really delightful to meet you.'

Marrer was a trim, muscular dragon, mostly amber-maroon in colour. His brow displayed a receding line of head spikes that made him look intellectual. But the main impression he created was one of *likeability*.

'The feeling is entirely mutual.'

'I apologize for our servants,' he said, smoothly. 'They're not terribly good, I'm afraid. We have troubles with retention.'

'Really?'

'They say that Doorbraak is haunted,' said Marrer. 'Imagine! They don't like it. This makes it harder than it might otherwise be . . .'

'Harder?'

'To retain good staff,' said Marrer, with a small sigh.

'It's nonsense, of course. The Island isn't *haunted*. But you know how firedrakes are!'

'Never having had servants . . .' Käal said, with an apologetic laugh.

'Oh, of course. Not every creature is as – *rational* as might be desirable. And firedrakes are particularly susceptible to mumbo-jumbo. Anyway, enough of our troubles. Have you settled in at Doorbraak? It can be a slightly disorienting place for visitors, I know.'

'I'm starting to get a sense of the place. I've, er, met your cousin – Asheila.'

'Aha!'

'She's lovely,' said Käal, loyally.

'So you two *hit it off*?' said Marrer. 'I'm delighted. She's a sweetheart.' He gave Käal a roguish look. 'Though she's something of a maneater, you know.'

'Really?' said Käal, impressed.

'Oh yes. She likes fine food. Not real men, of course – not your actual *hömös apes*. There aren't any of them left around. But there's a butcher in Starkhelm who cuts and dresses pork to look like an actual old-world man – puts him in the tin trousers and coat and so on and everything. Asheila likes to pretend she's the heroine of a medieval romance – dresses up in the gear, puts a woman doll in the top tower, and then eats the man.'

'Charming!' said Käal, with warmth. 'I didn't realize she had such a playful side.'

'And talking of eating, my friend, you must come and have supper with me. No, no, I *insist* upon it! My great-uncle has invited you here to write the Family Saga, I believe?'

'That's right.'

'Although everybody is saying that the real reason you're here is to investigate poor Hellfire's disappearance, all those centuries ago.'

There didn't seem to be any point in denying it. 'It's true.'

'My sister,' Marrer said, his expression growing briefly sad. Käal nodded, trying once again, and again failing, to visualize the complex netting of the Vagner family tree. 'I still miss her, poor little dragonette.'

'I have something of a reputation for *finding stuff out*,' said Käal. 'I hope I'll be able to uncover something about your sister's, uh, evanishment.' Was that a word?

'I hope I can be of some use to you.'

'Asheila suggested I talk to you, actually.'

'Did she?' said Marrer, his face breaking into a smile. 'My dear cousin! What else did she say?'

'Only – to spare your embarrassment – that you are very nice. A straight-up, honest, dependable dragon, she said.'

'I hope so!' said Marrer, laughing again. 'I try my best. I certainly *don't* maintain a secret dungeon beneath my apartment in which I imprison visitors, torturing them to death over months with a succession of wet and slimy creatures, on account of the diseased psychotic impulses writhing through my degraded brain!' He beamed at Käal.

In the far distance: the cawing of gulls.

'Right,' said Käal, shortly. 'Of course. Of course you don't. Of course you *don't!*'

'I mean,' said Marrer, grinning and rolling his eyes, '*that* wouldn't be very nice, would it?'

'No.'

'It wouldn't be nice.' Marrer put a claw on Käal's shoulder. 'And nice is what I am. Everybody says so! Shall I tell you something else I've never done? Committed incest with, and subsequently murdered, my sister Hellfire.'

'I feel sure that goes without saying,' agreed Käal, looking at the claw with some anxiety.

'Come inside. Come along.'

Käal followed Marrer in.

They went into the main hall together, and the heir of Vagner spent some time talking Käal through the various portraits of eminent Vagner ancestors. 'So there they are,' he concluded. 'All our illustrious dead, all illustrated here. Illustrious *and* illustrated. And all buried in the vault on this very island.' He smiled warmly at Käal. 'Right under our feet!'

'It's a little spooky to think of it,' observed Käal.

'Spooky?' repeated Marrer, raising one eyebrow. 'You think so?'

'I do,' said Käal, laughing nervously. 'It's as spooky as – as . . .' He searched for an appropriate simile. In truth he was a little jangled by Marrer's jokes. Or by what he genuinely hoped were Marrer's jokes – the torture basements and incestuous murder material. '. . . er . . . a bicycle wheel,' he finished, somewhat at a loss. 'All those dead family members just lying underneath your feet? It doesn't spook *you*?'

'I can't say it does,' said Marrer, thoughtfully. 'Although I've never really thought about it, if I'm honest. Come along. You must be hungry.'

They went out of the great hall and ascended to Marrer's spacious apartment. And there they were met by a firedrake: a younger one than the servant who attended Helltrik, but equally reticent. 'Come in, and say hello to my girldragon, Redsnapper. Red? Red! We have a guest!'

A comely she-dragon came out of a back room. Her eyes were nightsky, black with inset sparkles of fiery white; and her scales were of a remarkable silver hue. Even more strikingly, her wings were scarlet. It was hard to gauge her age, although there was something mature and settled in her manner. She padded over to Marrer, and the two put their mouths together and blew affectionate fire at one another.

'Pleased to meet you,' said Redsnapper. 'You are—?'

'Käal,' said Käal.

'Käal will join us for supper.'

'Excellent!'

'He is here to investigate my sister's death,' said Marrer.

'After all these years!' said Red, putting her foreclaws together. 'Well, it's about time.'

The three of them took supper on Marrer's balcony; a petal-shaped extrusion from the body of the castle built of white stone marbled with gold seams and whorls. The food was delicious: a starter of whole dog (shaved, basted, baked and served with a shredded cat stuffing), followed by a main course of tender mutton chunks, and for dessert crème brûlée, all washed down with some very serviceable firewater. As the small talk pattered agreeably across the table, and the sun went down in splendour over the western horizon, Käal came to the conclusion that all the stuff Marrer said about murdering his sister and torturing visitors to death had indeed been a joke. There was nothing suspect or dodgy about him. In fact, never in all his life had Käal encountered so deeply decent, reasonable and *nice* a dragon as Marrer. The worst that could be said against him was that he was not so skilled in properly judging the level of a joke. But surely, failing precisely to judge the level of a joke is an insignificant failing when set against the many courtesies, marks of intelligence and charm that Marrer displayed?

'So, Käal,' he said. 'You've been here a day?'

'Just a day.'

'Do you have any theories yet as to what happened to my sister?'

'Don't pressure him, Marr,' said Red.

'No it's all right,' replied Käal. 'In fact, I might turn the question back on you. Do *you* have a theory as to what happened to your sister? You must have given it a lot of thought.'

Marrer put his smile carefully away, folded his foreclaws and replied: 'I have indeed. Of course I have. I haven't become obsessed – if that's not too harsh a way of putting it – like great-uncle Helltrik. But of course it haunts me. I remember that last day so well! It was foul weather, perfectly impossible to fly. Impossible, even, to step outside. Drizzle for hours and hours, an uncanny, unsettling rainfall. Pretty much the entire clan had gathered, and since we couldn't go out things got a little – tetchy, I suppose you could say.'

'There were arguments?'

'You have to understand the tensions. My grand-father, Reekhard, had – certain unsavoury *political* sympathies. This was something my mother Isabella, Reekhard's daughter-in-law, could never quite under-stand. It was baffling to her, I think, and distressing. We were all gathered in the smoking room, passing round a number of old family eyes. Reekhard and my mother got into an argument. I honestly can't remember how it started. But soon enough they were calling one another all manner of horrible names, and suddenly my sister just snapped. She flew up to the ceiling, dived back down through the door and hurried off towards the Great Hall.'

'Did you go after her?'

'No.'

'How do you know she went in that particular dir-ection, then?'

'Asheila saw her.'

'And what was this argument about.'

'Oh,' said Marrer, glancing across the golden table at his girldragon. 'The usual. There's really only ever one argument in my family, endlessly repeated and varied. You see, Mon. Brimstön, there is . . . a guilty secret at the heart of Doorbraak.'

'I know,' said Käal, speaking up to spare Marrer's blushes. 'Your granduncle explained everything to me. I know that, despite heroic service in the Scorch Wars, several key members of your family displayed sympathy for the ideas of . . .' He lowered his voice. 'Democracy,' he concluded.

Redsnapper lowered her eyes. Marrer looked sombre. For a while nobody said anything.

Eventually Marrer went on: 'It wasn't the first time Reekhard and Isabella had argued. Each taking their traditional side in the fight. Oh, but it wasn't even the *content* of the argument that was so upsetting! If they'd had a properly dragonish flaming row, that would have been different! But it wasn't like that. It was this drip-drip whining *"yes you did"* *"no I didn't"* *"yes you did"* *"no I didn't"*. It was demeaning for both of them, really, although my grandfather . . . well he really should have known better.'

'And that was the last you saw of your sister?'

'It was.'

'And what do you think happened to her?'

'I honestly don't know. I have given it a lot of thought, obviously, and I've honestly no idea.' Marrer looked thoughtfully out at the thickening dusk light, and said: 'I know what *didn't* happen to her. She didn't commit suicide.'

'Oh!' said Käal. 'Do some people think she did?'

'The police investigated her disappearance, and that was the tentative conclusion they came to. The idea was: distraught, she rushed from the castle, straight into the rainfall, tried to fly, and instead fell a mile through the air to her death. But there are too many holes in that theory for it to be taken seriously.'

'The eye,' said Käal.

'Well, yes. The eye underneath the mountain didn't see anything. A dragon getting suddenly tangled up in her own wings and plummeting – that would be recorded. Like many others, I've had that eye in my own socket, and I have seen everything it saw. It didn't see that.'

'What did the police say? I mean, why did they conclude she had fallen when the eye shows that she didn't?'

'There was some chaff about poor visibility. Such nonsense! I mean, it was raining, but not hard, and you can see everything with great clarity. You should have a look yourself. The eye is kept in the Vagner Vault, now. Pop it in, and check.'

'I will.'

'The other problem is that, if Hellfire had fallen to the ground and been killed by the impact, then she would have left a pretty enormous crater. There was no crater – and no body.'

'And how did the police explain that?' Käal asked.

'They couldn't, of course. There was some talk of a second individual, somebody who retrieved the body and hid it, filled in the crater and so on. That's so nonsensical, it's *beyond* nonsense! It's . . . what do you call something beyond nonsense?'

'Sense?' offered Käal. Both Marrer and Red looked rather sharply at him. 'I mean – or, no, that's the opposite, isn't it. How about: nonnonsense? No, that's another opposite. Sensenon?'

'For one thing,' said Redsnapper, 'the police argued

for a spontaneous suicide. So where did this mysterious accomplice come from?'

'And for another,' said Marrer. 'The . . .'

'Supernonsense!' said Käal.

There was a pause.

'For another thing,' Marrer said. 'The ground underneath where the island was on that day has been thoroughly examined.'

'Ultranonsense?'

Marrer ignored this. 'If there had been a crater it would have been found. Even if there had been a crater and some mysterious third party had shipped in dirt and filled it in, that would have been discovered. Perhaps you don't know, my granduncle hired earthwyrms to search the lower portions of the island?'

'He,' said Käal, 'mentioned something.'

'Well, he also paid them to examine the land underneath Doorbraak too. They'd have spotted a recently filled crater: it would have stood out like a sore thumbclaw. Nothing.'

'Where was the island over at the time?' Käal asked. 'By which I mean: over where was the island that time at? No, wait a minute. Over which country did the, was the island, during the time at when over? Over whence did the island then be at, over?'

'Limbchopping,' said Marrer. 'The island moves, slowly but inexorably, you know, following a great oval. It passes north over Swedragen, loops round in Fangland, comes back south over Lizardania, Lostvia and Stonia, and sweeps back over Dustland and Dragonmark. It takes exactly a year to make one revolution.'

'How very remarkable!' said Käal.

The sun had set. Fireflies circled lazily over the table. 'Well,' said Marrer, rearing up. 'It's been very pleasant meeting you, Mon. Brimstön. I trust this is the start of a genuine friendship; and that I will not end up having to cut your head off with a magic dragon-slaying weapon!'

'Ah!' said Käal, likewise rising, uncertain at the abrupt termination of the meeting and not able to read the tone of Marrer's last comment. 'Well that would be . . . a shame.'

'Wouldn't it! Chopping your head right off! That would be terrible!' He laughed. 'I'm joking!' he added.

'Aha!' said Käal, with some relief.

'Of course I'm joking! Or—' His face abruptly fell. '—am I?'

'You,' said Käal, feeling his way, 'are?'

'Of *course* I am! Good night, Käal. Sleep well! Good luck with your investigation!'

11

When he got back to his room that evening Käal found a raven waiting for him on the end of his bed. It was from Beargrr, sent from the offices of the *Köschfagold Saga*. 'She wants you back in Starkhelm, tomorrow,' cawed the bird.

'What? But she just sent me *here*! Why do I have to go back?'

'She wants you ba-a-ack,' repeated the raven.

Now, the thing with ravens is: if their message isn't instantly clear, you must frame your question such as their small-as-a-piece-of-gravel brains can recognize, and to which they have been primed with an answer. If they don't recognize the question, they will just repeat the last thing they'd been taught. I'm sure you know that.

'Baack,' said the raven, rummaging amongst its own tailfeathers.

'OK, raven,' said Käal. 'Is it to do with the trial? Do I have to go back to Starkhelm because of the trial?'

The raven put his head on one side, in that insolent way ravens have. It did a little moonwalky dance with its asterisk-shaped feet. It fixed Käal with its blank eye. 'Back!' it cawed. 'Sta-a-a-rkhelm.'

'Yes, I understand *that* part of your message. But I don't understand *why*. Is it the Wintermute court case?'

'Back!'

'Is it the court case, though? Is it to do with me appearing in court.'

'B'kaaaak!'

'Is it some *Köschfagold Saga* business?'

'*Köschfagold*!'

'So – there's something. I have to go back to Stark-helm because the Saga need me to . . . what?'

The raven opened its beak very wide, soundlessly, as if yawning. Then it leapt into flight, and disappeared through Käal's window without another word. He thought of going after it, but there seemed little point.

There was a knock at the door. When Käal verbally encouraged whoever it was to push open the door, the knock was repeated. Käal reiterated his invitation to enter. 'Coo-ee!' said Asheila. 'Hellow-w-w, lover-dragon!'

'Ah! Hello, Asheila.'

The she-dragon pounced through the door with an arch expression on her lips. She was wearing a girdle belt of *or-massif*, a purse carved from a single giant ruby, and she had dabbed Sulphur behind her ears.

'My but you look glum!' she said. 'Why so sad, my love? How can there be any sadness when we have discovered between us the true love that only spirits of flame can share?'

'Oh!' said Käal.

'Our spirits have touched one another!' sang Asheila. 'Since the first sun poured pure fire upon the world, the

gods have been waiting for a love like ours to blossom!'
She flew up to the ceiling, and from her ruby reticule she
brought out a chiffon scarf in shape and colour, though
not in temperature of combustability, like a flame. She
then flew around the ceiling, singing 'Love is a Dragony
Splendour'd Thing' at the top of her voice.

'Erm,' said Käal, his eyes going to the open window.

Asheila settled, slowly, to the floor, the chiffon scarf
drifting down to drape itself over her snout. 'How have
you been? It's been ages since I saw you last!'

'Er,' mumbled Käal. 'Yesterday . . . ?'

'Oh but EONS pass when we are not in one another's
company! I cannot bear to spend a wingbeat apart from
you! To be in a separate room feels like I have been
banished to Hostileia!'

'Yes, look, now,' said Käal. He thought how best to
say what he needed to say. 'Erm,' he said.

'Let us seal our hearts together in the flowing magma
of our passion!' suggested Asheila.

Käal jumped up. 'I've got to go!' he squealed.

'Go?' A cloud passed across Asheila's face. Of smoke,
obviously. 'Go where?'

'Starkhelm – just got a raven – urgent business with –
thing – in Starkhelm.'

The arch banter vanished. 'You're not serious,' she
said, in a menacing voice.

'I'll only be gone a day. Two at most.'

'No,' said Asheila.

'I'm sorry?'

'We are meant to be together. If you are in Starkhelm
and I'm on Doorbraak, then we're not *together*. Think

about the logic. I think you'll find it unassailable.' She put her long face close to his, and repeated: '*Not* together. See? Hmm?'

'Well . . .' said Käal, trying to think of a way of countering what was, after all, a fundamental truth of the orientation of objects in physical space. 'Err,' said Käal.

'You shan't go.'

'I think I'd better, actually.'

Asheila's nostril's flared. Which is to say, fire came out of them. She rocked back on her hind limbs, and threw her wings wide for emphasis. 'Fly through that window,' she warned, 'and you and I are over. We are icing *done*. Through. Finished with!'

'Ah, OK,' said Käal, nervously.

'I'm serious! Do you really want to throw away all that we have built together?'

'Look,' said Käal. 'I hope you haven't got the wrong end of the stick. You're a super she-dragon, you really are. But I wasn't looking for a long-term relationship. It was just a fling, really.'

'Of *course* it was a fling,' yelled Asheila. 'But a fling of iron! A fling for the ages! A fling that minstrels will sing about for centuries to come!'

'But – a *fling*, yeah?'

'Well naturally,' said Asheila. 'I can hardly hamfast with *you*. The blood of Regin himself flows in my *veins*.'

'Mine too,' said Käal, a little peeved by her tone of automatic superiority.

'Yes, yes. But I am a Vagner! We are *lineal*

136

descendants of Regin the Royal! You're just a dragon. I mean,' she added, seeing his crest fall, 'you *are* a dragon, which is splendid, of course, one of the children of Regin – you're not a firedrake or lowly wyrm, or anything like that. But you must see there's a difference between *you* and *me*. I'm a Vagner!'

'Mmm,' said Käal. 'This seems to have shifted about a little from where it started. You were lamenting my going-away in operatic terms?'

'Indeed!' said Asheila. 'Just so that we understand one another?'

'I think so.' Käal smiled, thinking to himself: this is one unpredictable loon of a dragon. 'The thing to do, Käal-me-lad,' he said to himself, 'is to give this one a wi-i-i-de berth. Let her down gently, but then try never to have anything more to do with her.'

'So,' she said, 'want more sex?'

'Go on then,' said Käal.

Afterwards, as Asheila snored on the bed, and Käal moved quietly about his rooms picking up the knocked-over furniture, his mind went back to affairs in Stark-helm. Though he was not, in the usual course of things, a dragon much given to deep thought, he found himself worrying about the raven's message. If the *Köschfagold Saga* folded, it *would* be an inconvenience for him. He'd have to find another Saga to employ him. That was assuming the court case with Wintermute didn't go against him. A contrary judgement could cost him a great deal of money, and he didn't *have* a great deal of money. His was a modest hoard, stylishly designed, but made up of new-minted ingots rather than old treasure and far from heavy. He had never been able to raise much actual money on the strength of it. In a worst-case scenario he could actually go to prison. Decades in the stone wells of Hardland!

He went out onto the balcony and watched the night sky for a while. The stars were all clearly visible. The sublime transparency of night, through which we see the stars; before dawn comes to solidify the sky to a wall. Käal recalled to himself that Helltrik had promised him a great treasure, if only he could solve the mystery of young Hellfire Vagner's disappearance. Once he had *that*, he wouldn't need to worry about the court case, or about the Saga going bankrupt, or anything at all. 'What I need to do,' he said aloud, to himself, 'is solve this perishing mystery!'

It was natural, accordingly, that his thoughts turned to Lizbreath Salamander; for she would surely be able to supply the research to crack this case wide open. But though he had sent her several ravens, she hadn't replied. Käal permitted himself a certain righteous indignation at this fact. She was a researcher, after all! If she would only do her job, he could put her data to use, solve the case, collect his considerable reward.

'If I go to Starkhelm,' he told himself, 'I could look her up, chivvy her along. There's no excuse for laziness!'

Away to the north: a comet, like an icicle embedded sideways in the night. Käal watched it for a while. There it was, Käal thought: endlessly pulling its bridal train around the solar system. There seemed to be some symbolic significance in that; but he wasn't sure what it was.

Shortly he went back in and lay down next to the snoring she-dragon.

12

The following day Käal left the island and flew down to the ground. The nearest town with an airport was a neat little place called Burnlänge. From there he caught a slightly raddled Skylligator for the hop across to Starkhelm, arriving after lunch. He went straight to the *Köschfagold Saga* offices. Beargrr was there.

'Good,' she said, without preliminary. 'Our backing has pulled out.'

'Our backing? You mean, our financial backing?'

'No,' said Beargrr, sarcastically. 'Our musical backing. Of *course* our financial backing!'

'That's terrible!' said Käal. 'Why?'

'Oh I don't know,' Beargrr said, with sarcasm so heavy that light could not escape its gravitational pull. 'Maybe it has something to do with the fact that Wintermute is in the process of suing our *tails* off? That the legal liability we are almost certain to incur will not only seize *your* personal hoard, it will snaffle all funds legally associated with the Saga itself?'

'Only if Wintermute is successful in court,' Käal pointed out.

'Well I suppose our financial backers consider it likely

that he will be successful. They have indicated that by withdrawing all their funds.'

'That's terrible!' said Käal again. 'But how will the Saga continue?'

'We'll have to find alternate funding,' growled Beargrr.

'Wait!' said Käal. 'Ooh! Yes! I've got it! Helltrik Vagner has promised me the Siegfried treasure if I successfully solve the mystery of his grand-niece's disappearance! We can use that to bankroll the Saga!'

'I see,' said Beargrr. 'And have you?'

'What?'

'Have you solved it?'

'—solved the mystery? Not yet, no. I have found out one secret though . . .'

'Yes?'

'The Vagner family, though it is one of the wealthiest and purest-blood dragon nests in the world, has a shameful secret. Several important family members have a political commitment to . . . democracy.'

'I know,' said Beargrr.

'You do?'

'Loads of people know that.'

'They do?' said Käal, in a disappointed voice. 'It was news to me.'

'Well, you've never been a dragon who has kept his ear to the ground. It's been gossip on the Starkhelm journalistic circuit for centuries. Literally centuries. Have you found out anything else?'

'No,' Käal conceded.

'This Hellfire girl – *is* she dead?'

'I don't know.'

'So you don't actually *have* the treasure? You're not, for instance, carrying it about your person right now?'

'No.'

'Then that's not very much of an icing *solution* to our woes, is it!' she yelled. Visibly reining herself in, she went on with more self-restraint: 'There's only one thing for it. We have to go into the den.'

The blood in Käal's body dropped several degrees. He actually gasped. Blue smoke seeped from the corners of his gawping mouth. 'There must be another way of raising the money?'

'If can think of one, then let me know,' said Beargrr.

Käal spun his mental rolodex, but came up blank. 'But – the den? There *must* be another way.'

'There's not. We're going there right now.'

' "*We*"?'

'Of course you're coming. Why do you think I sent you that raven?'

'But why do I have to come?'

'Because you're a bloodline dragon.'

'Aren't you?'

Beargrr put her her face into her foreclaws. 'How long have you known me? We have worked in the same office, and had sex together. You may be the most self-absorbed individual I've ever known. No, I'm not bloodline.'

'But you *are* a dragon?'

'Of course I'm a dragon! Are you a *complete* idiot?'

'Then from whom do you claim descent?'

'Glaurung.'

'Glaurung? You're a Glaurungian? Well well!' Käal scratched his nostril, abstractedly. 'You learn something every day!'

'I'm glad this afternoon is proving educational,' said Beargrr, in a tone of voice that suggested, in fact, that *glad* was very far from what she was. 'And now you and I are going to the den.'

Käal started. 'What, right now?'

'That's right.' She took hold of Käal by his wing-elbow and steered him to the door of the office. 'We need this investment, Käal,' she told him. 'Or it's curtains for *Köschfagold Saga*.' Käal looked rather pitifully at the actual office curtains. But there was no help for it. The two of them were through the door and out on the street on their way to the den.

The den had once been an actual cave, reputedly both dark and dank. But the need for proximity to the centres of business and commerce had resulted in a move to an empty warehouse near the waterside. Simply stepping through the main entrance gave Käal the kollywöbles. As they waited their turn, he started hyperflameinating. Beargrr kept telling him to calm down. They were approached by Evildavis, a boss-eyed firedrake in charge of shepherding applicants before the den dragons. When he announced that it was time for them to go up, Käal almost passed out. Although, to be fair, this had something to do with the weirdly unbalanced orientation of his two eyes.

'It's too nerve-wracking!' Käal wailed. 'My nerves are

overwracked. I need to perform a nerve dewrack immediately.'

'You're being ridiculous,' hissed Beargrr. 'Pull your-self together. And most of all: *don't* say anything. Let me do the talking.'

'All right,' quavered Käal.

Up the wide stairs they came together, and onto the wide floor. The four den dragons sat, each on their own portable heap of gold, looking down on the new entrants into their domain with towering condescension.

'Hello, dragons,' said Beargrr. 'My name is Beargrr. This is my associate, the celebrated Saga writer Käal Brimstön.'

'Is he descended from Regin?' drawled the dragon on the far right: a plump dark grey creature with a smug face.

'He is.'

'How pure is his blood?' asked the smug-faced she-dragon in the middle.

'He is two-fifths pure . . .' Beargrr began saying.

'Can't he answer for himself,' interrupted the dragon second from left. He had a thick North Snakeland accent, and a smug fa— Look, I tell you what: rather than repeat myself, perhaps we can take it as read that the faces of *all* the den dragons could be described as 'smug'. 'Hasn't he got a tongue in his head?'

Käal blinked, and blinked, and looked about. An industrial-sized eye, hung from the ceiling, was watching everything. It was astonishingly nerve-wracking. He tried to keep his mind focused on what was being said to him, but it kept sliding away into irrelevance. 'I have a tongue!' he squeaked. 'Nobody's cut *my* tongue out and sent it through the postal system!'

The four dragons looked at him.

'By which I mean to *say*,' said Käal, trying for a smooth recovery, 'hello.'

The dragons continued looking at him.

'Hi,' said Käal. 'My name's Käal.'

'What's your pitch?'asked the fourth dragon: a sleek-scaled younger beast.

'We have come before you, dragons,' said Beargrr, glancing crossly at her companion, 'to raise funding for our publication, the *Köschfagold Saga*. We'd like to offer you a twenty per cent stake in the Saga for one hundred thousand crowns.'

'The *Köschfagold Saga*,' said the she-dragon. 'What's that?'

'We are Scandragonia's premier financial services Saga,' said Beargrr. 'We are a weekly publication, covering all the affairs of money-making and business investment in Scandragonia. You may have heard of us.' She looked from dragon to dragon, but they met her gaze with indifference. 'Seeing,' she prompted, 'as you are all financial players? Anyway, many of our readers are big financial players like, er, you yourself. We contain investment advice and, um. No? You don't read the *Köschfagold Saga*? No? Well, believe me, lots of rich dragons do. Also, we carry pieces of investigative journalism, written in the appropriately Saga style, by our star reporter, whose fame is really peninsula-wide.' She gestured to Käal. 'Monster Käal Brimstön.'

She looked expectantly at Käal, but his anxiety at actually being in the den – with the eye focused upon him, and the four den dragons glowering silently at him – was growing larger with each moment that passed. He started to speak, but the words underwent a peculiar transformation as they came up his throat, emerging as a sequence of bubbling gurgles. He stopped, grinned widely, coughed, and tried again.

'Hi,' said Käal. 'My name's Käal.'

'What my colleague means to say,' said Beargrr, 'is that with appropriate investment we feel that *Köschfagold Saga* could expand into new markets and maximize profit share.'

'What *are* your profits?' boomed the dragon on the left.

'Over the last quarter,' said Beargrr, 'our profits have been *broken through* the, er, midpoint on the number line.'

'What do you mean?' asked the she-dragon. 'The midpoint on the number line? That's zero, isn't it?'

'You put it *very* well,' said Beargrr, 'and if I may . . . your solid-gold chain adornment? *Very* chic.'

The she-dragon frowned. 'Your profits have *broken through zero* in the last quarter? You mean, in more conventional parlance, you have started turning a profit?'

'You could put it that way,' said Beargrr. 'Although, honesty compels me to add that if you *were* to put it that way it would not be, precisely, true. The breakthrough being in the, er, opposite direction. But *direction* is a relative concept, isn't it? From-me-to-you is a direction only from where *I'm* standing.'

'When you say you "broke through zero", are you saying,' said the dragon on the far left, looking, if possible, even crosser than normal, 'that you went *from* profit *into* loss?'

'Just so. That would be the to-you-from-me way of putting it.'

Käal became aware of an awkward silence, and wondered if he should say something. But his mind was dancing into wilder and wilder territories. He thought again of all those severed dragon tongues, delivered once a year to Helltrik Vagner on his lofty floating island. Surely the mutilation of so many dragons must have left *some* record in the official annals? Presumably the dragons who had suffered this horrible fate had died. The premature deaths of *three hundred* dragons, even over some centuries, would surely be a matter of international scandal! Assume that a serial killer were at work: perhaps whoever it was started with young Hellfire, and went on to murder a dragon a year, and cut out their tongues. That they sent this grisly token to Helltrik surely meant that the crimes had some connection with the Vagner clan. But what?

He became aware of silence. Everybody was looking at him. 'Hi,' he said, looking around. 'My name's Käal.'

'And that,' said the she-dragon, 'is why I'm out.'

'Wait,' said Beargrr, desperation evident in her voice. 'With investment the Saga would go from strength to strength! Or, if you prefer, from weakness to strength!

But that's still pretty good. Better than going from weakness to slightly-less weakness. Although that would still be going in the right direction! And we're not even talking about that!'

'What are your projections for the next four quarters?' asked the dragon on the far left

'A seven hundred per cent rise in profitability,' said Beargrr, with the air of someone too-obviously picking a figure at random.

'And where's that profitability going to come from? What's your advertising budget?'

'Advertising is vulgar,' said Beargrr. 'We don't stoop to it.'

'Then how are you going to attract new readers to your Saga?'

'Let me turn the question around,' said Beargrr. 'Our present readership is four thousand dragons. If you *don't* invest, we will go out of business. In that circumstance our readership will be zero. If, however, you *do* invest we will retain our four thousand readers – an *increase of four thousand* over the alternative situation. Now, surely you can't turn your snout up at such a massive increase?'

'Your market is shrinking,' said the dragon. 'You have no plans for increasing your customer base. I've never *heard* of you, despite the fact that I ought to be one of your core customers. You have no collateral at all, except your personal hoards which – you readily admit – are modest. For all these reasons, I'm out.'

'Me too,' said the third dragon.

Prompted by he-knew-not-what, Käal said: 'I have the Siegfried treasure.'

Everybody in the room, including Beargrr, turned astonished faces upon him.

'You *what*?' said the fourth dragon.

'The Siegfried treasure,' said Käal. 'I have it. Doesn't that count as collateral?'

'Käal!' hissed Beargrr.

'Well, I don't have it *yet*. But I've been promised it, and will have it by . . . the end of the week.'

The one remaining dragon studied Käal carefully. Of course, a dragon of the blood would never *lie*. Still: this statement seemed so extraordinary and fantastic it strained credulity. And although a dragon of the blood never *would* lie, he or she might joke, or use irony. 'You're being serious?' asked the fourth dragon.

'Yes.'

'This is . . . the truth?'

'Of course!' said Käal, bridling at the thought of his honour being impugned.

'Well this changes things. You can have your hundred thousand crowns. But in return I want a forty per cent stake in the Saga. And I want a portion of the Siegfried treasure as collateral, until the Saga begins to turn a profit.'

'Agreed,' said Käal, airily.

'Wait!' said Beargrr. But it was too late. The dragon lifted himself off his hoard, and came down to smack tails with the pair of them, thereby finalizing the deal. 'If I don't get my collateral by the end of this week, though,' he growled, as their tailends clacked together beneath the eye, 'I shall take your offices and stock, break it all down and sell it to recoup losses.'

'No problem,' said Käal.

Beargrr, though, seemed to think that there *was* a problem. 'What have you done?' she fumed, as they left the warehouse. 'You told me you only get that treasure if you solve the mystery! And from what you said earlier, you have no idea about this mystery whatsoever!'

'Ah,' said Käal. 'But something occurred to me, as we were standing under the bright lights, there, back in the den. A crucial element of this mystery that has been overlooked by the authorities but which, just perhaps, will crack it wide open. A kind of revelation, actually.'

'What? Tell me! What?'

Käal put his lips together and nodded sagely. 'As it happens,' he said, 'I can't remember. I definitely *had* the revelation. So it'll probably come back to me.' He nodded again. 'Something to do with *tongues*, I think.'

'You outrageous moron!' cried Beargrr. 'I sent you to Doorbraak to get you out of harm's way, not so that you could specifically endanger the future of everything I own and everything I've worked towards! You've tied the destiny of the *Köschfagold Saga* to your ability to solve – in one week – a mystery that has defeated the family concerned and the authorities *for three hundred years!*'

'I'm *pretty* sure I can do it,' said Käal, vaguely. 'More to the point, I missed lunch, though. Shall we go get something to eat?'

'Käal,' said Beargrr, in a calm voice. 'You're going to have to go away from me now. Because if you stay in my immediate vicinity, I'm afraid I will cause you lasting, painful physical damage.'

Käal tried his most winning smile, but that only seemed to outrage her further. In the end he took the hint.

13

Lizbreath Salamander went home via the office. Had she gone *straight* home, things might have turned out rather different. But, having spent several days out of official circulation, she figured she needed to check in.

Luckily for her.

The research department served a number of different Sagas, and was housed on the unfashionable ground-floor of a blocky building. Her line manager was called Dragan Intheoriginal-Noreally: a plump, senior beast, originally from Talonkey. 'Oh it's you!' he said, seeing her come through the door. 'They've just left.'

Immediately Lizbreath knew that something was wrong. Nobody ever came to see her at her work. None of her countercultural friends would be seen dead there. 'Yeah?'

'I told them,' Dragan said, 'you were probably at home.'

'And you told them where my home was?'

'They seemed to know already. They were not unpissed-off, Liz. If you see what I mean.'

'Who were they?'

'They told me they worked for Burnblast. He's your Guardian, isn't he?'

'Ex-Guardian,' said Lizbreath, but with a sinking feeling in the keel of her stomach.

'Well, they looked cross,' said Dragan. 'Burnblast is a pretty important dragon, you know – pureblood, a personal friend of the Dragonlords, wealthy. Not some-one to make into an enemy.'

'No,' said Lizbreath, in a pinched voice.

'Do you know what I would do, if I were you?' said Dragan. 'Lie low. For a while. Do you have friends you could go stay with?'

'None,' said Lizbreath, thinking rapidly, 'that my Guardian doesn't *know* about. I thought that he and I had reached an understanding.'

'We-e-ell,' said Dragan, stretching back in his chair. 'Reading between the lines, from what was said by the gentledragons who have just left this office, I wonder if your "understanding" wasn't based on the concept of blackmail?'

Lizbreath looked at him, unsure how much to trust him. 'As the philosophers are fond of pointing out,' she said, 'a thing either is, or is not.'

'Well, let's play with the hypothetical that it *is*. Let's imagine that you, a junior researcher in a run-of-the-mill Starkhelm office, tried to blackmail one of the most respected, well-connected, wealthy and powerful dragons in the country.'

'Be*cause* that senior dragon . . .' Lizbreath began to say.

Dragan put up both his hands. 'Seriously, Liz? *Don't*

tell me. I don't want to know. You need to understand: his provocation doesn't *matter*. Burnblast is powerful enough to shut down any Saga that even *thought* about running a story he didn't want. Whatever he did – and I don't want to know – it's never going to see the light of day. And if the story *doesn't* see the light of day, then a hypothetical blackmailer doesn't have any leverage. You see?'

'But,' said Lizbreath, in a small voice. 'I have proof.'

'It's not about proof,' said Dragan. 'It's about power. Any Saga you approach will already have been leaned on by Burnblast's goons. If you go to the police, I guarantee the inspector detailed to investigate will be a member of Burnblast's circle. Even if you were able, purely hypothetically, to go right to the top – to speak to the Dragonlords themselves – well: what are they going to do? Discard their friend and ally of centuries? Or side with a mentally defective underage female Salamander who lived her life deliberately and provocatively in opposition to all the solid values of dragofascism? I know,' Dragan added, in a conciliatory voice, 'that you're *not* mentally defective. I would hardly employ you here if I thought otherwise. But it's all about how you are perceived, by the general public.'

Lizbreath took a deep breath. 'I'm in,' she said, shortly, 'a pickle.'

'OK. But you can't hide here. When they find you're not at home, they'll come back. And if what you say is true, you can't hide with any of your friends. So you'd better make yourself scarce. Light out for the wilderness

– go south, go north, go anywhere, but make sure it's nowhere you have previous associations with.'

Lizbreath was no dawdler. In a moment, she had assimilated the truth that her plan had turned to sludge. Dragan was right: she had to get away. But at that particular moment, she had no idea where to go.

'Drag,' she said. 'Thanks.'

'Don't thank me,' said Dragan, turning back to his work. 'I'm not involved. I didn't see you. I don't know where you're going, or when you'll be back.'

She stretched her neck out, and kissed his ear. Then, without further ado, she curled herself about and walked out through the indoor.

The worst of it, she thought, was that she couldn't go home to collect her gear. Without her gear she was severely limited in terms of what she could do. It was not just a question of money; although money would obviously be a problem. It was all the other stuff.

At the building's main entrance Lizbreath almost collided with a well-proportioned middle-aged male dragon coming the other way. Her heart thrummed for a moment, thinking that he might be one of Burnblast's goons; but the way – after she knocked accidentally into his left wing – he leapt back with a mouselike shriek led her to believe that he was not possessed of the physical bravery and ruthlessness to work as a goon. 'Sorry,' she said.

'You could be a little more careful!' he noted.

'In a hurry,' she said, and started sliding past him.

'Wait!' he cried. 'Can you help me? I'm looking for a researcher.'

'Plenty of those inside.'

'I'm looking for one in particular. Lizbreath somebody. I've sent here several ravens, and she simply has not replied. It's, well it's rude but, more than that, it's awkward. I need this research doing, and . . . well.'

Lizbreath curled her head back round. 'Lizbreath Salamander?' she said.

'That's the name!'

'I'm her. Are you Käal?'

'How did you know that?' Käal returned, a little suspiciously.

'You sent me those ravens.'

'Ah,' said Käal, with a look of relief on his face, as if the workings of a baffling magic trick had been revealed to him. 'Yes. You didn't reply!'

'I've been busy,' said Lizbreath. 'But now I'm all yours. You're up at the Vagner place, aren't you? That floating island?'

'Yes. And it's *quite* important,' said Käal. 'Indeed, in light of recent developments, it's become *really* quite important, that you do some of that research thingie that you do.'

'So,' said Lizbreath, scanning the road up and down to check that Human – or any other Burnblast henchdragon types – weren't heading straight for her. 'Basically you want me to find out what happened to Hellfire Vagner, who disappeared without trace three hundred years ago. Is that right?'

'Spot on.'

'OK,' said Lizbreath. 'I'll do it.' Käal's face lit up. Literally. 'But,' Lizbreath added, 'I need to see the island. I can't research a paper trail here in Starkhelm. That won't get any closer to the solution of the mystery. I need to be there. On the ground.'

'Well, I don't know,' said Käal, looking perplexed. 'It's a terribly exclusive place. They've an eye above and another below to monitor who comes and goes. It's not the sort of place you just sneak onto.'

'I'm not suggesting I sneak on. I'm suggesting that when you go back you take me with you as your officially credited researcher. Introduce me to Helltrik himself. Once I'm there, I'll be able to help you solve the mystery. Otherwise – no deal.'

Käal pondered this. 'Well, all right,' he said. 'When do you want to come?'

'Right now.'

'Don't you want to go back to your place, pack an overnight bag, that sort of thing?'

'Nope,' said Lizbreath. 'I want to fly, literally this minute, to the airport, and get on a Skylligator and go straight to this floating island.'

'Well,' said Käal. 'All right.'

14

Right up until the moment when the Skylligator closed its capacious jaws over them and lifted off, it seemed to Käal that this young Salamander was a nervy sort of creature. But as soon as it got airborne, he found himself struck by how remarkably cool and collected she was.

'Are you all right?' he asked her.

'Fine and dandy, now,' she said, settling back against the tongue and making herself comfortable.

She was, he had to admit, attractive; despite being small and skinny, and having – Käal noticed – a weird picture painted on her shoulder. It took him a moment to clock this as a female hömös ape. *Such* a strange and, frankly, ugly piece of body adornment! Who would want a picture of an ape on their body? Might as well have a seaslug. 'What's that?' he asked, pointing at the tattoo.

'Glenda Larson,' said Lizbreath.

'An ape?'

'Friend of mine,' she said. 'Though I couldn't say I've ever actually *met* her.'

'Aren't you a little *old* to be having an imaginary friend?'

She looked straight at him. 'Aren't you a little old to be wearing Kelvin Climb eau-de-toilette?'

Käal glanced away and muttered something about it being *just* as popular amongst mature dragons as striplings. The hostess came by, offering them snacks. Käal, who still hadn't had lunch, took a whole live lamb and a bladder of burnt sack. Lizbreath limited herself to a bag of roasted hooves.

'I'd have thought most imaginary friends are at least, you know, dragons,' Käal said. 'Not mythological creatures.'

'The apes aren't mythological. They're real enough. There used to be loads of them, before the Scorch Wars.'

That, Käal thought, was rather beside the point. He drank his sack.

'So,' Lizbreath asked, looking at him out of the corner of her eye. 'You write Sagas, then, Käal?'

'That's right.'

'So, Käal. Is there a Mrs Käal? Is there a *Lady* Saga? A helpmeet, somebody who wears spectacles made of lobsters and a zebra-stripe bikini over a sarong?'

Käal blinked. 'I have no idea what you're talking about,' he said.

'A private joke. But are you really a lone Saga-sayer? All on your ownsome?'

'I have an understanding with a very large lady dragon, if you must know,' Käal said, stiffly. 'It is complicated, because she is hamfast with a very large, senior, very senior dragon.'

'Oho? Hamfast you say? And he doesn't mind you

getting your talons on his lady's hams?' Moments before she'd been a quivering nervous wreck on the streets of Starkhelm; now she was this superconfident hoof-crunching minx!

'They're very *shapely* hams,' said Käal, awkwardly. 'Wonderfully plump. Armoured like a bank vault.' As he spoke, though, he had a mental flash of the furious disdain to which Beargrr had treated him at their recent parting. Things, he realized, were not as happy between them as he was implying. 'What I have with her,' he pressed on, doggedly, as if saying made it so, 'is – special.'

'Isn't *special*,' Lizbreath said, 'a variant of the word *specious*?'

'You have a wide-ranging vocabulary,' noted Käal.

'Thanks!'

'Oh, it's not a compliment. I'm not sure that words are at their best free-range. Personally I've always thought that words should be like livestock: kept in pens, for when we need them, not galloping all over the countryside.'

'Spoken like a Saga journeydragon,' said Lizbreath, haughtily.

'And what do you mean by *that*?' Käal demanded, his backspines bristling.

'All the Sagas are just variants of older Sagas,' she replied, dismissively. 'It's the same story over and over. Dragons are afraid of novelty. It didn't use to be that way: we used to prefer to hunt wild livestock. Now that's seen as unhygienic and all our mutton is grown in sheds. Words are the same. Some poets *prefer* to chase wild words over the grass-clogged hillsides. Look at the way *I'm* treated. The legal position is that, effectively, I'm insane. Why? Because, every now and again, I try something new.'

'Like,' said Käal, trying to be withering, 'painting a female ape on your shoulder?'

'It's not painted,' said Lizbreath, in a tired voice.

Straight away Käal felt ashamed. It had been a cheap shot. Still, his professional pride had been hurt. 'Sagas are not as old and staid as you're suggesting, you know. Some newness, provided it is dignified and elevated, is not only permitted but actually required. It's just that, by the same token, Sagas are not Salamander gossip scrolls, or gnomic texts.' He was feeling a little awkward in his own half-adopted grand-old-dragon manner, and tried to soften it. 'I'm not so different to you, you know. I understand the appeal of the old wild hunt. But dragons are masters of the world, now. We have . . . responsibilities.'

For some reason this riled Lizbreath. 'Really? Because it seems to me that it's the most senior dragons who are the most *ir*responsible.'

'Come, Lizbreath, we've just met!' he said to her. 'Let's not get off on the wrong claw.'

'All right. Look, I'm sorry if I'm snappish,' she said. 'I've had a hard few days.'

'I understand,' said Käal.

They landed at the airport, and Käal and Lizbreath made the rest of their journey under their own steam, smoke and fire – a pleasant cross-country flight northward. Soon enough the enormous bulk of Door-braak became unmissable in the sky.

They landed at the main entrance. 'Right,' said Käal. 'Let's tell Helltrik that you're here.'

He asked a passing firedrake where Mon. Vagner was. The firedrake gestured loosely in an upward dir-ection and slunk off, leaving the two of them no better off.

As they crossed the main hall they encountered Marrer. 'Hello!' said the young dragon. 'Who's this?'

'Lizbreath Salamander,' said Lizbreath, bringing her tailend up and round to tap his. 'I'm Käal's research assistant. I'm here to help with . . . his project.'

'Oh! Well – splendid,' said Marrer, although his expression rather implied that it wasn't splendid. 'In that case, I'm pleased to welcome you here to Door-braak!'

'Thank you very much.'

'So Mis. – Salamander, is it? Mis. Salamander – will you be staying in Käal's room, or would you like a room of your own?'

'Would it be too awkward to ask for a room of my own?' said Lizbreath, batting her eyelids at Marrer so as to generate a pretty little series of snare-drum noises.

'Not at all,' said Marrer, distractedly. He clapped his hindlimb on the floor, and a firedrake appeared instantly. 'Can you show Mis. Salamander to the,' he asked, his eye falling for the first time on the design on Lizbreath's shoulder, 'to the guest room on the thirteenth floor?'

'Too kind, *thank* you,' Lizbreath gushed.

'If you'll excuse me,' he said, his eyeline on the girl tattoo. 'I hope to meet you properly later, Mis. Salamander.'

'I'm looking forward to it,' she said.

The firedrake took them, silently, up to the thirteenth floor, deposited Lizbreath in a rather small room, before slinking off with a 'things-will-only-get-worse' expression on his face. Lizbreath, by contrast, was very cheerful. 'Well this is nice,' she said, stretching herself on the bed to try it for size. It was small, though plenty big enough for her. 'Better than the alternative, at any rate.'

'You're not here to lounge about on a bed,' said Käal, severely. 'You're supposed to help me solve this mystery.'

'Absolutely!' said Lizbreath sitting up. 'Well let's crack on! So, the mystery is that this young, wealthy, pureblood she-dragon vanished into thin air three centuries ago. She couldn't get off the island, because it was isolated by prolonged drizzle, and besides the two panoptic eyes would have seen her. But she might have been murdered here, and smuggled off by some means at a later date. Or she might still be alive, in which case we need to work out how why and where. Plus, somebody is sending severed dragon tongues, one a year, to the head of the Vagner family.'

'The first one was Hellfire's,' Käal put in. 'So she either is dead, or else she's alive in an, er, tongueless sort of a way.'

'Right! That's as much as I know. What have you done?'

'What?'

Lizbreath arched her back and opened her wings. 'What have you *done*? What investigations have you undertaken into the disappearance, and likely death, of this young she-dragon?'

'Ah!' said Käal. 'Well, I've looked about.'

'Looked about?'

'Yes. All over the island.'

'All over?'

'Well, not in Helltrik's private hoard chamber, of course. It would be pretty unseemly to go poking through his gold after all! And I, and I haven't been *permitted* to go into the Vagner family burial chamber, which is in the centre of Doorbraak, of course. But apart from that . . .'

'You haven't been permitted?' said Lizbreath, sharply.

'No. That's the one part of the island that's out of bounds. But everywhere else . . .'

'Interesting,' Lizbreath said. 'So the tomb is the *one* place they said you couldn't go? We will have to go there.'

'Well!' said Käal. 'I don't know if that would be very respectful . . .'

'Don't be stupid. We're investigating a mystery. The currency of mystery is the secret. We have a duty to poke our snouts into any and all secrets, like this burial chamber. I'll bet we'll find what we're looking for in there.'

'Well,' said Käal, uncertainly. 'If you really think so . . .'

'But that will have to wait until the island's asleep,' said Lizbreath. 'Meanwhile, tell me what you've found out.'

'Found out?' repeated Käal. 'How do you mean?'

'In your investigations. Looking around the islands. What have you discovered?'

'Ah!' Käal thought for a bit. 'Well, the gardens are very nice.'

'Come now – the mystery! What have you discovered about the mystery?'

'Not,' said Käal, speaking very slowly, 'a *great* deal . . .'

'Did you look through the eyes?'

'You mean the ones above and below the island? No.' When Lizbreath made a surprised face, he added: 'The police did all that. I'm sure there's nothing we can learn from them.'

'*We're* investigating this,' said Lizbreath. 'Not the police. Well, we'll do that tomorrow. You take the top eye, and I'll take the bottom. What else? What did you find in Hellfire's old room?'

'Where?'

'In Hellfire's old room? The one she lived in, before she disappeared? Were there any clues in there?'

'I haven't, exactly, checked the room . . . look, once again, I'm confident the police checked all that sort of thing out. There's nothing to be gained from reinventing the wheel . . .'

'Hard to believe you're quite as much a berk as you appear,' Lizbreath said, pleasantly. 'Come on. That'll be our first stop.'

They went into the main hall. A firedrake was sweeping the marble tiles in a desultory sort of way. 'Hello!' said Lizbreath, brightly. 'Can you tell me where we might find the rooms formerly occupied by Hellfire Vagner?'

'Haunted,' said the firedrake, glumly.

'Are they?'

'Whole castle is. Bad things happened here. Young Hellfire?' The firedrake shook its skinny head. 'Dead and gone.'

'We'd still like to look in her room, please.'

'Unsettled spirits in this place,' the firedrake said, doomily. 'The whole island. Stra-a-a-ange goings on! It's down those stairs, seventh floor, northside. Nobody's been in there for three centuries.'

'Surely,' Käal said, feeling he had to make the point, 'surely the police looked through them, after her disappearance?'

The firedrake settled its blank eyes on Käal. 'They didn't find nothing,' he said. 'Disappeared, they say!' He clucked, disapprovingly. 'Disappeared *from life*,' he said. 'Appeared amongst the *dead*.'

'Thank you!' said Lizbreath, chirpily.

Käal and Lizbreath descended the stairway together. 'I'm impressed you manage to get those firedrakes talking,' he said to her. 'They're not so chatty around me.' As soon as they emerged on the seventh floor the location of Hellfire's old room was obvious: the door was layered in three centuries of dust. 'Untouched in all this time!' said Lizbreath, putting her claw on the door-handle. 'What *will* we find inside?'

The door opened with a creak so creaky it sounded as if the air itself needed lubricating. Inside was a spacious apartment. Light, coming through a large crystal window, fell on all the furniture you would expect to find in a young she-dragon's lair, and every surface was covered with dust, like a skin. Stepping into the space was eerie. And spooky. And sneezy.

'It obviously hasn't been touched since her disappearance,' said Lizbreath. 'It's like they've kept it – as a shrine to her.'

'I'm sure they'd keep a shrine cleaner than this,' said Käal, as he sneezed spikes of flame from his nostrils. 'You ever see a dusty shrine? I think not.'

Lizbreath was at the bookshelf. 'All the usual scrolls and Sagas,' she said. 'Exactly the sort of thing a respectable young she-dragon would read: *Adventures of Huckleberry Fang*; *The Tail of Peter Dragon*; *Treasure Flying Island*; *The Wonderfully Chewy Wizard of Oz*; *Fiery Potter and the Goblet of Gold*.

'What's this?' said Käal, at the desk. 'A television, is it?' He puffed air from his nostrils, and blew a cloud of fine dust in the air off the object.

'Ah!' cried Lizbreath, delighted. 'Now that is *very* interesting.'

'A clue?'

'It's a computer.'

'A what?'

'Come, Käal,' said Lizbreath, banteringly. 'Don't tell me you haven't heard of computers?'

'I'm guessing from the *come* prefix that they have some sexual purpose?'

'No!' said Lizbreath, shocked. 'Computers have nothing to do with any of that! Well,' she added, scratching her chin, 'not *entirely* to do with that, at any rate. *Computers* are data-processing devices. They run programs to make virtual scrolls, play games, and even connect with other computers to generate a web.'

'Like between a frog's toes?'

'Well . . . I suppose you could say so.'

'So why haven't I heard of these computers, then?' Käal asked. 'Are they a young person's toy?'

'Pretty much,' said Lizbreath. She reached a claw round to the back of the 'computer' and scrabbled around for a while. 'They're fairly common in the counterculture. But I suppose a respectable dragon like yourself would have nothing to do with countercultural shenanigans.'

'Indeed not! Neither shenanigans, nor henanigans. I have my reputation to think of.'

'Exactly,' said Lizbreath. 'Which makes it all the more intriguing that a respectable young she-dragon, a member of the clan in which the blood of Regin flows purest of all . . . that such an individual would own one of these. Ah!'

The screen was suddenly lit from within. 'Oh!' said Käal. 'You've . . . what, switched it on?'

'Let's have a look,' said Lizbreath. She pulled a shelf out from underneath the desk, upon which Käal saw a rectangular tray in which a series of molars had been arranged in rows. Lizbreath's claws clattered and sclattered across this strange tray, and the whiteness of the screen filled with writing.

'That's clever!' said Käal. 'How are you doing that?'

'I'm trying to drag-log-on,' said Lizbreath. Several rectangles appeared on the screen, each one plastered on the others, and each heralded with a 'ding!' noise. Käal peered at the screen. 'What does "Error Code 404" mean?' he asked.

'It means this software hasn't been upgraded in four hundred and four years,' said Lizbreath, through gritted teeth. 'It's an old system.' She pressed some more buttons, and a new rectangle appeared: 'SERPENT NOT FOUND'. 'Well, I should be able to see the sites she was drag-logged-into.' There was more tippity tappity.

Bored, Käal strolled about the room. 'Spooky,' he said. 'Being in here.' He picked up a paperweight: a crystal globe, containing a tiny model of a landscape. He shook it, and red-and-yellow imitation flames filled the inside of the sphere. He put it back on the side, and watched them slowly settle again, leaving the scene in the globe as still and tranquil as it had been when he first saw it. On the far wall was a Michael Dragson poster. 'Hmmf!' said Käal. 'Remember him?'

'That does rather date the room,' agreed Lizbreath. She appeared to have finished with the 'computer', and was looking through Hellfire's adornment wardrobe. 'Find out anything useful?' Käal prompted.

'Well, she was clearly a young she-dragon with a wide range of interests,' Lizbreath replied, absently. 'A shame she was cut off on this island. If she'd lived in a big city, like Starkhelm, she might have found some like-minded dragon to hang out with.'

'Like – you did?'

Lizbreath flashed a smile. 'At least I'm still alive.'

'Maybe Hellfire's still alive,' Käal said.

'Maybe. But if so, then where is she?'

'Not on this island any more, certainly,' Käal mused. 'It's been pretty thoroughly searched, not once but many times. So – if she's alive – she must be somewhere else.'

'On the mainland, maybe,' said Lizbreath. She looked to be searching for something specific; but if she was, she didn't find it.

'Not in Scandragonia, I think,' said Käal. 'Her family has put up enormous rewards, and hired flights and flights of private investigators. Scandragonia's not that big a place. If she were here, I think she'd have been found.'

'Further afield, then,' said Lizbreath, standing up straight in the middle of the sepulchral room. 'Even the Vagner millions can't sieve the entire world.'

'You think she *is* alive, then?'

'I don't know. But I doubt it. Why should she hide? The obvious reason would be; because she is afraid. But what makes a dragon afraid?'

'Something very terrible.'

'So on the one hand we need to calculate the odds that she has not only escaped this something terrible, but also successfully evaded it for three centuries. On the other hand we need to work out the odds that the something terrible *got* to her and snuffed her out. Balance of probabilities is with the second of those two, don't you think?'

'Poor Hellfire!' said Käal, looking around the dismal space.

'Hey,' said Lizbreath, bringing out a metallic tub or box of some sort. 'Well well!'

'What is it?'

'An ice-cream maker, I *do* believe.'

'You're *kidding*!' gasped Käal. 'Surely those aren't legal?'

'Perfectly illegal. Ice cream is a very dangerous substance.' The smile on Lizbreath's face rather contradicted the tenor of what she was saying. 'Still, a lot of the wilder kids like to muck about with it.'

'In heaven's name – why?'

'The thrill, the danger, the *taste*,' said Lizbreath. 'You make a lump of it, and a friend – wearing gloves, of course – tosses it at you. You have to blast it with fire and eat it. If you get it right the dangerous ice turns into cold but just about edible slurry, very sweet, rather nice. But if you get it *wrong*, then you'll suffer a scarring freeze-burn that you won't forget in a hurry.'

'Hellfire had one of those burn marks on her tongue,' Käal remembered. 'That's how Helltrik recognized her severed tongue when it was sent to him. I guess she played that game one too many times.'

'I'm more interested in what a respectable well-bred pureblood young she-dragon like Hellfire is *doing* with a piece of kit like this in her room.' She put it back. 'Come on,' said Lizbreath. 'I'm hungry.'

They went down to the gardens, and asked a firedrake to release a couple of sheep from the larder pens. The beasts waddled slowly towards the trees. Lizbreath swooped and plucked hers in one easy moment, and took its head off with a single bite. Käal, not so nimble, had to chase his about a little. 'I assume you have a "computer", then,' he said.

'Perhaps you've heard the stories,' Lizbreath replied, staring into the distance, where the late afternoon clouds gathered eighty shades of red and yellow on their plump western sides. 'That I sleep on a hoard of silver?'

'I did hear something,' Käal conceded. 'It sounded like a pretty . . . wacky sort of thing to do. Counter-cultural, is it? An act of rebellion against normalcy? Seriously – a hoard of *silver*?'

'It's not strictly true that I sleep on a hoard of silver,' said Lizbreath. The last of her sheep disappeared, legs-last, into her maw. 'Although I do sleep on a hoard of silver-*coloured things*. And I certainly wouldn't ever con-template sleeping on a hoard of gold. What would be the use?'

'Use?' asked Käal.

'Gold is inert.'

'Inert? It's extremely valuable!'

'Its value only exists in the context of exchange,' said Lizbreath. 'The irony is that dragons hardly ever use it that way. Instead they accumulate a great mass of gold, and then have to go through the financial contortions of raising paper-money loans mortgaged upon their hoards, at punitive rates of interest, and so on, and so forth. Me, I prefer just to use the gold. Since everybody is desperate to get gold, and I'm one of very few people spending it, my purchasing power is tremendous. I'm still young, but I've been able to buy some of the most sophisticated tech gadgets available in the world – and one or two out of it.'

'And, let me guess: this tech happens to be silver-coloured?'

'That's right.'

'And you sleep on it?'

'A girl's got to sleep somewhere.'

'So, instead of curling up in a comfortable bed of gold, you sleep on a big pile of "computers" . . . yes?'

'Only *some* of my gear is computers,' said Lizbreath, distantly. 'I have other sorts of tech, too.'

'Oh I'm not mocking,' said Käal, picking a hoof from between his front teeth, 'You know what I sleep on? Ingots. It's supposed to be modern and stylish: fresh-minted gold ingots in a sparsely furnished bedroom. Supposed to be up-to-the-minute Scandragonian. You know what it *really* is? Uncomfortable.' He shook his head. 'I don't know why I do it, really.'

'Why *do* you?'

'I'm a slave to convention, I suppose. In a way I envy you – that you're not a slave in that way, I mean.'

'It has advantages and disadvantages,' said Lizbreath, looking west and speaking in a queerly passionless voice.

15

That night Käal slept uneasily. He kept waking from half-remembered dreams, many of which concerned Lizbreath. Not his type at all, of course. And yet he found he couldn't get her out of his dragon brain.

The morning came, and Käal did not feel rested. Lizbreath, knocking on his door with her hind legs, seemed filled with enormous energy. 'Where does a hungry young dragon get breakfast round here?'

They descended to the gardens, where chickens and pigs were being served up to various dragons. Helltrik was there, reading a *Saga Telegraph* with crystal lenses, held in a queer O-O shaped structure, balanced on his snout. Marrer and Redsnapper were there too. Käal even caught sight of Ghastly, lurking in the foliage, jumping out to grab a piglet, and then retreating from public view.

'Ah, Käal,' said Helltrik, putting his Saga down. 'Good to see you. And is this your new researcher? Marrer told me that you'd hired some dragon to help you with your enquiries.'

Lizbreath fluttered forward and tapped her tailend against his very politely. 'It's an honour to be here, sir,' she said with what (although he'd only known her for a

day) Käal could tell was wholly uncharacteristic deference. 'Doorbraak *is* beautiful!'

'Thank you!' said Helltrik, evidently pleased.

'I'm only sorry to be here under such disagreeable
circumstances,' said Lizbreath, demurely. 'The tragic
evanishment of your grand-niece. I hope Käal and I
are able to shed some light on this mystery, for the
sake of your peace of mind, and that of your whole
distinguished family.'

' "Evanishment"?' said Käal.

'What a well-bred she-dragon!' Helltrik said to
Marrer. 'Rarer and rarer in this day and age. What's
your name, my dear?'

'Lizbreath Salamander,' said Lizbreath.

'Delighted to meet you Lizbreath,' said Helltrik,
repositioning his crystal lenses and picking up the *Saga
Telegraph*. 'If there's anything, anything *at all*, that I can
do to help your researches, don't hesitate to ask,' he said
in the tone of a man who wanted to be left entirely alone
to read his paper.

'Thank you, sir! Actually, there *is* one thing.'

Without removing his gaze from his paper, Helltrik
arched one eyebrow.

'We were hoping to look in the tomb of your ancestors.'

'The Clawsoleum?' said Helltrik, in a stony voice, and
still without taking his gaze from the Saga he was reading. 'I'm afraid not, my dear. It's strictly out of bounds.
Nobody goes in there.'

'That's one reason why we were hoping to look

inside . . . it strikes me, strikes us, as one place that was never searched – for Hellfire's body, you know.'

'In point of fact it *was* searched, after the fateful day,' said Helltrik, in a low voice. 'And nothing was found. Nothing except what is supposed to be in there – the bodies of fifteen score dead Vagner dragons, laid to their sacred rest, and *not* to be desecrated. It's out of the question, my dear.'

'Of course,' said Lizbreath, looking abashed. 'I apologize for asking. It was insensitive of me.'

'Don't mention it,' Helltrik drawled, dismissively. Käal snaffled a chicken and ate it in one bite. 'Shall we get on, then, Lizbreath? Lots of stuff-finding to be done, after all. Good morning, Helltrik.'

'Good morning, sir!' said Lizbreath, brightly.

As they were moving away Helltrik spoke again. 'Lizbreath Salamander,' he said.

Lizbreath stopped. 'Yes, sir?'

'Where have I heard that name before?'

'I'd be very surprised if you've heard it anywhere, sir. I'm very far from being famous. I'm a humble researcher, a nobody.'

'Nevertheless, I'm sure I have heard it,' said Helltrik. 'And recently, too. One of my friends was . . . never mind, it'll come back to me. Good day!'

'Good day.'

When they were back inside the castle, Käal tried asking 'what was *that* all about?', but Lizbreath ignored it. 'One thing we learned there,' she said. 'We absolutely have to get a peek inside that Clawsoleum.'

'Our employer just told us not to,' Käal pointed out.

'The person paying the bills. The dragon who wants us to solve this mystery. He said no, so we won't.' Käal thought about it. 'Beside, how are we supposed to get in there? It's a Clawsoleum. It will be locked.'

'They *must* open it up, sometimes,' said Lizbreath. 'To put new corpses in, for instance.'

'Lizbreath,' said Käal. 'You're talking about desecrating a tomb.'

'I know! It's exciting, isn't it?'

'No,' said Käal, from the heart. 'No it isn't! It's the *opposite* of exciting! The very thought of it makes me feel sick in my stomach, and tingly under my scales! It makes my heart race! Exciting is the *last* thing it is!' He thought for a moment, and added: 'Oh. Ah . . .'

'Dragonkind needs a little desecrating from time to time,' said Lizbreath, with an offhand blasphemy.

'Helltrik Vagner is our host. We'd be violating his courtesy.'

Lizbreath gave him a big, reeky grin and darted down the main stairway. Käal lumbered after her. 'You don't trust him!' he called after her. 'But how can you not trust him? He hired me to solve the mystery! He wants the mystery solved. He'd hardly want to put obstacles in our way!'

'And yet he specifically forbids us from looking inside his Clawsoleum.' They emerged on the lowest level; a dimly lit hallway, coped in onyx-granite and lit by a central glowglobe. The floor was covered with a huge mosaic – Regin the King, the family's ancestor, standing in a heraldic pose, with a stern expression in his orange eye.

178

'It must be under here,' said Lizbreath, scouting the design. 'I'd say that Reggie's head lifts up.'

'Don't call him Reggie!' squeaked Käal, genuinely spooked by the offhanded ease of his companion's disrespect for the pieties of dragon tradition.

'He's long dead,' Lizbreath said, peering closely at the image. 'He doesn't care. Here! Look! The old boy's right nostril is a keyhole.'

'Don't call him the old boy – he is the *pater draconis*,' Käal started saying, until he was distracted by the oddity of the set-up. 'Seriously? His nostril?'

'I'd say: insert the key and turn it, and the whole thing lifts up. To reveal steps down to the Clawsoleum.'

'Well, we don't have the key,' Käal noted. 'So that's where this trail ends. I can't pretend I'm sorry . . . it saves us from committing terrible sacrilege.'

From her reticule Lizbreath brought out a tapering sliver of stone. There was no mistaking what it was.

'Where,' Käal demanded, 'in the name of wild *Woden* did you get that?'

'Hellfire's room.'

'Well that could be *any* key, to any room! It probably opens her secret diary.'

'It has Vagner Clawsoleum written along the shaft, in small runes.'

'You're kidding?' Käal sat back on his tail. 'What was she doing in her bedroom with a key to the family tomb?'

'That's a good question. Shall I try it?'

'No!' said Käal, looking guiltily around.

'Come on, Käal! Don't you want to see the last

resting place of all those legendary dragons? Regin's son, Deas, is down there, you know.'

'Helltrik specifically said we were not permitted to – Lizbreath I forbid you to put that key in that keyhole.' She slid the key into its slot. 'Liz! Lizbreath Salamander, I *forbid* you from turning that key in that . . .' She turned the key.

Nothing happened.

'Oh,' said Käal, disappointed despite himself. 'It's not the key, after all.'

'No,' said Lizbreath, thoughtfully. 'It went into the mechanism. I think it is the right key. It just won't turn. I wonder why?'

'Maybe the mechanism is stiff? After all, it's not often used.'

'I don't think it's that,' said Lizbreath. 'I think it's one of those magic locks. I think the key only works if it is being held by a certain person. Presumably somebody with Vagner blood in their veins.'

'Well that's that! Nothing more we can do!'

'We need to find a family member who will help us,' said Lizbreath. 'We absolutely have to get down there.'

'Why?'

'Käal, listen to me. I am convinced the solution to this whole mystery is there, just beneath our feet. There's a secret at the heart of the island, of the Vagners – and if we can get down there we'll understand everything.'

'Golly,' said Käal, picturing himself *that very day* claiming the Siegfried treasure, achieving personal wealth, saving the *Köschfagold Saga* and redeeming himself in the eyes of Beargrr. 'Well,' he said. 'Perhaps we could ask Asheila?'

'Asheila Vagner?'

'Yes. She and I have become – shall we say *friendly*.'

'Friendly? Do you mean what I think you mean?'

'That depends on whether you're thinking what I think you think I mean when I mean that.'

'You and Asheila Vagner – you've been drilling the dragon with *her*?

'We have something rather special,' said Käal, awkwardly.

'What about the special thing you've got going with that she-dragon in Starkhelm?'

'Look, the point of me mentioning it wasn't to give you the chance to make fun of me,' said Käal, stiffly. 'It was to suggest a way of getting into the Vagner tomb.'

'*Excellent* idea, Clawsanova. Let's nip upstairs and see if the lady can be persuaded.' Lizbreath tried to take hold of the key and remove it from the keyhole, but it would not budge. 'Hmm,' she said. 'Well, that's awkward.'

'Give it a proper yank.'

'That would only break it. I'm certain, now, that this is a magical device. Now that it is engaged, it will only move if a Vagner touches it. Come on! No time to lose! We need to try and persuade your girldragon to help us.'

Having suggested this way forward, Käal was now having second thoughts. He could almost hear Asheila's voice saying 'No!' in that implacable way she had. On the other hand, the thought of solving the Vagner mystery that very day was too intoxicating for him.

The two dragons had only just started up the stairway when a loud click behind them, like the bolt sliding across on a rifle, stopped them. Slowly they both snaked their necks so as to bring their heads right around. The hallway was empty.

A line of shadow had appeared, haloing Regin's mosaicish head.

They went back down. By grasping Regin's ear it was possible to swing the whole portion of floor up and round, revealing a curl of downward stone steps. 'I don't understand,' said Lizbreath.

It was the first time since meeting her that Käal had seen her completely wrongfooted. 'I guess it wasn't a magic lock after all,' he said. 'I suppose it was just a little stiff.'

'It can't be that.'

'You must have turned it almost enough to spring the mechanism, then it got stiff so you stopped. But us walking away must have shaken it past its tipping point, and spung! There you go.'

She looked at him. 'Spung?'

'As in, the noise a lock makes when it is opened.'

'Except that it wasn't *stiff*,' she said. 'It was completely motionless.' She looked puzzled. 'I could have *sworn* it was a magic key!'

'Anyway,' said Käal. 'It's good news. We can go down, sort this mystery out, and I don't have to try and recruit the, to speak frankly, unstable Asheila.'

Lizbreath didn't lose her puzzled expression, but she said: 'True. Well, let's go down.'

The stairs were small, and curved sharply round; they had to proceed by walking awkwardly on their back legs only. 'It must be quite a squeeze getting the corpse of a full-grown dragon down here,' Lizbreath noted.

There were seven turns in the stone stairway, and finally they emerged into a vast space, as wide as was the main trunk of the castle itself. Tiny windows sparsely arranged around the edge of the space admitted a thin, chill light, unpleasantly blue in tint. The sepulchre was a huge circular space, and around the edge were arranged the bodies of great Vagners of the past.

Käal and Lizbreath alit upon the white marble flags. 'How many did Helltrik say?' Lizbreath said, in a hushed voice. 'Fifteen score?'

'It's amazing!' whispered Käal.

All the dragons were interred, according to dragon tradition, laid upon stone pyramidic structures meant to represent their hoards. They were not otherwise enclosed. In the few days after death, the ferocious internal chemistry of any given dragon parched and mummified the majority of the softer flesh; and the outer scales were, of course, perfectly imperishable. So these once great figures looked in death pretty much as they had done in life, save only their eyes, which melted from their sockets during the first year or so post-mortem.

They were laid snout inward, and their names were inscribed in gold letters upon the cold marble of their monuments. Käal felt the awe of their presence.

Hundreds of dead Vagners! Thousands of years of family lineage!

'Right,' said Lizbreath, brightly, clacking her fore-claws together. 'It must be in here somewhere!'

'It?' repeated Käal. 'What?'

Lizbreath went low on all fours and made a complete circuit of the space. She darted from tomb to tomb, tapping each monument in turn with the hard point of her tailend.

'What are you *doing*?' Käal hissed.

'It's not here!' she replied. 'But it must be! Hidden . . . hidden . . . But where? Not inside the monuments . . . that wouldn't work at all.'

Doubts about what they were doing were starting to intrude into Käal. 'What are you talking about? And, wait a minute. You said the solution to the mystery would be down here! There's no solution to the mystery here! It's just a ring of mummified dragon corpses!'

With increasingly frantic motion, Lizbreath ran from monument to monument. 'It must be here!' She eeled to the centre of the room, and fished some device or other from her reticule.

'I think we should leave,' said Käal, his anxiety getting the better of him. 'Before somebody finds us down here.'

Lizbreath angled her handheld whatever-it-was in a sweep all about the room. 'Nothing!' she said, as if it were a swear-word.

'There's nothing here! Come on, Liz, I don't like this . . . not at all.' Käal made his way back towards the central stair-stem.

Lizbreath hurried back to one of the monuments. It was the corpse of Deatheagle: scowling and eyeless, his bulky tail coiled round to lie across his neck, he glowered down at her. She took hold of the creature's upper lip, and levered open its mouth.

'Liz! What are you doing?' Käal cried. 'That's tantamount to desecration!'

'Well well,' she said.

'What? What is it? Have you found what you were looking for?'

'No,' she said. 'But I have found a clue.'

'What clue?'

'The tongue has been cut out of this dragon.'

'No *way*!' said Käal, his excitement overriding his apprehension. 'Is that where *all* the tongues came from?'

Lizbreath went along to the next dragon, and pulled open its mouth. 'Looks that way,' she confirmed.

Between them, they checked a dozen or so of the illustrious corpses. Every single one had its tongue removed. 'Extraordinary!' said Käal. 'Wait until we tell Helltrik that this is where his tongues have been coming from!' Then he added, second-thoughtishly: 'Wait, if we tell him, he'll know that we've been inside his family's Clawsoleum.'

'That's true.'

'That's awkward. He specifically told us not to.'

'I suggest we don't tell him. Let's solve the whole mystery, first. This is an important clue, after all. Let's assume that whoever cut out Hellfire's tongue is the same dragon who cut out all these *other* dragon tongues. That means it must be somebody on the island! If the entrance had been guarded with a magic lock, like I thought, that would have narrowed it down to a Vagner family member. But,' the puzzled expression crossed her eye again, 'I guess it's a regular lock, so it could be anyone. But somebody on the island!'

'Why, though?'

'Good question. Answer that, I'd say, and we'll be able to wrap this mystery up.'

'Hey,' he said. 'What were *you* looking for?'

'What?'

'You were looking for something, and you didn't find it. You waved that strange device about, from your reticule – what *was* that? What were you looking for?'

'You really want to know?' said Lizbreath.

There was a loud bang, a burst of smoke, and the dragon's corpse beside them exploded. Käal yelled out sheer terror. Lizbreath's reactions were quicker. She threw herself into her companion's torso with such force that, though she was much smaller than he, Käal was bundled out of the way. They skidded together along the marble, both got their footing and leapt as one for cover behind a funerary monument. From the corner of his eye Käal glimpsed a blast of fire stretch from the staircase towards them – but it was a strange fire, unlike any he had seen before: an oddly muted shade of red, thin as a blade of metal. He pulled his head down and the fire collided with the monument podium. Chunks of stone flew outwards through a swelling cloud of masonry dust. Shards clattered against Käal's scales. 'What *is* that?' Käal asked.

'It's something *not* to get hit by,' said Lizbreath,

pulling Käal by his left wing. Together they ducked behind the nearest memorial.

'I've never seen fire like that! Who's blasting it?'

There was a third clunking explosion, an instant rosebloom of pale pink smoke and the sound of debris spattering to the stone floor. 'How does he keep the stream of fire so thin?' Käal wondered aloud. 'I saw a dracrobat from the Fangish Circus last year blow some amazingly-shaped smoke rings. Is it a trick like that?'

'It's not coming from any dragon's nostrils,' hissed Lizbreath, trying to peer round the memorial.

'It's not?'

'It's from a device! Now be quiet!'

'Like – a flame-thrower?' said Käal, disbelieving. 'I still don't see how it keeps the line of flame so skinny, though. Or that colour. And why is whoever-it-is trying to shoot us . . .'

'Shh!' said Lizbreath again.

Käal pushed one eye around the edge of the funeral monument. He caught a glimpse of somebody scuttling from the base of the stairs away to the left; but through the slowly drifting rags of smoke, and in the dim blue light, he couldn't make out who it might be.

'When I say go,' whispered Lizbreath, who was bracing her back against the rump of the mummified remains of an ancestor Vagner dragon, 'go.'

'What do I do?' asked Käal, slightly wild-eyed.

She paused. 'What?'

'What do I do when you say go?'

'Go!' she hissed.

'Yes, *go*, I got that bit. But what do I *do* when you say go?'

'Go!'she hissed.

'Do you think I'm deaf?' he snapped back, crossly. 'I *heard* that bit. When you say go – right, sure. But *when* you say it, what are you expecting me to do?'

'When I say go – go! It's not a complicated utterance.'

'Oh, so *now* you're going to say go-go? Make up your mind.'

Lizbreath looked at Käal very closely. 'I'm amazed your brain hasn't collapsed under the weight of its own colossal idiocy,' she whispered.

'Charming!' he said.

'Go – *now!*' she yelled, suddenly, pushing her hind legs with all her might and leaping into the air, flinging her wings wide at the same time. The mummified body of Bullar Vagner was propelled into the air – much larger than she of course, but lighter too. It flew through the air, caromed off the ceiling and started falling. Its dead wings fluttered, caught the air and opened wide. The corpse glided lurchingly forward in a grisly approximation of life.

Lizbreath ran-flew straight for and up the stairs. Käal was a heartbeat behind. As he crossed the floor he caught sight of one, then two, then three of the strange lines of red light blasting at the freakily airborne corpse. The lights played upon the body, and then Käal saw something impossible. He saw the flame break *through* the scales that lined Bullar's vacant body.

But of course, he couldn't have seen that. You know

as well as I that *no* fire can penetrate the scales of a dragon.

It was so incomprehensible a sight that it almost stopped Käal on the spot. But the instinct for self-preservation carried him on. He reached the foot of the stairway just as the corpse of Bullar crashed enormously into the floor. He threw himself up, and a moment later he was in the hallway above.

16

'Keep going,' Lizbreath hollered at him. 'That weapon is not to be trifled with!'

They dashed up the main stairway, through corridors, past a startled firedrake carrying a shovel. They did not stop until they burst out through the main entrance and into the gardens.

'Did you *see* that?' Käal gasped. 'That burst of fire broke straight through the scales on that old dragon!'

'Unless you want,' Lizbreath snapped at him, grabbing his wing-elbow, 'to explain to all the Vagners that you've just desecrated their Clawsoleum, I *suggest* you keep your voice *down*.'

'Oh!' said Käal, looking around. 'But,' he went on, in a quieter tone, 'that guy was trying to kill us . . . wasn't he?'

'Yes, he was,' said Lizbreath, looking carefully around her.

'I saw his fire go straight *through* the scales of that dead dragon's body!' Käal said. 'I must have hallucinated that. Nothing goes through dragon scales.'

'Käal—' Lizbreath started to say. But she was distracted. 'There!' she cried, pointing.

A dragon was spying on them, from the shrubbery by

the main entrance. Both Käal and Lizbreath turned to look, and the creature knew itself observed, and got spooked. It broke from the foliage and dashed for the castle entrance.

There was no mistaking who it was. 'Asheila!' Käal called. 'Asheila!'

She vanished inside the building.

Käal made to go after her, but Lizbreath held him back. 'She might be armed.'

'Asheila?' he said, astonished. 'You don't think she was the one who blew fire at us, down there, do you?'

'She was following us!' said Lizbreath. 'She was spying on us. All I'm saying is – she might be armed.'

'Armed?' said Käal, breaking way. 'Don't be absurd.'

'Somebody was *shooting* at us, Käal!'

'Asheila? No.' He hurried inside the castle.

17

Asheila was nowhere to be seen, but Käal guessed that she had gone back to her room. He raced up to her apartment and knocked on the door. 'Asheila?' he called. 'Asheila!'

'Go away!' she replied, through the closed portal. Her voice sounded tearful. 'Just go away! Go all the way to Hostileia for all I care!'

'Asheila, were you . . . following us?'

'You and your girldragon!' she wailed.

'Asheila, open the door! It's daft trying to have a conversation this way.' Nothing. 'You know, she's not my girldragon. Really!'

After a pause, Asheila said: 'You seem very intimate.'

'Is that why you were following us?' He thought back to the Clawsoleum, and tried to think of a way of asking her about it without tipping his hand. 'Did you . . . wish us harm?'

'Of course!' she howled. 'I want you both buried in Antarctic ice! I want her drowned in the ocean! Oh woh-woh-woh!'

'Asheila, it's not *like* that. She's not my girldragon. I'm not interested in her . . . like that at all.' Not *exactly* a lie, this last one, and so not a violation of his draconic integrity. 'She's only here for one reason . . . to help me solve the mystery!'

'You're in such a hurry to solve this sludging mystery!' she howled. 'So you can leave Doorbraak and go back to Starkhelm with your skinny little girldragon!'

Käal tried again. 'For the last time – she's *not* my girldragon! She's a researcher. You do want me to solve your family's plaguey mystery, don't you?'

'I don't *want* you to solve the mystery,' she screamed. This pronouncement was followed by various tantrum sounds, vividly suggestive of a forty-tonne dragon thrashing with furious abandon about her rooms, indifferent to the damage she might cause on her furniture or furnishings.

Käal thought this a good moment, quietly, to withdraw.

Coming back down the stairway, he had an epiphany. Suddenly, like a lightning strike to the top of his head, he understood what the mystery was all about.

I don't want you to solve the mystery, Asheila had said. The words clanged a gong inside Käal's mind. *Why* didn't she want to solve the mystery?

There were two possible answers. Because she was the murderer, and didn't want to be exposed. Or because *Hellfire was still alive* – and she was *protecting her secret location!*

Of those two possibilities, only one made sense to Käal. Whatever else she might be, Asheila was no killer.

Things Asheila had said came back to him. *It almost*

makes me want to run away, she had told him: *all the way to Hostileia.*

Or that other time when she had said: *to be in a separate room from you feels like I have been banished to Hostileia*!

How could Hellfire have remained undiscovered all these centuries? What better hiding place than . . . the opposite side of the globe?

It all clicked in Käal's head.

Of course Asheila had access to the vault. She had been resident on Doorbraak throughout the previous three centuries. She could have been going down, once a year, to cut out the tongues and send them to her uncle, in mute, symbolic rebuke. Why? And why had she never left the island?

Why else but to protect her niece?

Käal felt the intense, brain-buzzy feeling of having *solved* the problem. Of having – himself, unaided – found the stuff out. Not every detail was in place yet. For instance: why had young Hellfire felt she needed to leave? (Something to do with the family's dark secret, probably.) How had Asheila smuggled her out past the Eyes? Perhaps she had cached her in her rooms whilst the searches were made, and then smuggled her out in the mouth of a cargo Skylligator. But the missing details did not diminish Käal's giddy sense of joy at having seen through the murk. 'With what splendour,' he said aloud, 'it all coheres.'

He had to tell Asheila that he knew the truth. Her door was obviously a no-go. So he hurried across the main hall and outside. He flew up the side of the building, looking for her balcony. This proved harder than he first imagined it would: it was difficult to correlate the outside of the castle with its interior layout.

He picked a balcony and landed on it, only to see Asheila emerge on a completely different balcony, away to his left and two floors down.

He almost called to her, but something in her demeanour held him back. She no longer seemed upset. Indeed, she possessed an unusual purposefulness. Creeping to the edge of his vantage point, he watched her bring a raven out of a cage. Then she released it.

The revelation broke in his mind like a sunburst. 'She's *warning* Hellfire!' he gasped.

Käal knew it was time to act. He waited until Asheila had gone back inside again, and threw himself into open space.

It was a bright day, and the sky was littered with numerous plump white clouds, like scatter cushions. Visibility was good: Käal could see the raven soaring its way south. There was no time to lose. Now, Käal was not the fittest or fastest flier in the world, but he reasoned he could catch up with a small bird if he put his wings into it. And in fact he covered the first stretch easily, disguising his approach as best he could by flying from cloud to cloud. One minute the bird was a diacritical mark, nothing more, shifting regularly from V to Λ. Then, with a gasping swoop, Käal dived down out of the sun. The bird turned its raveny ('ravenous', should that be?) head, its inkdrop eyes wide. Then Käal had him, in a swirl of squawking and threshing feathers.

'Got you!' cried Käal, in triumph. Attempting to turn

and rise holding the bird in his claws, he immediately dropped it.

'Awwwk!' said the raven, falling straight down. With a yelp of fright Käal tucked his wings back and fell after him, grabbing the bird with his teeth, and straining to pull out of the dive. It was the kind of descent that dragons called the *Stuka*. Because it was the sort of downwards trajectory one was liable to get *stuck* in.

With a mighty heave, Käal flattened his trajectory, pulled up, and was finally able to fly more calmly on. He picked the raven from his jaw with his left hindleg.

'Hey!' the raven said. It did not sound happy.

'You were sent with a message,' said Käal, gasping a little, for the rapid flight had taken his puff away, rather. 'Admit it!'

'Nay,' said the raven.

'Don't play the innocent with me,' gasped Käal. 'I know all about it! Tell me the truth.'

'Go drown yourself in the sea,' cawed the bird, unhelpfully.

'You don't need to tell me the whole message,' Käal said, finding it hard to fly, hold the wriggling bird still and speak all at once. 'Neither do you need to tell me who sent you. You don't even need to tell me who you've been sent to. I know all that.'

Quoth the raven: 'Nay! Vamoose!'

'Don't be unreasonable!'

'Push-off! Yar! Boo!'

'The game is up,' said Käal. 'I've *found out* all the *stuff*. I know everything except one piece of the puzzle. I need to know *where you were going*.'

'Hostileia,' said the bird, with a frantic wriggle to get free.

'I knew it!' cried Käal. 'It is exactly as I suspected. But where exactly – Malborn? Sadney?'

'The moon!' spat the bird.

'Don't be ridiculous. Where in Hostileia?'

'The North Pole!'

'I'm warning you!' The bird hissed, and wriggled, but when Käal added 'I'll release you if you tell me' it conceded: 'Tssa! Nay!'

Sadney?' cried Käal. He opened his claw, and the bird lurched and flapped away, its feathers disarrayed, uttering a frankly disrespectful sentiment as it departed. Käal did not care. He was filled with dragon-glee, for he, *he*, the Käal Brimstön everybody underestimated, had solved the mystery.

18

He made it back to Doorbraak, and alighted on his own apartment's balcony gasping like a displaced fish. It took a while to get his breath back. Lizbreath had seen his approach, and flew up to him from the garden. 'Are you OK?'

'I've solved it,' he said. 'I've solved the mystery! Me! *I* did it! You stay here. I need to get to Hostileia.'

'Hostileia?' Lizbreath asked. 'Why?'

'You'll see!' said Käal.

'Don't be tedious, Käal. Just tell me. Why do you want to go all the way to Hostileia? It's on the other side of the planet!.'

'I'll be back in a couple of days. And I think you'll be pleasantly surprised.'

'Don't tell me that Hellfire has been alive all this time and now is living in Hostileia?' groaned Lizbreath, her wings drooping. 'How rubbish is *that*?'

'Don't say it's rubbish!' said Käal, crestfallen, something literally possible for dragons. 'Why is it rubbish? It's brilliant. It's certainly brilliant that I'll get the Siegfried treasure. And it's especially brilliant that I worked it all out for myself.'

'*Is* that what you worked out?'

Käal felt a spurt of annoyance. 'You'll see,' he said, stubbornly. 'I'll be back soon.'

Lizbreath looked as though she was going to press him for the answer, but then seemed to change her mind. 'OK,' she shrugged, and went back into the apartment.

Käal had got his puff back. He fetched his purse and attached it to his dragon belt. Then he slipped back into the broad sky, and flew in a leisurely helix down to the ground. The floating island was near the Fangland now, and it was a short hop by Skylligator to the Fangland capital city, Sink-of-Hell. There, pausing only to eat a single bleating sheep from a roadside booth, Käal made his way to the International Airport.

It was busy. Whilst he queued to buy a ticket, he had second thoughts. More specifically, he wondered whether he shouldn't have gone first to Helltrik, explained the situation and got the old dragon to pay for the flight. But it would work much better as a dramatic reveal. Doubt reasserted itself when he actually bought the ticket, for it was very expensive indeed. But he consoled himself with the thought that, after all, he *had* solved the mystery. That meant that the Siegfried treasure would soon be his, and he would be wealthy beyond his wildest dreams.

He took his ticket to the waiting area, and sat with the other passengers in a tall crystal-walled room that overlooked the runway. The International Skylligator was being readied, and fuelled: two Airsprites were pouring great buckets of small fish into its maw. Even Käal, who had travelled by Skylligator many times, was impressed by the size of this one. Specially bred for its business, its pale green body with the crenellated spine and fat body was no more than eight hundred yards long. But its prodigious jaws were half as long again, and wide enough to accommodate three dozen adult dragons in comfort.

Finally it was time to board. Käal queued, presented his ticket, and flew down the loading chute to take his seat on the plump red flesh of the beast's upholsteryish tongue. Excitement was growing in his belly. The chute was withdrawn and the jaws slowly closed, whilst flight attendants (all firedrakes) lit the glowglobes and passed amongst the passengers settling everybody for take-off. Up at the tongue-tip, the pilot was making the usual safety announcement:

'. . . and as I'm sure I don't need to remind frequent fliers, soot from your nostrils can irritate the sensitive mucus membrane and linings of the Skylligator, so please keep your sootbelts fastened over your snouts during take off and landing. Thanks for flying Brutish Airways . . .'

He was barely listening. In his mind, he was already arriving in the glory of a Hostileian morning, stepping from the opening jaw into antipodean sunlight, ready to complete his brilliant investigation.

The Skylligator rumbled, loped down the runway and lifted into the air. Impatience made Käal fidgety, and elongated the first hour or so of the flight prodigiously. But food was served, which helped; and an in-flight play (a puppet production of *Dragon with the Wind*) began. Worn out with his own excitement, Käal dozed. He woke after an indeterminate time, and lay still, soothed by the whooshing sounds of flight, and almost monkish murmuring of the crew and passengers. Around him, most people were sleeping. It was all so soothing that Käal fell back asleep. He woke only when the Skylligator began its final descent.

Sadney airport was a bigger structure than Sink-of-Hell, although there were far fewer people around. Indeed, Hostileia had always been a relatively under-populated country, for reasons Käal had never quite understood. Because – he stepped into the air and flew leisurely over the city, glad to be able to stretch his wings after the long confinement – it seemed at first blush little short of paradisical. It was very hot and dry, with enormous skies and wide open countryside. Better still, it was possible to farm sheep on a large scale. Why did so few dragons choose to live there?

Käal moved through this new country and was amazed. The sun was ferociously bright and hot. Dust blowzed over the road in spectral tan-coloured folds. The mountains tucked their tips into the pleats of bleach-white clouds. Beautiful!

Hostilea! He was really there!

He took a room for the night in a hotel whilst pondering how best to track his target. In the bar that night he struck up an interesting conversation with the bardragon. 'Why do so few dragons live here?' he asked, with tourist ingenuity. 'It's my first visit, but it looks to me pretty much perfect.'

'It's a good question, mate,' said the bardragon. 'My theory – it's too *happy* here.'

'Too happy?'

'Sure, cobber. The entire population of Hostileia comes from the northern hemisphere. This was wholly open territory, mate, with only a very mild hömös infestation. And like you say: paradise for dragons.'

' "Cobbler"?' Käal queried, weakly. The bardragon didn't seem to hear.

'The thing is, dragons are a gloomy bunch. They don't know what to make of contentment. They'd rather mope around Scandragonia – tell me it ain't so.'

'But I can't tell you so,' said Käal, with a serious expression on his face. 'It clearly *is* so. Is it in our genes, this addiction to gloom?'

'Nah,' said the bardragon. 'Look at me. I'm perfectly well adjusted.'

'Tell me,' said Käal, 'have you heard of the . . . Vagner clan?'

'I read the Sagas, just like anybody,' said the bardragon, cleaning the used crystal goblets by breathing fire into them and rubbing the soot off with a rag.

'So you *have* heard of them?'

'They've got that Floating Island, yeah? A-*may*-zing, that. How does it stay up?'

'Magic,' said Käal, 'so I'm told.'

'That's a crap kind of answer, though, mate, ain't it? Magic is fair enough, for day-to-day getting-along. But keeping millions of tonnes of rock and earth in the air, year in, year out? That's something more than magic, I reckon.'

'I daresay you're correct,' said Käal, vaguely. 'But I

have a question for you. Have you heard of any members of the Vagner clan settling over here?'

'Over here? What? In Hostileia?'

'Yes. Specifically, here in Sadney.'

'Nah, mate. They all live on their island. You should check that out.'

Käal thought to himself: but of course she would be here under a false name. 'Nevertheless, I heard that one of that clan came down here to live – several centuries ago.'

'Nobody's come to Sadney for half a millennium, mate,' said the bardragon. 'Back of beyond, down here.' For a flickering moment Käal's confidence wavered. What if he was wrong? But then the bardragon added: 'Apart from that one woman. What was she called? Firehell, that's it.'

'Who?'

'She's called Firehell. Came down about three hundred years back. She runs a sheep factory, just north of the city, if memory serves. Came down under slightly mysterious circumstances, in fact. But she's a nice enough bird. Why?'

Käal's heart caught fire, and joy danced in his eyes. 'I need to pay her a visit tomorrow. That's all.'

'Owes you money, does she?'

'Nothing like that!' said Käal; and then, thinking of the Siegfried treasure, effectively his own possession now, he added: 'Although money has *something* to do with it.'

He went to bed intoxicated with firewater and slept heavily. The sun had been up for a long time when he eventually emerged from his room and settled his bill. He asked the desk clerk, a strangely grinny firedrake, about the sheep factory north of the city, run by the she-dragon who'd arrived in town three centuries before.

'You mean Firehell's place?'

'That's the one. What's it called?'

'It's called the I Was Betrayed By My Pig Of A Brother farm. Funny name, really.'

Käal flew into the bright sunshine and took a bearing straight north. It didn't take him long to find the factory: a complex of large sheds and a single tall house in the middle. He circled it, noticed activity in the loading area, and flew down.

He landed beside a great heaving mass of sheep, all being directed along penned ramps into the large body of a food cart. Three dragons were occupied thuswise; one of them clearly the driver of the cart. Of the other two, one was a young male dragon; the other a mature female dragon. Just looking at her, Käal could see the family resemblance.

Looking up from her work, she asked Käal, in none too friendly a voice: 'Can I help you?'

'I hope so,' said Käal. 'I've travelled a long way to see you.'

'To see me?' She stood tall on her hind legs, stretching high. 'Why?'

'Because, Hellfire, it's time to come home. Time to stop hiding down here.'

The woman looked at him. 'Say what?'

'You are Hellfire Vagner. It's all right, I know the

204

whole story. I was hired by your granduncle to find out the requisite, er, stuff. And I did.'

'You're one coal short of a whole fire, mate,' said the woman. 'My name's Firehell.'

'You can drop the pretence anymore, Hellfire. It's all over.'

'You're bonkers, cobber.'

'Come! Why carry on this fruitless charade?'

'Shall I wring his neck, Ma?' said the young he-dragon, coming alongside.

'Is this your son? How wonderful! Helltrik will be delighted.'

'Who?' said the woman.

'Your granduncle. He's been obsessing over your disappearance for three hundred years. There's only one part of this whole mystery that I still don't understand: *why* did you send him the tongues?'

For a long minute nobody said anything. There was no sound at all except the massed bleatings of the sheep. 'Tongues?' she said, eventually.

The he-dragon took a step towards Käal.

'You, er,' said Käal, watching the young male dragon approach with some small trepidation. 'You *know* what I mean. You . . . shall we say *removed* the tongues of three hundred dragons and posted them to your granduncle on Doorbraak, one a year. I still don't understand why.'

Firehell put her head on one side. 'You're off your chump,' she opined. 'You must have ice for brains. Sling him, Brute.'

The young male – this, evidently, was Brute – took hold of Käal's neck. He didn't, humiliatingly enough, use his hindleg. His forelegs were muscled enough to turn Käal's well-modulated voice into something that sounded more like a sheep. 'Wait! Wait!' he gasped. 'Don't be hasty! Let me explain!'

Firehell nodded at her son, and the grip was released just enough for Käal to be able to say: 'This farm *is* called the I Was Betrayed By My Pig Of A Brother farm, yes?'

'Check the main gate,' said Firehell. 'It's called the My Brother Has Pigs So I Thought I'd Trade Sheep farm.'

'Ah,' said Käal. 'Conceivably I misheard. But you *did* come here three hundred years ago, in slightly mysterious circumstances?'

'Three hundred years? How old do you think I *am*?'

'Erm,' said Käal, his own feeble foreclaws gripping Brute's long, muscular forearm and feeling the hold on his throat tighten. 'Ah, I thought that . . .'

'I wasn't *alive* three hundred years ago! Came here a hundred and ninety year ago – from Faraway Land.'

'From Faraway Land? Not from Scandragonia?'

'Never been to Scandragonia in my life.'

Now that he listened, he could hear a distinctive West Coast Faraway-Landish accent to Firehell's words. 'Mmm,' he said. 'That's – ah. Look,' he added, trying for a mollifying grin, 'it is just conceivable that I've somehow got hold of the wrong end of the stick. If I may summarize: you're a successful sheep farmer, who came to Hostileia a little under two centuries ago from Faraway Land. Which would mean, logically, aha! Ha-ha-ha. Which would mean, you're *not* Hellfire Vagner living in Hostileia under an assumed name having fled Scandragonia *three* centuries ago for shameful and terrible reasons, and that you *haven't* sent three hundred severed tongues to your granduncle by post.'

'Brute,' said Firehell, to his son. 'Chuck him in the midden.'

The midden, it turned out, was a reservoir of sheep dung. Since sheep dung is fairly dry, being chucked into it was not quite the dangerously humiliating experience it might otherwise have been. Still, it was *pretty* humiliating, as I'm sure you can imagine.

'You come back here,' said Brute, 'or bother my ma again *in any way*, I'll chain you at the bottom of the midden for a week.'

'I believe you,' said Käal, brushing as much of the ordure from his scales as he could, and flying away.

Käal went back to his hotel and moped for a long time in his room. Eventually he went back down to the bar. The bardragon recognized him at once. 'Did you find the bird you were looking for? The one at the My Brother Has Pigs So I Thought I'd Trade Sheep farm?'

'Didn't you tell me,' he replied, 'that it was called the I Was Betrayed By My Pig Of A Brother farm?'

'Nah, mate. That doesn't sound like a farm name at all.'

'I must have misheard you. It turns out the owner came over here about two hundred years ago, from Faraway Land.'

'I could have told you that, mate. She came over with her brother when they were both Salamanders.'

'Were there any *other* females, who came to Sadney from . . . and this part is quite important . . . from *Scandragonia* maybe three – rather than two – hundred years ago?'

'Nah, mate.'

'You're sure?'

'You could check the public records office. But I don't reckon you'll find anything.'

The following day, Käal proved the correctness of the bardragon's reckoning; he spent half an hour in the public records office with a sinking heart. That evening he boarded the return Skylligator, a night flight back to Starkhelm, in a state of considerable mental discouragement.

19

He arrived at Sink-of-Hell airport, feeling foolish and grumpy. His own flat was cold and damp, which did not enhance his mood. He lit a fire, and broodily stared at the flames for a long time. He tried not to think about the enormous dent he had made in his hoard, buying a short-notice first-class return Skylligator ticket to Hostileia for no reason. But, as you'll have observed yourself, trying not to think about something is an excellent way of focusing your thoughts precisely upon that something.

There was no avoiding his return to Doorbraak. He sent a raven to Lizbreath saying he was on his way back, and got himself a drink. His annoyance and embarrassment was pricked by the realization that the mystery remained unsolved. It seemed that Hellfire had *not* snuck away from the Floating Island, made her way to Hostileia. So what *had* happened to her?

He decided he was too exhausted and despondent to fly himself to Doorbraak. So outside Sink-of-Hell airport, he hired a sedangerous chair, pulled through the air by a muscular young workwyrm. It took nearly half an hour to reach Doorbraak, travelling slowly and inexorably south over Fangland.

Käal paid the chair with a resentful sense of how depleted his funds now were. He jogged through the air on aching wings, and landed – finally – on his apartment balcony with a sigh.

He stepped through the door ready to lie down and sleep. But the chamber was crowded with dragons. Somebody at the back called 'here he is!' and a great, flame-garnished cheer burst from those assembled. Käal was so startled he tripped backwards, fell over, knocking the sideboard over with a snare-drum clatter with his tail as he struggled to get back to his feet. When he got himself upright again, Old Helltrik Vagner was standing right in front of him.

'What?' said Käal.

'Well done, my boy!' the old dragon said. There were tears in his eyes – actual, hot-phlegm tears.

'What?' said Käal. He looked at Helltrik, and then at the crowd of other dragons in the chamber: Asheila was there, looking tenderly at him; Lizbreath was clinging easily to the frame of the kitchen door. Marrer was there, and Redsnapper, and four or five other inhabitants of Doorbraak that Käal, his mind jangled, recognized but couldn't immediately name. He looked at Helltrik. 'What?' he asked that august dragon.

'My trust in you has been *well* repaid,' said Helltrik. 'Where is she? Out on the balcony?'

'She?' said Käal, not quite grasping what the old dragon meant, but with a sinking sense of the situation. 'What?' He looked around, tried, 'she', and then reverted to 'what?'

'Hellfire,' said an elderly female dragon, whom – as

she spoke – Käal recognized as Greendragon. Helltrik's venerable older sister.

Käal understood what had happened. Lizbreath must have told them that he, Käal, had located Hellfire, alive after all these years and living in Hostileia. More, she must have passed on the information, somehow, that he was bringing her back. The full sickening weight of his circumstances hit him. He looked about, tried to formulate a sequence of words that would communicate to this roomful of expectant dragons that they were mistaken, that he had not located Hellfire, that the mystery was as far from being solved as ever. The sequence of words refused to coalesce in the speech centres of his dragon brain.

'What?' he said, instead.

Marrer went out onto the balcony, and came back a moment later looking puzzled. 'She's not there.'

The mood in the room shifted, marginally, but palpably.

'What's going on?' asked Greendragon.

'What? Right,' said Käal. 'It looks like you're expecting something. I'd say that you're all expecting . . . something.'

'We are expecting,' said Helltrik, looking hurt, 'you to arrive here having brought back Hellfire from Hostileia. Did you leave her in that country?'

'Right, well I don't know *why*,' Käal said, 'you might expect such a bizarre thing.'

'Because your researcher told us that was what you were doing,' said Helltrik.

Everybody twisted their heads about to look at

Lizbreath. 'It's true,' she said. 'You told me you have discovered that Hellfire was in fact living in Hostileia.'

Everybody turned their heads back to face Käal.

'Well, all right, that's true, I did,' he admitted. 'I reasoned that Hellfire must have survived. If she were dead, then she couldn't move her body, so she would have been found. The fact that she hadn't been found must mean that she did move her body – so as to avoid being found, you see. That must mean she wasn't dead.'

The looks in the eyes surveying him did not seem as persuaded by his logical inference as he was himself. He tried again. It was important to convey to them how watertight his logic was on this. 'If she died, then how did her body move? A third party? But who would move a dead body? Nobody would! Anybody would notify the authorities!'

'Unless,' said Asheila, as if to a child, 'you had just murdered the person, and didn't want the body to be found?'

Käal pondered this. 'Well, that makes sense, I suppose,' he conceded.

The room was filled with groans. 'You idiot!' snarled Greendragon. 'I knew it!' said somebody else.

'Now, look,' said Käal, trying to muster a small quantity of his own outrage. But it wasn't easy. 'I didn't *ask* you to gather here, in my apartment . . .'

'You went all the way to Hostileia?' asked Marrer, incredulous.

'I did, yes,' said Käal.

'And it was a dead end? A wasted journey?'

'Well, yes, I suppose you'd have to say it was.' Käal

was conscious that this made him look foolish, so he added: 'I paid for the ticket with my own money, too.' Once he had said this, he realized that it made him look more, not less, foolish.

'You consummated *berk*!' fumed Greendragon.

'Why did you think she was in Hostileia in the first place?' Marrer asked.

'Well, I saw somebody send a raven. I thought it was a message for Hellfire, so I intercepted it. When I asked it where it was going, it . . .' He trailed off. He could see, in retrospect, how stupid this sounded.

'And it said it was going to Hostileia?' Marrer finished.

'Yes.'

'And you,' said Marrer. He paused in the middle of utterance, paused for long enough to look slowly around the room and note every single dragon inside it. The silence stretched. '*Believed* it?' he finished, eventually.

'Well . . .' said Käal.

'Was it a long-distance raven?' asked Helltrik, in a baffled voice.

Käal made the sort of face you make if you have bitten into what you thought was an orange only to discover that it is actually a lemon. 'No,' he conceded. 'Also, when I asked it where it was going, its full answer was: go drown yourself, nay, never, Hostileia, the moon, the North Pole.'

'You *are* a proper fool,' said Asheila with tremendous and perhaps excessive vehemence.

The room broke into uproar. Everybody was talking at once. Everybody except Lizbreath, who clung comfortably to her doorframe, watching everybody with sardonic pleasure.

'I knew it!' cried one elderly female dragon voice, piercingly enough to silence the rest. 'I knew this – fraud – would not return with my daughter.' Käal recognized Isabella, Marrer's mother. The old she-dragon was coming to the front, poking out her wings to shove dragons out of the way. She stood next to him. 'Do you *know* how I knew?'

Nobody took the cue, so Käal felt obliged. 'How did you know?'

'Because I *have proof* my daughter is dead.'

Everybody was staring at her. For a moment, Käal thought she was about to confess to murdering her own offspring. But instead she said: 'I know this because she has communicated with me – from *beyond the grave.*'

'Oh!' said Käal. It was more of a squeak than anything. 'No? Really?'

'Yes.'

'OK, yes, right,' said Käal. 'But, you know. *Really*?'

'Really, young dragon. There are more things in heaven and earth,' she said, in a thrumming, uppy-down voice, opening her wings and putting her throat up like a thespian, 'than are dreamt of in your philosophy, Horror-show!'

'Oh,' said Käal again. 'Horror-show? Really? Me?'

'Stop a moment,' said Asheila. 'Aunt Bella, are you saying that you have had communication with Hellfire from *the other side*?'

'Oh we all know the island is haunted!' said the old she-dragon, dramatically. 'We pretend it isn't, we avert

214

our eyes, we go about our ordinary lives. But we know it is! We've all seen the poltergeist evidence!'

'Horrow-show just seems,' said Käal, to nobody in particular, 'a little – harsh.'

'Come now, Mother!' said Marrer. 'That's just super-stition, and you know it. Firedrakes and workwyrms might believe in all that bells-and-whistles . . . ghosts and charted-accountants and the boogeydragon, but *we* are above it, surely! You'll be telling me next that you believe in Santa Claws!'

'Hush!' said Isabella, turning on the spot and sweep-ing her still-open wings around the room with a great rustling sound. Several dragons had to pull in their heads to avoid being struck. 'Hush, my foolish son. I have *spoken* to my daughter! Nobody here can deny that I have. Nor can they deny that this means she is dead!'

'Isabella, my dear,' said old Helltrik, mildly. 'We've all been very upset by Hellfire's passing. We all know I have! Could it be that, in your grief, you have *imagined* speaking to the dear girl? Perhaps imagined it *so vividly* that . . .'

'Helltrik, you old cinder,' snapped Isabella. 'Shut your snout. You really don't know what you're talking about. I didn't imagine it! I *spoke* with her.'

'But . . . how?'

'I used a "yes-yes" board. Sometimes called, by more linguistically cosmopolitan dragons, a *Ouija* board.'

'Mother!' said Marrer, astonished. 'Really?'

'It's not the *horror* part, I suppose,' said Käal, despite the fact that nobody was listening to him. 'Horror is a reasonable draconic quality. It's the *show* part. As if I'm just a sort of play-actor.'

'Through the medium of the yes-yes,' Isabella announced to the room, 'I have communicated with my daughter! She has told me that life on the far-side is nothing to be afraid of! When we die, there is a bright point of heat – we must go into the heat! There is peace and contentment in . . .'

'Mother,' snapped Marrer. 'Stop all this nonsense.'

'Nonsense? Nonsense!' said Isabella. 'By which I mean,' she clarified, looking a touch flustered, 'that *nonsense* is a nonsensical thing to say. It is nonsense to call it nonsense. Because it's *not* nonsense.' She addressed the room as a whole. 'Hellfire spoke to me. She told me she was dead – and that she had been murdered!'

This created a small sensation. Voices clamoured together: 'No!' 'I can't believe it!' 'Beyond the grave?' 'I knew it!'

From her reticule, Isabella brought out a piece of paper. 'In my last communication with the dear departed dragon, she gave me the following message.' She held the piece of paper up. On it, in quavery letters, was written the following:

A FINGER THE HINGE OF WORLDS!
BURNT FINGER!

It took a moment for everybody in the room to read this. Then it took another moment to digest it, and perhaps half a moment before they realized that it was gibberish. 'What on earth does that even *mean*, Mother?' demanded Marrer, in an exasperated voice.

'What's a *finger*?' asked Käal.

'It's an antique word for claw,' the old she-dragon explained. 'I looked it up.'

'It's gibberish,' said Helltrik, firmly. 'That's the basic problem with all Ouija technology. You get a lot of words and letters randomly assembled, and they tend to make gibberish. Why would you think this garbled message came from Hellfire in the first place?'

Isabella turned the paper over. 'I asked,' she said, 'and I wrote down the answer.' On the verso of the scroll was written:

HI THIS IS HELLFIRE EVERYTHING FINE HERE HOW R U? THE SILENCE MUST STOP, MURDER AND LIYS, LIES, NO, LIYS, AGH!! SPELLING!!! ANYHOW THERE'S A MESSAGE AND IT IS IMPORTANT! I FOUND OUT THE TRUTH!

'So,' said Käal, 'you got this message, and then the other one?'

'Yes.'

'Turn the scroll over, and let's have a look at the second message again.'

Isabella did so.

'I think it's the "hinge" that throws me,' said Asheila, after a while. 'Looks almost but not quite like "finger". Should it *be* "hinge"?'

'What else would it be?' snapped Isabella.

'Maybe "hinger"?' said Asheila.

'Don't be ridiculous. "A finger the hinger of worlds"? That doesn't make any sense at all.'

'Oh, when "finger the hinge of worlds" does?'

'If she means claw, why doesn't she say claw?' asked Greendragon.

'Finger doesn't mean claw,' said a voice from the back of the room. It took a moment for Käal to realize that this was Lizbreath, contributing to the discussion for the first time. Several dragons turned to look at her.'

'The young Salamander is correct,' said Isabella, stiffly. ' "Fingers" is a technical term, to describe the claw-like digits of certain reptiles and squirrels.'

'And these squirrel claws are the "hinger",' said Käal, pronouncing this last word with a hard 'g'. 'What's a *hinger* again?'

'No, no!' said Isabella. 'You're getting distracted.'

'Is it a misprint for "hunger"?' asked Asheila. 'That would make more sense.'

' "*Squirrel claws are the hunger of worlds*" makes more sense?' asked Marrer.

'Well, it's no more nonsensical than the original message!'

'It doesn't say anything about squirrels!' said Isabella, crossly. 'Squirrels are not mentioned.'

'Reptiles, then,' said Old Helltrik. 'What else has fingers?'

'Bats have fingers,' said Greendragon, displaying a surprising knowledge. 'I happen to know quite a lot about bats. They have fingers. Their wings are attached to them.'

'This message has nothing to do with bats,' snapped Isabella.

'The message *is* bats,' was Marrer's opinion.

'Racoons have fingers, don't they?' said Greendragon.

'They're just another kind of squirrel,' said Helltrik, dismissively.

'Oh,' said Greendragon. 'Really? I wouldn't say so. I thought they were a separate species from squirrels. Or do I mean race? A separate race from squirrels. No. Species. I mean species, do I?'

'Shut up!' screeched Isabella, her ancient vocal chords audibly creaking with the effort. 'Stop this idle chatter! We have been blessed with a communication from beyond the tomb! And all you can do is bicker like hatchlings!'

'Fingers!' said Asheila. 'Why would a poltergeist specify fingers?'

'Human beings,' said Lizbreath, in a clear and resonant voice. Heads turned in her direction. 'The hömös apes. *They* had fingers.'

'And?'

'That's what the message means,' said Lizbreath, shrugging. 'That's all.'

'How can you possibly know that?' said Isabella, crossly. 'Why would my daughter struggle back from the afterlife to communicate information about an extinct race of disgusting apes?'

'I recognize the allusion, that's all,' said Lizbreath.

'I'm kind of surprised nobody else in this room does. Though I'd guess one or two of you *do*.'

'I don't need a mentally unbalanced Salamander from Starkhelm telling *me* I don't recognize allusions. There are no allusions in that gibberish,' said Asheila.

'Yes there are.'

'In the squirrel-claw hunger? Don't be ridiculous. Or, since you are inherently ridiculous, you scrawny insane Salamander, don't be more ridiculous than you already are.'

'Well that's not very polite,' said Lizbreath.

'Hey!' said Käal, weakly.

'Let's stop this,' said Marrer, going onto his hindlimbs and standing up tall. 'Come along! This is all non-sense, and we all know it. We have been gathered in this chamber under false pretences. We allowed our hope to fool us. We all miss Hellfire so much that the faint chance that Mon. Brimstön here could be bringing her back, alive, from Hostileia was enough to get us all to gather in this place. But we have to accept that she is not here.'

'Maybe she *is* here.'

'Oh, Mother,' snapped Marrer, crossly. 'Stop with all the spectral nonsense! Hellfire is *not* present. There's no such thing as ghosts!'

'I didn't say anything!' retorted Isabella, haughtily.

'What? Who said that, then?'

'I did,' said Lizbreath.

'So you believe all this ghostly idiocy, do you?'

'I didn't say anything about ghosts. But I have a question for Isabella, though.' She put her foreclaw in front of her nose, and blew a quick blast of red flame upon it. Then, using the soot on her talon, she reached up and drew a simple shape over the door. 'Has your daughter ever drawn this for you?'

The shape looked like this:

$$+$$

Isabella puffed a series of little blue smoke baubles from her nostrils. 'I don't see how you know that, young Salamander – unless you've been going through my private papers.'

'I assure you I haven't done anything like that,' said Lizbreath, cleaning her talon against her scaly side.

'What is it?' demanded Asheila. 'What does it mean?'

'I recognize that,' said Greendragon. 'I have lots of those in my hoard. Little tiny ones. The old hömös made millions of them out of gold.'

'That's right!' said Käal. 'It's an old ape letter. It's equivalent to our "t". For some reason, the apes used to like to wear that letter around their neck on little golden chains.'

'I read in a Saga once,' said Asheila. 'It was a Gossip Saga, and they had one of those "Interesting Facts" sections. *It* said it was because so many of the apes liked imbibing a drink called, oddly enough, "t". Whenever you saw an ape wearing one of those things, they were announcing that they really liked drinking "t".'

Isabella was rummaging in her reticule. 'Here.' She brought out a second piece of paper, and held it up for everybody to see. 'This came – from the other side.'

It was a little hard to take in what the paper represented: there was quite a lot of complicated writing on it. The central + was obvious, but there was writing in each of the four quarters that this shape created. The dragons in the room all leaned in to take a closer look.

Then, without warning, Marrer sneezed. A lance of fire connected his mouth and the upheld scroll. A moment later Isabella was holding aloft nothing more than a charred corner of scroll, and fat black ashes floated down, like snowflakes wearing mourning.

'Oh!' said Marrer. 'Sorry!'

'Marrer!' snapped his mother. 'You destroyed it!'

'I do apologize.'

'Is it too much to ask you to put your hand in front of your snout when you sneeze?'

'Anyway,' said Marrer. 'That's gone. And I suggest we all disperse. There's nothing more to see here, after all. No Hellfire, no solution to this mystery, and certainly no strange glyphs passed over from beyond the grave.'

There didn't seem anything else to do. People slowly filed out of the chamber, chatting amongst themselves. Isabella said in a cross voice: 'That was my only copy!' and Marrer, laying a hand on the back of her neck, said: 'Come along, Mother, let me take you back to your room. You need a little lie down, I think.'

Soon, only Käal, Lizbreath and Helltrik were left. The old dragon, sighing heavily, seated his venerable rump upon the room's single sofa, fitting his tail neatly through the slot.

'Wait,' said Käal, his brow still creased. 'Did Marrer just burn that scroll – on purpose?'

'He sneezed,' said Helltrik. 'That's all.'

'But that scroll – it had the t, and all sorts of writing. And now we'll never know what it said!'

'It was certainly gibberish. Forget it.' Helltrik rubbed his eyes with his forelimbs. 'Leave it alone, Käal.'

'But what if it was the solution to this whole mystery?'

'Come now! You're clutching at straws, Käal, you really are.'

Käal gulped, for he recognized the truth of this. He *was* clutching at straws. The whole fragile edifice of the last few weeks teetered in his mind, teeter-tottered, and started tumbling down. Sadness swelled in his heart. It had all come to nothing! He had blithely accepted the commission, had come to Doorbraak with a fool's baseless confidence, believing he could solve the mystery. But of course he could not. He lacked the capacity. 'You're right, Helltrik,' he said, in a small voice.

'I don't know what strange nonsense Isabella had written on that scroll,' said Helltrik. 'But how could it possibly contain the answer to this mystery?'

'It's hard to see how it could,' Käal agreed,

'At any rate, it's gone beyond restoration now. And to think I actually got my hopes up! Came trotting along here, thinking I'd see my grandniece again!'

'I'm sorry,' said Käal, 'Sorry about that.'

'I can't pretend I'm not disappointed,' said Helltrik, mildly enough. 'I *had* hoped you could find out what happened to my grandniece. But I've lived with not knowing for three centuries. I daresay I can live with not knowing for a few years more.'

Exhausted from his pointless trip to Hostileia,

battered down by circumstances, and supplied by his nature with a considerable reservoir of self-pity at the best of times, this was too much for Käal. He began to cry. 'I'm sorry!' he said. 'I'm so sorry!'

Helltrik looked embarrassed. 'Don't do that,' he said.

'I just thought I could solve this mystery!' Käal wailed. 'I really thought I could.'

'There there,' said Helltrik, awkwardly. 'I suppose some mysteries are beyond solution. Some puzzles are never to be unpuzzled. We must accept that, and get on with our dragon lives.'

Käal's tears were making the stone floor smoke. He wiped his eyes with the back of his talons, and sucked in a deep, slightly shuddery breath. 'I have failed you, sir.'

'No positive harm done,' said Helltrik. 'After all, I only promised to pay you if you *solved* the mystery!'

Käal began to sob again.

'You had a fair run at the challenge,' said Helltrik. 'So we'll never know what happened to poor Hellfire, all those years ago! So what!'

'*I* know what happened,' said Lizbreath.

Helltrik paused, looked at her, and decided to ignore her. 'We'll never know what's behind the annual delivery of severed dragon tongues . . .'

'I know,' said Lizbreath again.

'Please, my dear,' said Helltrik. 'Don't interrupt. I'm trying to have a conversation with Käal, here.'

'This mystery you're both on about – I know the solution,' said Lizbreath, climbing down from the doorframe to stand on her hindlimbs on the floor. 'And what's more, *so do you.*'

Helltrik and Käal both looked at her, in silence, for a long time. 'I can see why you have your reputation for mental instability,' said Helltrik, evenly. 'If I know the solution to this mystery, then why would I have retained the services of Mon. Brimstön?'

'Oh,' said Lizbreath, 'you don't know what happened to your *grandniece* – that's true. You don't know *that*. I guess you hoped that, maybe, Käal could find out something new about her. But I'm not talking about *that*.'

'Then what,' said Helltrik, severely, '*are* you talking about?'

'All the other stuff,' she said.

20

'There's a secret at the heart of this family,' said Liz-breath, moving about the chamber with impressive nonchalance. Indeed, her lack of chalance was so extreme it looked, to Käal, to be rather studied. Certainly the rhythm of her skinny flanks and the sine-wave action of her tail drew the eyes of both the men in the room.

'I know all about the Vagner secret,' said Käal. 'Helltrik told me *all about* that, almost as soon as I arrived.'

'I doubt that,' said Lizbreath.

'Well that just shows what you know, Mis. Salamander,' said Helltrik, with considerable asperity. 'Mon. Brimstön and I did indeed talk about the Vagner nest's shameful secret. Didn't we?'

'We did, Lizbreath. Really.'

'And what did he say it was?'

'Certain members of the family have espoused . . . democracy,' said Käal, glancing nervously at Helltrik. 'You can see why they might want to keep that secret.'

Lizbreath thought about this, nodded, and then said: 'Nope. That's not it.'

'That's not *it*?' gasped Helltrik.

'What?'

'Democracy. No. There *is* a secret at the heart of this family, but that's not it.'

'And what is it, then, pray?' snapped Helltrik. 'What is this secret that is so much more terrible that the politics of democracy? Fingers, I suppose?' He snapped his claws together dismissively.

'Well – yes. Fingers, yes,' said Lizbreath, with a knowing glance at each of the two men in turn.

'I think we have indulged you long enough, Mis. Salamander,' said Helltrik, drawing himself up, and slipping his forearm into his belt-slung satchel. He kept it in there, and looked at Käal. 'I rather regret permitting this she-Salamander onto our island, to be frank. You know she lies on a hoard of *silver?*'

'You heard about that?' said Käal.

'It's *well* known. She's insane, I'm afraid. Dragon rectitude and honour, and her own descent from good family, has meant that her insanity is treated with great leniency. But, although I am, I hope, as sympathetic as the next individual, there comes a point where we are not helping the afflicted individual.'

'Maybe she has her reasons for lying on a hoard of silver,' said Käal, feeling awkward to be talking about Lizbreath in the third person when she was right there.

'Beyond mere insanity? I believe it to be a counter-cultural affectation, Käal. But I think it means we can disregard any crazy theories she spins out of her brain.'

'Yes,' said Lizbreath. 'I lie on an unconventional

hoard. But I'll say this: *my* hoard is a lot more use to me than a pile of old gold jewels stolen from the extinct race of hömös.'

'Is that some barb aimed at me, Mis. Salamander?' frowned Helltrik. 'Only *some* of my hoard is ancient Vagner treasure, from the time humans walked the earth.'

'Like the Siegfried treasure? The one you promised Käal, here?'

'If he could solve the mystery of my grandniece's disappearance! He has not done so.'

'The treasure you inherited from your illustrious ancestor?'

'From Regin the Great, yes. Regal Regin. Father of our house, and of all true dragons as well, yes.' Helltrik looked increasingly uncomfortable.

'But missing a piece, I heard?'

'Just a small thing,' said Helltrik, grumpily. 'Hardly even a thing. A nothing, really.'

'A ring?'

'Lucky guess,' Helltrik snarled.

'There're not many dragons who would be so blithe about missing even the tiniest portion of his hoard – wouldn't you say?'

'The Siegfried treasure is a mighty haul!' boomed Helltrik. 'One tiny ring is neither here nor there! My ancestor, Regin the Great, won it in honourable contest with Siegfried Dragonheart!'

'Ah, yes, Siegfried Dragonheart. Slain by Regin,' said Lizbreath. 'Siegfried Dragonheart. Do you wonder why we call him that?'

'I don't see why we have to talk of these old mythic stories,' said Helltrik, clacking his talons together impatiently. He really did look extremely uncomfortable. 'I'd rather we discuss the present day. In fact, let us discuss the immediate future. I would like you to leave my property, Käal, and I would like you to take your . . . associate with you.'

'Monster Vagner . . .' Käal said.

'Siegfried Dragonheart,' interrupted Lizbreath. 'Wasn't he called that because, of all humans, he was the one who was closest to approximating a dragon – in courage, strength, violence and so on?'

'That's right.'

Lizbreath went to the window. 'I've heard otherwise.' There seemed to be some mark or blot upon the crystal, for she brought out a rolled-up wad of something from her satchel and rubbed at it. The crystal squeaked and complained under the action.

'Mon. Vagner,' said Käal, in a mollifying tone of voice. 'I understand your disappointment. And I apologize for the – eccentric behaviour of my associate. You want us to leave Doorbraak, and of course we shall.'

But Helltrik wasn't paying attention to him. Instead, he was peering past him at Lizbreath.

'Young Salamander,' he said, with choleric emphasis. 'What are you doing?'

'There,' said Lizbreath, stepping away from the window and depositing whatever she had just been using back in her satchel. 'There you go.'

'What did you do?'

'I drew something on the window.'

'On the crystal?' Both men came closer. And indeed a design *had* been carved upon it – actually cut into the fireproof crystal. 'Hey, that's neat!' Käal said, wonderingly.

'What is it *of*?' demanded Helltrik.

'Unless I'm very much mistaken, it is what Old Isabella had written on her scroll,' said Lizbreath. 'And it's the *real* secret of Doorbraak. Or are you going to keep pretending that I'm insane, Mon. Vagner?'

'No,' said Vagner, in a pinched and weary voice. 'No, Lizbreath. I can no longer pretend that.'

This is what Lizbreath had carved into the crystal:

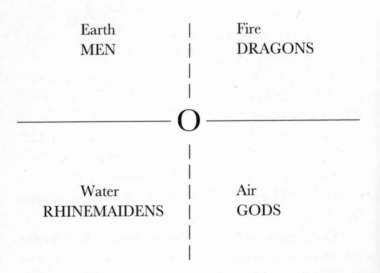

| Earth | | Fire |
| MEN | | DRAGONS |

| Water | | Air |
| RHINEMAIDENS | | GODS |

'How did you *do* that?' Käal asked. 'That's solid crystal! Did you gouge it with your fingers? Wow! Just

– wow. And,' he added, looking again, 'what does it . . . mean? The diagram? What's . . . uh . . .'

'It is a great shame' said Helltrik, in a tight voice.

'I thought it was just written on the top!' said Käal, still doing his wow!-voice. 'But it's actually *scratched* into the crystal! And crystal is really tough! Fireproof, and very hard to break . . .'

Without warning, Vagner leapt up, threw his wings wide, knocked his head against the ceiling and swung his body round. Kicking out with his hind legs, he smashed through the window with a cacophonous smash. Shards of crystal flew out and glittered through the air. The firewood frame splintered and broke into two separated pieces, thudding out of its space in the wall and falling away.

Vagner's legs continued through the trajectory of their kick. Then he lowered them again, drew in his wings and settled back on the floor.

'. . . and very easily *broken* ,' Käal finished, 'with one forceful backleg kick from a mature male dragon. Hey! Why did you do *that*?'

'Same reason Marrer burned the scroll,' said Liz-breath. 'Because nobody must be allowed to see it.'

'Quite right,' said Helltrik. 'It is much too harmful.'

'But *I've* seen it!' said Käal. 'It didn't do me any harm!'

'On the contrary,' said Helltrik. He brought his right forearm out of his satchel. In his claws was a bulky letter L, which he was holding by the shorter of its two limbs. 'I'm afraid that seeing it will do you a great deal of harm. I'm afraid that seeing it will . . . *kill* you.'

Käal saw Lizbreath, standing as she was beside him, stiffen. She drew in a long breath.

'I really don't understand what's going on,' Käal announced to the room.

'We can take that *as read*,' snarled Helltrik. 'It's been obvious for quite a while that you don't understand anything very much.'

'Hey!'

'Käal, be quiet now,' said Lizbreath, with calm authority. 'Do you see that device Mon. Vagner is holding in his hand? Believe me when I say it is capable of killing us both in two seconds. It emits a kind of fire from its end, in a concentrated straight line, and that line will go directly through your scales and cut your heart in two inside your chest.'

'So you recognize my little toy?' Helltrik asked.

'I know enough to take it seriously,' said Lizbreath.

'Good. Because you *should* take it seriously.'

'*Through* my scales?' said Käal.

'Käal, think back,' said Lizbreath. 'Back in the Clawsoleum?'

'I'd hardly forget that!' Käal said. 'Oh, wait a minute. Was *that* what was fired at us? One of *those*?'

'And *by* me, yes,' said Helltrik. 'You were profaning our most sacred space! Defiling the tomb of my ancestors! I couldn't have you poking around down there, pushing the corpses of my noble dragon-ancestors off their pedestals.'

'But it's not *down* there, is it?' said Lizbreath. 'I know. I looked.'

'Oh you're a *clever* girl,' said Helltrik, disdainfully.

'Not clever enough, it seems,' Lizbreath replied, grimly. 'I thought it would be there, but it wasn't. So where is it?' A look of revelation passed across her face. 'Your hoard! Of course!'

'It seems I was right. You're clever enough,' said Helltrik. He was aiming his peculiar device directly at Lizbreath's forehead.

'But *why* the hoard? Is it . . . wait, shielding?'

'Very good. You've done a lot of work on this, haven't you? It's a shame to have to kill you. Shielding. It emits a great quantity of quantum radiation, as you might expect. A human would use *lead* to shield it. But you can't very well imagine me, the head of the Vagner nest, sleeping on a hoard of lead, now, can you?'

'What *are* you both on about?' asked Käal. 'I'm utterly and completely baffled.'

'Mon. Vagner,' said Lizbreath, ignoring him. 'I'll tell you what I think. I think that if you were going to kill us with that, then you would have done it already. I think you want to keep us alive for something. So perhaps we should get to it? What do you want?'

'Ah,' said Helltrik; and there seemed genuine sorrow in his voice. 'I'm afraid *there* you are wrong. I don't want to keep you alive. I am going to kill you both, now. I pause only for one thing. And that, because I am not a cruel dragon – precisely because I am *not* a human. It is because I wish to apologize. I'm sorry for what I am about to do. I wish it could have been otherwise. Believe

233

me, I take no pleasure in this. But, believe me: there is no other way.'

He raised the device in his hand, and aimed it directly at Lizbreath's face. Käal had time for only one thing: a yell of 'Wait!' and then—

Then several things happened at once. Helltrik's device discharged its weird fire – a bright plumb line of ruby-red brilliance – but *not* at Lizbreath. Helltrik yelled in surprise. The ceiling exploded into big chewy chunks of stone that clattered all about them as an indoor hailstorm. Käal felt an impact from the side, and it was Lizbreath. She had launched herself at him with such energy that he was almost bowled over. 'Come on,' she gasped, her mouth right up against his head, pushing with her legs. Wide-eyed, Käal looked back and got one last glimpse of Helltrik: he appeared to be dancing, or perhaps having a conniption fit. The forearm that was holding the device pointing straight up, the other forearm gripping the wrist, the hindlegs thrashing, incoherent bellowing noises coming from his mouth. Then, with one last heave of her legs, Lizbreath managed to push Käal onto the balcony, and a moment later they were out in the plain air.

'Up!' Lizbreath called. 'Don't fly straight or you'll be an easy target! Up the castle, and curve round.'

He was so discombobulated he almost didn't follow her advice. But she slithered away through the air, sticking close to her own shadow on the wall, and her tail tapped him on the head as she went; and, for some reason, this prompted him to action. He pointed his head straight up, thrust his wings back with one

234

powerful stroke, lunged forward, smacked his belly against the stonework of the castle wall. With a 'hurr!' he flapped again, and then again, and oared himself upwards. Below, on the receding balcony, he saw Helltrik emerge and lift his device towards him. Exactly enough dragon-sense remained in his brain for Käal to jink sharp right. A perfectly straight red-gleaming pole appeared in the air where he had been, and then vanished. A piece of the castle's exterior stonework the size of a Moomin broke away just above and to the left of Käal, and fell away in a mist of masonry dust.

That put vim into Käal's flight. Adragoline surged through his bloodstream, and he flapped vigorously, hurtling upwards and following Lizbreath's path. In moments they were round the other side of the tower. Lizbreath alighted on the intersection where one of the smaller towers jutted from the main central structure, like a branch from a treetrunk. Gasping for breath, Käal landed beside her.

'What *is* that device?'

'It's a laser pistol,' said Lizbreath, as if this were the most natural thing in the world, looking behind her, and in front, above and below.

'I've never heard of such a thing!'

'Then you're not reading the right Sagas – *look out*!'

Helltrik came rearing up through the air, his wings broad behind him, the fire tugged into downward tendrils coming out from his nostrils by his upward momentum. The device was in his outstretched claw. Lizbreath leapt straight up. Käal, though, panicked somewhat. He tried to jump to the side, banged his head against the

235

tower, half-fell from his perch, and went head-over-rump. There was a sharp pain in the end of his tail, and simultaneously the crump of masonry breaking. And then, out of control, he banged into Helltrik. The old dragon cried in alarm. Käal, in pain from his tail, and disoriented, thrashed his wings to right himself. When he got upright again he saw Helltrik, empty-handed. They looked down together. The device, turning over and over, was falling through the sky.

'You fool!' cried Helltrik. 'You complete fool!'

He lowered his head and pushed off, flying hard straight down, beating his wings desperately to try and catch the falling artefact.

Treading air, Käal watched his descent feeling stupid. Lizbreath was at his shoulder. 'You knocked it out of his claw with your tail! What a hero!'

'I'm afraid my heroism was entirely inadvertent,' said Käal. 'And my *tail*—' he brought the tailend round to where he could see it. 'My tail *hurts*.'

'He shot through the tip of it,' Lizbreath observed.

'Through my scales! Right through, and out the other side! It's incredible!' Black blood oozed from a tiny hole, welling into inklike droplets and falling singularly into the wide air.

'You'll be all right,' said Lizbreath. 'There are no vital organs in the very end of your tail.'

'It hurts!' said Käal, again.

'I have friends who did that to themselves. For fun,' said Lizbreath.

'What? Shot themselves?'

'Not shot. But drilled holes in their scales, using a laser.'

'In the name of Woden, *why*?' Käal cried.

'Body adornment. You can put metal pins and hoops through the hole you make. It looks hot.'

'This is just – insane! I never heard of such a thing!'

'Oh we don't have access to laser pistols. Nothing so powerful as Mon. Vagner's little toy.' Helltrik was still visible, below them, much diminished in size. Then the low-lying cloud swallowed him. 'Nothing so compact. I have a device – though I need a large satchel just to carry the generator around in. It's how I made my tattoo. The difference between a tattoo and body-painting is that painting just goes over the surface of the scales, where a tattoo puts pigment actually *into* them. If people stopped to think for a minute, knowing what they know about dragon scales, they'd realize that we're talking about more-than-draconic technology.'

'Where did you get your tattoo machine from?'

'A friend of mine built it. But he was working on a blueprint. And the blueprint came from the same place that Helltrik got *his* device. And that place is not the world of dragons. Come on!'

'But,' spluttered Käal. 'But – with a device like *that* . . . if it fell into the wrong talons . . . think of the damage it could do! Lizbreath, it shot a beam of fire *right through my scales*!'

'I saw.'

'*Nothing* goes through scales! Scales are impenetrable! If there's a weapon that just slices through them, like an incisor through a sheep – well, wow! Wow! This changes *everything*!'

'Belatedly,' said Lizbreath, 'you are starting to get it. Come on!'

21

'We need to get inside Helltrik's hoard chamber,' Liz-breath said, as they alighted on the balcony to Käal's chamber.

'Helltrik aimed that device, his . . . lazy piston . . .'

'Laser pistol.'

'Exactly. He aimed that *right at your head*! He aimed at your head and fired the weapon. You should be dead. That beam would have gone right through your skull! It would have killed you.'

'You don't need to tell *me* that.'

'So why didn't he shoot you? He shot the ceiling. Why spare you?'

'I don't think he intended to spare me.'

'So what happened?' Käal asked.

'I don't know,' said Lizbreath. 'But I've got a notion. Come on, though. We haven't much time. Helltrik is doubtless on the ground below, right now, retrieving his weapon. And when he finds it, he *will* be back. And when he comes back, he will shoot to kill. Make no mistake, he means to kill me and to kill you too.'

'I don't want to be killed! Being killed would be very inconvenient *indeed*!'

'Then we'd better get a move on.'

They scuttled through the inner door and down the main castle corridor. 'Where are we going?'

'I thought it was in the Clawsoleum! Stupid of me, really. Of course it's in the hoard chamber! They've been using his huge pile of gold to mask its output.'

' "It"?'

'It's – complicated. A kind of hole. A sort of doorway.'

'OK. So that's *it*. And . . . "they"?'

'The Vagners. More specifically, Helltrik and that grandnephew of his, the one he's appointed his heir . . .'

'Marrer!' shrieked Käal.

'I know his name,' Lizbreath snapped back. 'You don't have to scream.'

'No – I mean – there's Marrer!' Not only was Marrer there: he was holding in his foreclaw another one of the freaky dragonscale-piercing weapons! Käal didn't get all this out before the wall-tiles broke into pieces and scattered in all directions. 'Down!' This time Käal got a close look at the beam of the device's weird fire, straight as a painter's line. It chopped a triangle off the end of one of Lizbreath's spinal plates and gouged a hole in the far wall with a bang and a blurt of stone pieces. Lizbreath, pressing her belly to the floor, slid his way with remarkable celerity. Not the vegetable; that's celery. Celerity. It means *rapidity*.

The two snuck round the corner as a third blast of the mystery weapon turned a portion of wall into a tumbling risotto of stone.

You know: *quickness*.

'Whichever dragon clan invented that weapon will

240

surely conquer the entire world!' gasped a hyper-ventilating Käal.

'No dragon invented it,' said Lizbreath, laying her long face lengthwise along the corner-edge of the wall, so as to angle her eyes just enough to see round the corner.

'No dragon? Did it just tumble, fully formed, out of the lap of the gods?'

'It was made by humans.'

'By,' said Käal, '*humans*? Did I hear you say humans? The vermin that used to infest the world, a sub-species renowned for their cruelty and barbarism? The creatures that lived in wooden houses that were effectively unlit bonfires, that ate vegetable slime and spent their time mocking one another? *Those* humans? Yes. *That* makes sense. So, I suppose, the apes somehow mocked up a superweapon capable of punching right through *dragon scales*, and then just forgot to use it during the Scorch Wars, eh? And it's lain unnoticed in one of the desert lands until the Vagners came across it? Pull the *other* one.'

Lizbreath pulled her head back in. 'It's the truth. But never mind about that now. Marrer has gone. But he won't have gone far. In fact, he wouldn't have fired at us unless he'd spoken to Helltrik first. That means that the old dragon is back on the Island. Probably he retrieved his weapon. If he didn't, well . . . well, obviously Marrer has got one as well. Either way, we're in trouble. They'll be back, and they intend to murder us both.'

'But *why*?'

'Because we saw the diagram.'

'Well thanks a *lot* for scratching that into the crystal, for me to see,' said Käal with what he hoped was 'pointed sarcasm' but suspected was actually 'whiny dickishness'. 'That was *very* thoughtful of you. Now they're going to kill me!'

'They don't want the secret of this place getting out. That makes it even more pressing. We *need* to get into that hoard chamber.'

'The most solidly locked and inaccessible room in the whole of Doorbraak,' said Käal. 'It's a stupid plan. And why do you want to get in there, anyway? You itching to steal some of the Vagner gold?'

'Don't be stupid,'said Lizbreath. 'Who can help us? What about your girldragon?'

'Asheila? She won't help us.'

'You're sure? We need a hand.'

'I'll help you,' said a creaky voice behind them. For a heartstopping moment, Käal thought that Marrer had crept up behind them and was about to drill dirty big holes through their body with his miracle weapon. But it wasn't Helltrik: it was his battered-old-bird of a brother, Ghastly.

'Who are you?' Lizbreath.

'Ghastly Vagner,' said Ghastly, 'party *CONF*erence.'

'What?'

'Couldn't help but notice that my bound-ary comm-*ISSION* brother and grandnephew are trying to kill you.'

'Er,' said Käal. 'Yes. They do seem to be trying to . . . eh, kill us.'

'Is that because – CAUCUS – you've stumbled across the secret at the heart of my sorry family?'

'You know about that?' asked Lizbreath.

'Of course,' said the wizened old dragon. 'I've been trying to tell the world for centuries; but because of my – *grassroot*-party-activISTS! – little problem, nobody takes me seriously.'

'Democratourette's,' said Lizbreath, wonderingly. 'I've read about it, never seen an actual case in the flesh.'

'Might I just say,' Käal put in, 'that I'm still not sure what's going *on* . . . except that two leading members of dragonkind's wealthiest family are trying to kill me.'

'We have to get to the vault where Helltrik keeps his hoard. Can you help us?'

'Is that where *it* is?' Ghastly asked. 'I've lived here all my life and never known. Ma-a-a-a-ani*festo*!'

'I think so. We need to get in there, to be sure.'

'Why do we need to get in there?' Käal asked. 'Wouldn't it make more sense for us to fly far away from Doorbraak? They are trying to kill us, in case you've forgotten. And in *case* you've forgotten, my tail hurts.'

'Oh!' said Ghastly, noticing the hole in Käal's tailend for the first time. 'Well – look at that!'

'We need to get into the chamber so that I can record what is inside with this eye.' She pulled a small eye from her satchel. 'Nobody will believe my word, or yours, but if we can give them *ocular* proof, then we can tell the whole of dragonkind about the secret at the heart of the Vagner hoard.'

'You want to break into the chamber and record Helltrik's pile of gold – with an eye?'

'No. I want to record what the pile of gold is *hiding*.'

'You're crazy. We need to get out of here, not go deeper.'

'Believe me Käal,' said Lizbreath, 'we will not be safe until this is made public. Where would we fly? Starkhelm? Back to Hostileia? Wherever we went, assassins would follow. This goes right to the top! Even the *Dragonlords* know about, and are complicit in, this conspiracy! Only by breaking the story public can we keep ourselves safe; because then there would no longer be a secret that killing us would protect.'

'Well,' said Käal, uncertainly. 'Even if I agreed with that logic, and I'm not sure I do, I don't see that we can do any good going for the vault where Helltrik keeps his gold. It *will* be locked. And we don't have the key. Your computers won't help you there.'

'I have a key to the chamber,' said Ghastly, clacking his jaw startlingly and adding, 'first nationwide *then* on a constituency by constituency basis.'

'Thank you!' said Lizbreath, embracing him. 'Thank you!'

'Oh,' the dragon replied, taken aback by this expression of gratitude from an attractive younger creature. 'Don't mention it.'

'It will be dangerous, down there,' said Lizbreath. 'Do you want to give *me* the key, and stay out of it?'

'That won't work, I'm afraid, it's a magical key. It must be placed in the lock by a member of the Vagner family, or it *won't* work first past the post.'

'Will you do it?'

'Of course I will. All this secrecy hasn't been good for

our family. Get it out in the *open* once upon a time famous for radical legislation elevated debate forensic scrutiny of laws turned to giant franking machine that stamps whatever Acts the government wants sometimes hardly even.'

'I'm really not convinced that I,' Käal started to say. Then, without warning, the wall beside them exploded: fire, dust and stony shrapnel filled the air. The dust sizzled as the laser-beam zapped through it. The beam missed Käal's head by a talon's-width. 'Let's go,' he yelled.

The three of them ran, all-fours, down the corridor, their necks low and level with the floor. The air over Käal's ears was disco-crisscrossed with two red lights. Behind him he heard a voice calling: 'Ghastly?' It was Helltrik, calling at the top of his voice: 'Ghastly! Get out of the way!'

'Looks like he found his device,' Käal called to Lizbreath. She was at the downward spiral of stairs. 'This way,' she cried.

'Ghastly, what are you *playing* at!' yelled Helltrik. And Marrer's voice could be heard too: 'Granduncle, be careful! You might get hit!'

At this, the crotchety old dragon stuck his neck high, turned his head backwards and shouted: 'I won't get hit if you stop *shooting* you *idiots* principle of elective subsidiarity.'

Käal saw clearly what happened next. A gleaming ruby beam swept in an arc through the air, met the old dragon's scrawny neck, and passed on. Where it intersected the scales fizzed and melted. A line of black ooze appeared suddenly, like a tight necklace. The expression on Ghastly's face was blended of equal portions of surprise and annoyance. Then the head tipped forward, coming clean away, and hitting the ground with a clump. The neck remained upright, converted now into a hose for spurting out intermittent gushes of acid black blood.

'Oh no!' cried Käal.

Disregarding the danger, Lizbreath had leapt, half flown through the air to the dragon's body, weaving to avoid the darting, deadly lines of red that drew a thrillingly random series of lines through the air. 'There's nothing you can do for him now,' Käal yelled at her. 'He's dead!'

'I know he's dead,' Lizbreath called back. 'I'm not administering Blast Aid, for Woden's sake! We need the *key* . . . there!' She hauled his satchel from his belt by main force, and then ran, jinking and weaving, to the stairway. Käal was there too, in a moment.

An unlucky shot hit a stone lintel, shattering it and collapsing the whole portion of the wall, door included, just after they had gone through. The light vanished. Big chunks of stone tumbled down the stairs after Käal and Lizbreath, and several struck Käal painfully upon the pate. 'Blocked,' gasped Lizbreath, pausing to look up through the mirk and dust, and spitting a piece of stone from her mouth. 'But that won't hold them for long. Come on!'

22

They picked their way past debris, and emerged on the lower floor. 'There's no point in going down to the hoard chamber now,' Käal observed. 'Neither of us are Vagners – we can't work the key.'

'Then we need to find a Vagner who can,' said Lizbreath. 'Come.'

They found a rear stairway, and scrabbled desperately upwards, until they reached the level on which Asheila's apartment was located. 'Stop a bit,' he said. 'Look, I really don't think this is a good idea.'

'You have a better one?'

'It's just that – Asheila and I parted on . . . poor terms. She was, to be honest, very cross with me. She thinks that you and I . . . well, never mind what she thinks. My sense is that she never wants to see me again. I guarantee you one thing . . . she won't help us.'

'Who else should we approach? Helltrik? She's your girldragon, after all.'

'She's not my girldragon! Believe me when I say that knocking on this door would be the worst thing we could do.'

Lizbreath knocked on the day.

'What are we going to do now?' cried Käal. 'How can

I possibly talk her round? She'll spit in my eye, slam the door and . . . probably call the police.'

'Simply explain the situation,' said Lizbreath. 'Tell her that you've discovered the malign secret at the heart of the Vagners, that it's nothing to do with democracy, but that now Helltrik and Marrer are trying to kill you, using a new technology called "laser pistols" that can send a beam of energy that penetrates even dragon scales, that your life is in danger, and that everything depends upon getting into Helltrik's hoard vault, for which you have a key, but for which you need somebody with Vagner blood in their veins, and will she help you? I'm sure she'll understand.'

'You don't know her . . .' Käal started to reply, at exactly the moment the door opened. He flipped his head round from looking at Lizbreath to meet Asheila's angry-looking face.

'You!' she said. 'Well, you've got a *nerve*. What do you want?'

'Asheila,' he said. 'The truth is . . . I've discovered the malign secret at the heart of the Vagners, which is nothing to do with democracy, but now Helltrik and Marrer are trying to kill me, using a new technology called "laser pistols" that can send a beam of energy that penetrates even dragon scales – look!' He held up the end of his pierced tail. 'My life is in danger, and things are desperate, and *everything* depends upon getting into Helltrik's hoard vault, for which we do have a key, but for which we need somebody with Vagner blood in their veins, and will you help me?'

Asheila gave Käal a hard look. He simpered. 'Please?' he tried.

'All right then,' she said.

This caught Käal off guard. 'Oh. Really?'

'To be honest,' she said. 'You had me at hello.'

'I didn't say hello.'

'You know what I mean.'

'We're talking about – solving the case, you know,' he pointed out. 'And the last time we spoke you said you didn't want me to solve the case.'

'Only because that would mean you'd leave Door-braak. That's what I don't want, silly. After our silly little fight, I felt full of remorse. I assumed you would leave and never come back. I even sent a raven to your Starkhelm apartment! Apparently it never made it there . . . can't *imagine* why.' She tut-tutted Käal playfully.

'Ah!' said Käal.

'But you haven't deserted me!' said Asheila, gooily. 'That's the important thing. You're still here!'

'Uh,' agreed Käal. 'Eh,' he added.

'Mis. Vagner,' said Lizbreath, coming forward. 'We need to hurry. Time is of the essence.'

'Let me get my handbag,' Asheila said. 'And you've *really* got a key to uncle's vault? How very exciting. Come on then. There's no time to lose.'

They went down by the back stairway, and emerged in the main hallway. The hoard chamber was below. The three of them crossed to the entrance to the lower stairway, proceeding very cautiously. 'Wait here,' said

Lizbreath as they came to the corner. 'I'll check the way's clear.' She darted round the corner and was gone.

'Why are we creeping?' Asheila asked in a loud voice.

'I told you,' hissed Käal. 'They have these weird little, uh, devices. They shoot out a special kind of fire. The beam went right through my tailend. Look!'

'Oh yes,' said Asheila. 'That does look nasty! Poor little Käaly-Wäaly. And it's Helltrik's hoard vault you're wanting?'

'Yes,' said Käal.

'Because the mysterious *thing* is inside? The secret at the heart of our clan?'

'Yes,' said Käal.

'And what is it, this mysterious thing?'

'To tell you the truth,' said Käal, 'I'm not entirely sure. Something worth trying to kill us over, though. It must be something, uh, importantly secretive.'

'I love secrets!' said Asheila. She seemed very jolly.

Lizbreath hurtled back round the corner. 'They're both down there – it's no go.'

'Well, all right,' said Asheila, matter of factly. 'Why don't we take the back route down?'

'There's a back route?'

'Of course. It's along here.'

They went, one after the other, down a broad stairless chute. It was tricky, since there wasn't much room to move your wings, but there was a fireproof rope attached to one wall to help steady yourself with, and quickly enough they dropped three floors. 'What's this for?' Käal gasped.

'The servants. But it's not used much. Uncle is very secretive about his vault.'

'Asheila . . .'

'Yes?'

'I'm . . . sorry we had that fight.'

'That's all right, darling,' said Asheila.

'Very sweet,' said Lizbreath, through gritted fangs. 'But we need to get on.'

They crossed a wide marble antechamber, looking about them in all directions and slinking like commandos. 'Here it is,' said Asheila. 'Give me the key, and I'll open it.'

They were standing before a tall door of stone polished so smoothly it looked like metal, upon which was written, in the ancient, venerable runes of the dragon alphabet: SPEAK, FRIEND, AND PISS OFF – MY GOLD, THIEVING SWINE, MINE I SAY. It was a traditional inscription.

'I can hear somebody coming,' said Lizbreath, looking across the wide floor to the main staircase. 'Some-several, in fact.'

'Well let's get inside,' said Asheila. Lizbreath gave her Ghastly's key: a long tapering sliver of stone. She put it into the teardrop-shaped keyhole. The door creaked, and a crack appeared with a whipsnap sound all around its rim. Then the heavy portal heaved, and swung out towards them. At exactly that moment Helltrik and Marrer came clattering down the main stairway on their hindlimb claws. 'There they are!' cried Helltrik. 'My vault! The dogs!'

'Hello uncle!' cooeed Asheila, waving her tail.

'Shoot them!'

Käal grabbed Asheila by the left wing, and hauled her round the door. Lizbreath, with commendable presence of mind, plucked the magic key from its keyhole, and dived after them, pulling the heavy door to behind her with her hind limbs. There was the sound of a detonation on the far side, and the door slammed shut.

They were in complete darkness, save for a single strand of light coming through the keyhole. Lizbreath, thinking quickly, groped about until she found a wall-torch. She lit this by breathing on it, and by its flickering, quickening light she thrust the key back into Asheila's hands.

'Lock it!' Lizbreath told the she-dragon. 'Put the key in the lock.'

'Helltrik's got his own key you know,' said Asheila, bridling at the Salamander's tone, but complying. 'He can unlock it, even if I lock it up.'

'Not if we leave the key *in the lock*,' said Lizbreath. She leapt-flew to the base of Helltrik's enormous pile of treasure, picked up a massy golden bowl, blew hard into it to soften the metal, and then threw it, with impressive strength and accuracy, straight at the door. It stuck to the inside of the keyhole with an audible splat, like chewing gum.

'That won't keep them out for ever,' said Lizbreath. 'But it'll hold them for a minute, and that will have to do.' She ran quickly all the way around the circular inner wall, breathing on the wall-torches one by one, until the whole space was illuminated.

They were in a vast bell-shaped chamber, vaulted in

great keystone granite blocks. In the middle was the biggest pile of gold Käal had ever seen. The apex of the roof was very high, but the hoard almost touched it nonetheless. 'So,' said Asheila, in an awe-struck voice. '*This* is what uncle has been sitting on, all these centuries!'

'I can hear them,' Käal reported, his ear to the door. 'They're bickering amongst themselves. But they can't seem to get Helltrik's key in place.'

'Whose key is this?' Asheila asked.

'Ghastly's,' said Käal.

'Oh! I haven't seen him in ages. How is he, the cranky old dear?'

'He's had a . . . choppy sort of day,' said Lizbreath.

'He did rather *get it in the neck*, didn't he?' said Käal.

'At least he's not *running around* like a *headless chicken*,' said Lizbreath.

'He had his head *sliced off his neck*,' agreed Käal, 'by Helltrik's deadly laser.'

There was a moment of silence. Eventually Asheila said: 'Oh,' in a small voice.

'We can't hang about,' said Lizbreath. 'With the weaponry they have it won't be long before they break through.'

'So, I'm assuming there isn't another way out of here?'

'No.'

'So, we're trapped.'

'If you want to put it like that.'

'It's been an awfully jolly adventure,' said Asheila.

'But oughtn't one of you to tell me exactly what is going on?'

'We,' said Lizbreath, 'are going to move that hoard.'

The three dragons looked at the enormous heap of gold. 'It's bigger than my house,' Käal noted.

'Yes.'

'And you want to move it by hand?'

'Yes. And quickly.'

'In the name of Woden, why?'

'Because it's sitting on top of what we're looking for. Now you're going to ask me: *what are we looking for?*'

'Not so much ask it,' said Käal, 'as shout it at the top of my voice. But, yes.'

'I'll explain. But we'll have to work as I talk. Start shifting the bigger pieces. Pile them over there, by the door.'

23

They began gingerly, picking the larger pieces – a gold table, a huge golden shield with complicated relief images of hömös warriors fighting some unimaginable war – but as they got into the rhythm they began kicking great scoops of loose gold coins, bracelets, helmets, necklaces and odds-and-sods.

'You thought the secret of the Vagner family was democracy,' Lizbreath told Käal. 'It's not. By its nature, democracy is a *rubbish* secret. It's not like autocracy. A democracy, by its very nature, can only seize power if all the people want it to. That puts it at an automatic disadvantage to autocracies, such as the Fascist Union of the Dragonlords, who can seize power whether the people want it or not. In short: democracy is not a threat to the Dragonlords. There's a,' Lizbreath scratched a nostril with her foretalon as she searched for the right word, 'a certain social *stigma*, it's true. But the super-wealthy, like the Vagners, can afford not to care about that. No, the whole "democracy" thing was chaff, designed to obscure what was really going on here.'

'And that was?'

'How does this island stay up? People say – magic. But that hardly answers the question! Getting a dragon into the air, with our power-to-weight ratio and our small-by-comparison-with-birds-and-bats wingspan . . . that takes magic. But magicking a dragon is one thing. Magicking an entire million-tonne island, quite another.'

'So how *does* it stay up, then?'

'Good question,' said Lizbreath. 'And whilst we ponder that one, here's another question to go along with it: why does the island drift through this year-long oval trajectory over Scandragonia and Europe?'

No answer. 'I give up,' said Käal.

'The island stays up because it is, in effect, hooked on something – like a cape on a peg. And the thing it is *hooked* on moves, relative to the ground: moves in the year-long oval we see. Because the hook moves, the island moves. Simple as that.'

'And this hook is . . . ?'

'It's more than just a hook. It's a point of connection. It is called a *wyrmhole*.'

Asheila, half way up the goldheap, sent a scree-tumble of golden shingle glittering down in the torchlight. 'A what?'

'Wyrmhole.'

'I've never heard of such a thing.'

'It's not a regular thing.'

'It's a point of connection, you say?' she said, piling many smaller gold pieces into a gold cauldron, then discovering that this made the cauldron too heavy to move. 'And what does it connect?'

'Worlds. There are *four* worlds. As far as we can tell, two are barren, or almost barren: one is of air, and its great winds have long since torn up its landscapes and churned its oceans to muddy turmoil. Another is of water, and the fishpeople who live there have no interest in us. But two are *not* barren. One is ours, the world of fire. And the other is – a world of men.'

'Gracious,' said Asheila, straining against the cauldron with her two hind legs, and her back against the angle of the mound. 'Fancy!'

'These four worlds were created at once, we believe,' Lizbreath went on. 'They were all set on their ways together, with only these slight biases. You see, just as our world of fire is not exclusively fiery – we still have earth, and water, and air – so the world of earth has its fire, water and air too. It's a question of balances between them. Now, when the four were created, I think the wyrmhole was a stable point linking all four. But over the many hundreds of thousands of years these worlds have gone on, rolling inexorably about their four bright sun, I think it has come loose. Slight differences have crept into each world's orbital trajectory, and so the point of connection has started its circling, small at first, larger later.'

'But why do you call it a wyrmhole?'

'I don't call it that. The humans do. They call it that because it links their world with the world of wyrms.'

'By that logic,' said Käal, 'we should call it the *apehole*.'

Lizbreath looked at him. 'It might catch on,' she said, in a way that suggested that it wouldn't.

'I can't get used to you talking about the hömöses in the present tense,' said Asheila. 'They all died out centuries ago, you know.'

257

'The world of water – I can only guess what happened in its history. The world of air: well the gods of the air were too powerful, I think, and wrecked the other elements: snuffed the fire, gouged the earth, vexed the waters. But the world of earth was just like ours – humans and dragons, and many other animals. But one thing changed.'

'What happened?'

'Somebody – a human – burnt his fingers.'

'Fingers!' said Asheila. 'There it is again! I hadn't heard the word until today. Now we keep going on about it.'

'Fingers,' Lizbreath explained, 'are the human equivalent of talons. They're soft and fleshy, as human bodies all are.'

'Ugh!' shuddered Asheila.

'I don't deny it's a little repellent,' said Lizbreath. 'But it's how they are.'

'Go on: what was it about fingers?'

'I'll tell you the story. But it means going back before the Scorch Wars, into that place where myth and history are twined each about the other, and the truth is hard to see. Back to the time of Regin the Great, father of all the dragons.'

'I thought this had to do with the world of, what did you call it? The world of earth . . . the hömöses.'

'Yes. And our world too. Because – and this is the really crucial thing – until this point, our two worlds were basically the same. There were differences, but only minor ones. There was a Regin the Great in both

258

worlds, and a Siegfried Dragonheart too, although the humans don't call him that.'

'Go on.'

'As you know, Siegfried was so strong and mighty he almost deserved to be called a dragon. Humankind has not seen his sort since. So mighty he was, he could conceivably have posed a threat. His weapon was called Nothung – that's the archaic word for "Nothing". Does anybody here know why his weapon was called "Nothing"?'

'Because it was – invisible?' suggested Asheila.

'Matter is mostly nothing,' said Lizbreath.

The others looked at her. 'Perhaps you mean "matter is something"?' said Käal.

'It only *seems* that way,' said Lizbreath, eagerly. 'In fact, matter is mostly . . . nothing at all! Isn't that re-markable?'

'Remarkably *unlikely*, I think you mean,' said Asheila.

'I know it's counterintuitive. If you had a computer, I could send you the link to a really interesting website that explains all this in accessible vocabulary . . . look, never mind. All you need to know is that *at a subatomic level* matter is mostly nothing.'

'She's talking,' Käal explained airily to Asheila, 'about the atoms that, er, submarines are made of.'

'And those are made of nothing?' Asheila replied. 'Well that would explain why submarines float. Or – wait, are submarines the ones that sink?'

'Both,' said Käal, confidently, although he was noisily creasing his brow.

'Can I get on with my story, please?' said Lizbreath. 'Siegfried—'

'The ape?'

'Exactly: the hömös, Siegfried.' She went on, tossing items in time to the rhythm of her words. 'Well he was a – genius, really. He discovered through magical means what the technicians of the human world would not *re*discover – through science – for another three thousand years. He discovered how to turn the nothing of matter into prodigious destructive energy . . . atomic energy. This was the force that powered his weapon, his Nothing. It was more than an ordinary apean sword. For one thing it could cut straight through dragon scales. Provided, of course, that Siegfried could get close enough to wield it . . .'

'Cut *through* our scales!' shuddered Asheila, picking up Käal's tail and poking a talon into the hole at the end. 'It's – just – horrible.'

'Well, after Siegfried's death the skill to make weapons like Nothing was lost. As we know, Regin, the Father of Dragons, slew Siegfried. The hömöses fought against our kind for millennia, but we were ultimately victorious.'

'History.'

'The history of *our* world. But to go back to that moment when Regin slew Siegfried. Do you know why we call him Dragonheart?'

'Because he was so brave that he was almost worthy of being called a dragon?' said Asheila. 'I'm sure I did this in school.'

'That's not the reason. Siegfried was a mighty king

among humankind, and was possessed of a vast golden treasure. At that time, there was truce between dragon-kind and the apes, and peace there was upon the land.'

'Why are you talking like that?' asked Käal.

'Like what?'

'You're going all uppy-downy with your intonation, all singy-songy. And you're diction has become strange and rather stilted.'

'I'm trying for an appropriately mythical effect!' said Lizbreath. 'Shut up! Where was I? Oh yes – Regin's brother, Fafnir. The evil brother dragon. He stirred up dissension between the apes and the dragons.'

'Stirred up what?' asked Asheila.

'Dissension.'

'The stomach bug, with all the diarhhoea and every-thing?'

'No,' said Lizbreath, after a moment. 'Not that.'

'My tail hurts,' said Käal.

'Fafnir *stole* Siegfried's gold, and then made up some story to cover his tracks, about inheriting it from his father. But nobody was fooled. War threatened the land. Worse, Fafnir used his new-stolen hoard to lure dragons to his cause – for he hoped to overthrow his brother and assume the "Regal" title. So Regin made common cause with Siegfried. He agreed to show the ape-king where Fafnir had hidden the treasure.'

'You mean he *betrayed* his brother to the hömöses?' said Käal.

'You could put it like that. But then he betrayed Siegfried too. The deal was: Siegfried would go into Fafnir's lair, kill him, and use his Atomic Sword to cut

out the dragon's heart. Then he would cook it, and
Regin would devour it, acquiring his brother's magic
and becoming the most powerful dragon the world had
yet seen. In return Regin would return the treasure to
Siegfried, and swear undying peace between apes and
dragons. *That* is why Siegfried is known as Dragonheart.
And he did it too – killed wicked old Fafnir, and cut out
the fellow's heart.'

'Ugh!' said Käal.

'But once he had eaten the heart, Regin went back
on his word. He did what he had always intended
to do – blasted Siegfried with his hottest flame, and
then crunched up his scorched, screaming body into
tiny morsels.'

'I don't see why you have to put this relentlessly
negative spin on Regin's actions,' said Asheila. 'Too
many dragons these days think it's "hot" to denigrate
the achievements of our great leaders. Regin made the
world safe for Dragofascism, and preserved dragonkind.
He's a hero! Let's hear less of these so-called "betrayals"
and a little more about his solid and lasting achievements, eh?'

'He won, at any rate,' Lizbreath agreed. 'And history
is written by the winners. Right?'

'I think you'll find,' said Asheila, condescendingly,
'that history is written by *the historians*. Hence the name,
you see?' She smiled, nodded. 'Anyway, don't let it put
you off. We all make mistakes. Go on.'

Lizbreath looked sternly at her. 'Right,' she said,
eventually. 'OK. Anyway, that's the founding myth of
our modern world. Because Siegfried trusted Regin, and

cut out the dragon's heart. Because he cooked it. Because he was careful when he cooked it.'

'Your point is?'

'Through the wyrmhole is another world, just like ours, except – well, except that it's all *different*. And the difference came about because of Siegfried's fingers.'

'More finger gibberish!' said Käal.

'It's important,' said Lizbreath. 'Here's a different version of the story: Siegfried agrees to Regin's deal, creeps into Fafnir's lair and kills the dragon. Then he cuts out the heart, spits it on the sword, and cooks it over an open fire.'

'You've shifted into the present tense,' noted Asheila.

'Dramatic licence. There he is, Siegfried, in the red-orange sunset, his long shadow flicking across the turf as he moves, smoke from his fire climbing into the sky like ivy. He turns the spit.'

'He'll scorch it!' said Käal. 'Why doesn't he just eat it raw, like a civilized creature?'

'That's not how apes like their food. They prefer meat cooked.'

'They *like* scorched food?'

'Not scorched. I said cooked. There's a difference. To stop the heart charring, he takes some fat from the carcass he has just cut open . . .'

'Ugh!' said Asheila. 'Do you mind? Gross.'

'It's an important detail,' said Lizbreath. 'Before he cooks it he takes some fat, and smears it on the meat. Then he washes his hand in the river . . .'

'What river?' Käal put in, trying to catch her out.

'The Rhine. Then he puts the heart on the fire, and

turns the spit. The fat has melted, and is dribbling over the meat. He catches the dribbles of scalding juice in his shield, and pours it back over the top of the meat.'

'Scalding juice sounds quite tasty,' said Asheila. 'I'm starting to feel peckish, actually.'

'He turns the meat. He smells the savoury smells of cooking. His mind wanders – thinking of the great treasure he has won back, the greeting his ape-people will give him when he returns with news of the peace he has negotiated. He reaches out to turn the spit again. The hot fat, licked by the flames, spits and flies.' Suddenly she yelled: 'Ouch!'

Käal and Asheila jumped. 'Hey!' said Asheila. 'You startled me!'

'Siegfried's hand was burnt by the hot fat,' said Lizbreath, in a more matter-of-fact voice. 'Instinctively he put his fingers into his mouth to cool them.'

'Why did he want to cool them?'

'Because he was made of ape.'

'Ah!'

'Those burnt fingers changed everything. Once he put them in his mouth, he tasted the flesh of slain Fafnir. He took into his body a small amount of the magic of dragons – only a small amount, but it was enough. He understood the nature of the creatures with whom he was treating. He could see like a dragon, and smell like a dragon. And he smelt – Regin, creeping through the meadowgrass towards him, with murder in his heart. He leapt up and grasped the handle of his sword, pulled it from the two supports, and with a mighty roar of effort and strain, spun about. The sword was heavy at the best of times, but now he was carrying the immense weight of a dragon's heart upon the blade! It took all his strength to hold it up.'

'Wait,' said Asheila. 'You're in the past tense now. Weren't you in the present a moment ago?'

Ignoring this, she went on: 'He flexed his muscles to pivot about, holding the sword in front of him. The centrifugal effect slid the half-cooked heart along the metal, and it flew free and clear. The motion distracted Regin for a moment. Remember, he hoped to devour his brother's heart and gain his powers. For one fatal moment he was caught between destroying Siegfried and catching the heart. He chose unwisely. Freed of its weight, Siegfried's sword, Nothing, was swift and deadly in his hand. The ape-king leapt, and the magic sword pierced the thick scales of Regin's neck , here!' Lizbreath slapped herself noisily under her chin, talons on scales, 'In at the throat! Regin had his brother's heart in his jaws, and though he reared up in agony and rage he made no sound, nor put out any fire. Siegfried gripped the hilt, his feet on the writhing neck, and he didn't let go. When the mighty dragon fell back to earth, Siegfried leapt free. After the death agony, he took his sword again and cut the head whole from Regin's body.'

'Just like poor Ghastly,' said Asheila, in a small voice.

'Golly,' said Käal. 'That's quite a story.'

'It's not a story. It's real. It's the history of the place on the other end of that wyrmhole.'

'The apehole!' said Käal. 'Really?'

'*Please* stop calling it that,' said Lizbreath. 'And, yes, really. From that point on, history diverged. In the earth world, Siegfried led the apes to victory. Dragons were scarce back then, and after Regin's death there was no mighty father to lead the species' population expansion. Siegfried hardened his resolve, and never again trusted one of us. He hunted us, and his sons and daughters hunted us after his death.'

'So dragons are the minority in that other world?' asked Asheila.

'There *are* no dragons in the earth world. They were all hunted down and killed.'

'Great Woden!' gasped Käal. 'That's horrible!'

'It *is* horrible,' said Lizbreath, soberly. 'It is precisely as horrible as what we did to the apes during the Scorch Wars.'

'Oh I hardly think the comparison is just!' said Asheila, horror-struck. 'You can't seriously be making it.'

'No?'

'Of course not! Don't misunderstand me – I hold no truck with cruelty to animals, and I'm sure the hömöses are very clever and everything. But they were not dragons! Maybe purging the world of every ape was going a little far – but to kill *all the dragons*? That is to rob the world of its grandeur! Take away all the apes and what have you left? There are plenty of other small animals that creep about through the grass and clamber in amongst the trees. But take away all the dragons, and you leave a world without the majesty and splendour of dragons in flight – a world without fire, and magic! It is a crime against the cosmos!'

'Perhaps you can see it from the apes' point of view?'

offered Lizbreath. 'Surely they would see it exactly the other way about?'

'No,' said Asheila. 'No! I don't accept it. Because however fond you might be of the soft-fleshed humans, you must accept that they never *did* possess majesty and might. Perhaps the apes consider apes attractive, yes. Even beautiful, perhaps, in their own eyes, at least, however repulsive I find them! I grant it, for the sake of argument. Maybe the apes *were* beautiful, at least to other apes. But they themselves must accept the truth: *they were never sublime!*'

'You know, the hömöses have a word for the deliberate destruction of an entire people,' said Lizbreath. 'Genocide.'

'Of course they have a word for it!' said Asheila. 'They need a word for it! It's what they do! Everybody knows that humans were wicked, destructive, vindictive cruel, violent – and not in a good way.'

'Let's not get into a fight, please,' said Käal. 'It's ancient history, after all.'

'But that's just it!' cried Asheila, spreading her wings and leaping into the air. 'It's not ancient history at all! It turns out it's right here, right now! If Mis. Salamander here is right, and this chamber really does contain an apehole—'

'*Please* stop calling it that!' squawked Lizbreath.

'Then there's a whole other world in which dragons were hunted to extinction by savage apes! Maybe Helltrik is right to try and hide this portal . . . maybe we're wrong to try and uncover it? What if we open it, and

267

swarms of grublike apes come bundling through, to finish the job?'

'That's hardly likely to happen,' Käal said; although the thought *was* unnerving. 'Is it?' he asked Lizbreath.

'No,' said Lizbreath.

Käal cleared his throat with a healthy blast of fire and added: 'Surely you're not scared, are you, Asheila? Scared of a few apes? You'd cook them with one sneeze.'

'Unless they all come, grunting, squeezing out of this apehole, armed with their deadly lazy pistols? Eh? Like the ones Helltrik and Marrer are running around with? What then?'

'OK,' said Lizbreath, rearing up in the air herself, and spreading her wings as wide as possible for emphasis. 'Two things. One, neither of *you* have been in contact with the human world. My friends and I have. We've been monitoring it, as best we can, downloading as much from their internet as possible. That means I know quite a lot about it, and you don't, so maybe you'd better listen to me. And two: please stop calling the wyrmhole the "apehole"! It's . . . just foul.'

The door shook with a heavy detonation. From the far side came Helltrik's voice. He must have found himself a megaphone, or something similar, because his voice boomed. 'You in there!'

Lizbreath went over to the door. A small pile of gold was heaped at its base, still a pitifully small portion of the main hoard. 'Hello Helltrik.'

'You've no business being in there!' Helltrik boomed. 'That's my vault! My hoard!'

'We know about the apehole!' yelled Käal, at the top of his voice.

'I don't know what you're talking about!' boomed Helltrik,

'The wyrmhole, Helltrik,' said Lizbreath.

'Oh,' said the figure on the far side of the door. 'That.'

'Hello Uncle!' called Asheila, from the main heap. 'Cooee! What larks we're having!'

'Asheila!' boomed Helltrik's voice. 'I'm sorry you had to get yourself caught up in this, my dear. It is regrettable.'

'He means he's going to kill you,' Lizbreath told Asheila.

'No!' said Asheila, opening her eyes wide. She scrambled down the heap of gold, and came over to the door, putting her snout close to the stone. Shadows, thrown by the torches, stretched and shrivelled in pulses. 'Is that true, Uncle? Are you going to kill me?'

'I'm afraid I have no choice now, my dear,' said Helltrik. 'Now that you know about the wyrmhole, I will have to silence you – for ever.'

'But . . . I'm family!'

'I'm afraid that doesn't make any difference.'

'You didn't kill Ghastly,' Käal pointed out.

'Actually,' Helltrik boomed, through the door, managing nevertheless to convey a sense of regret, 'I did.'

'Well, yes, technically you did. But that was just now!' Käal said. 'I mean – before. For all those centuries, you let him live. Why not let *us* live too?'

'Nobody believed a word Ghastly said,' Helltrik

snorted. 'It didn't *matter* if we let him live. Everybody thought he was just a mad democrat. But you three . . . yes, even you, Asheila, my dear girl. If we let you out, the world might listen. And we cannot have that.'

'Still,' said Asheila, her voice trembling a little. 'Killing me seems a little . . . extreme.'

'I am sorry,' came Helltrik's disembodied voice. 'You'll have your place in the family tomb, though. We'll blame your death on those other two, the Salamander and the idiot Saga writer. But you'll get burial with full honours.'

'I suppose that's something,' said Asheila, wistfully.

'Idiot?' cried Käal. 'You hired me, Helltrik! If I'm an idiot, that makes you an idiot-hirer. Hah! Which is obviously, um, *worse*.'

'That's telling him,' said Lizbreath, sourly.

'I hired you to find out what had happened to Hellfire!' the old dragon's voice came back. 'Something you completely failed to do!'

'Didn't you think it was dangerous,' Käal asked. 'Hiring a world-famous finder-outer-of-things to come and poke around your island? Weren't you worried that I might find out about the one thing you didn't want me to find out about?' He looked from Asheila to Lizbreath. 'If you see what I mean?'

'I had you checked out, of course, before I approached you,' said Helltrik. 'The consensus was that you were an idiot.'

'So why hire me at all?'

'After three hundred years, it was starting to look . . . suspicious . . . that I hadn't done anything to discover poor Hellfire's fate. And all these tongues kept arriving, one a year! My initial interview with you reassured me that *you* weren't likely to get very far in the investigation. Of course, one reason why the *police* investigation into Hellfire's disappearance didn't proceed very far is that I used my influence with Detective Superintendent Smaug to make sure that the police didn't get too close to the *real* truth. Still,' he added, wistfully, or if not *full*, perhaps, then at least with a certain percentage of wist, 'I did want to know what happened to the poor girl!'

'You know what happened to her,' said Lizbreath, vehemently. 'You know because you killed her.'

There was a moment of silence. When Helltrik's voice was heard again, through the closed door, it sounded wounded. 'No I didn't,' he said.

'She found out about the apehole, didn't she?' said Käal, with sudden insight. 'She discovered that you had a secret apehole you didn't want the world to know about! She threatened to shine a light on your secret apehole, didn't she?'

There was a second pause. Finally, Helltrik's voice came back, sounding more baffled than anything else. 'What?'

'She found out about the wyrmhole,' said Lizbreath.

'She did,' said Helltrik. 'The clever little creature. I tried to talk to her – to convince her to keep the family secret. I thought she might do it, as well. She was a sensible young dragon, at heart. But she grew upset . . . ran off.'

'So you killed her!'

'No! It might have come to that – I'll admit that much. But it hadn't yet.'

'So—' said Käal, genuinely puzzled. 'If that's so, then . . . where is she?'

'I don't know!' barked Helltrik. 'That's what *you* were supposed to find out!'

'Oh,' said Käal. 'Right.'

'But I doubt she is alive,' boomed Helltrik. 'If she was, then I have to believe she would have gone public about the wyrmhole.'

'If she were,' shouted Käal, through the door.

'What?'

'You said "if she was", but that's incorrect.'

A pause. 'What?'

'It's the subjunctive. Unfulfilled wish or condition. You said "if she was", when the grammatically correct idiom is "if she were".'

'I must say you're making the decision to kill you much *easier* for me,' said Helltrik, through the door,

The door shook. Käal couldn't help but leap back. 'It won't be long now,' Helltrik boomed. 'I've called in reinforcements. We'll soon have this door down – and then it's curtains for the lot of you!'

'Oh Uncle!' wailed Asheila.

Lizbreath was scuttling, head down, all the way round the inside of the broad circular wall. The many chuckling torches played games with her shadow as she moved, casting it wide from her back like a black cloak, drawing it in tight as she came under the light and then drawing it out on the far side. Several half-shadows accompanied the main one. Having completed a circuit at the bottom, she jumped in the air and flew round the room again higher up. Asheila and Käal watched her with fascination.

The door boomed again, and shook in its stony frame.

'What are they *doing*?' said Asheila. 'Are they head-butting the door?'

'Shooting it with their guns,' said Lizbreath, alighting beside them. 'It'll take them a long time to break through like that. If that's the best they've got, then maybe there's time. But I tend to believe Helltrik has summoned heavier ordnance.'

'So we're trapped in here. Like rats in an, uh, bucket, or something. There's no other exit?'

'I was wondering if any of the keystones could, per-haps, be dislodged,' said Lizbreath. 'But it's very solidly built, all round. Unsurprisingly.'

'So there's only one exit,' said Asheila. 'If we opened it, suddenly, perhaps that would give us the element of surprise . . .'

'Helltrik and Marrer both have laser pistols,' Liz-breath reminded her. 'They have them trained on this door. We wouldn't get four steps into the antechamber.'

'We can't just wait here! Wait to die like rats in a cage?'

'There's another way,' said Lizbreath. She looked at the hoard of gold. The other two dragons followed her gaze. 'Underneath all that gold, in fact, I'd wager, right in the *middle* of it, is . . .'

'The apehole!' cried Käal, with sudden joy.

'Oh,' gasped Lizbreath, exasperatedly.

'No – you're right, that's brilliant!' said Käal. 'We can climb up the apehole! I assume it can fit three dragons, up there, can it? Maybe it'll be a tight squeeze, but . . . well it's a matter of life or death, isn't it? It might not be my first choice, but I'd rather force myself up an apehole, however uncomfortably, than *die*. Who's with me?'

Asheila was looking at him with an expression that could best be described as *aghast*.

'There is the slight problem that the *wyrmhole*,' Lizbreath put particular emphasis on the word, 'is presently blocked by several thousand tonnes of gold.'

'Well, let's clear it out of the way!' said Käal, filled with sudden eagerness. He scampered over to the hoard, and began picking up goblets, crowns, doubloons, triploons and swords, chucking them one after another in the direction of the door.

'It'll take us too long doing it by claw, like that,' said Lizbreath. 'They'll break through the door and kill us before we get anywhere near the hole itself. We need a quicker way! We need to clear all this junk *out of the way* in one giant . . . blast . . .'

'But how?' asked Asheila.

'How indeed? I don't know! There must be a way . . .'

'Explosives?' said Käal, from the hoard.

And as he said so, with rather nice timing, the door broke from its frame and clattered into the room, propelled by a massive blast, an ear-dinning roar, and a roiling sphere of fire. Flame bulged through and sank back, leaving behind huge gouts of smoke. The massive door, flying free, tipped right over, bounced on the granite floor and embedded itself a third of its length into the pile of gold. Käal reacted instinctively as it caromed towards him, darting backward, losing his balance and falling completely off the hoard. He scrambled to his feet, the high-pitched mosquito whine of tinnitus in his ears, and looked for his companions. It was not easy to see, since the space was full of smoke, but after a moment he saw Asheila lying, prone, on the floor. He looked frantically about and saw Lizbreath curled in a heap beside the heap, her tail straight up. 'Are you all right?' he called, but he couldn't hear his own voice, and that meant that he wasn't sure if he had spoken at all.

The naked doorway sent a shaft of light through the dust; and through it came three large dragons. Small fire licked around their feet as they moved. Lizbreath stirred, dropped her tail and sat up. Asheila lay motionless.

24

'Asheila!' cried Käal, in dismay. The whistle inside his ear went up a tone, then a semitone, and then it popped and the sounds of the outside world flooded in.

'Look what you made me do!' declared one of the dragons by the door. It was Helltrik, and he was holding his lazy pistol in his right claw. 'You made me break my own door! It'll be a major job repairing this – I hope you realize that.'

'Sorry,' said Käal, automatically.

'Not to mention the expense,' said Helltrik.

Käal looked at the other two dragons. The smaller was Marrer, and he too had his lazy pistol. But the third was a stranger to Käal: a very large, evidently old and important beast. He was not carrying a weapon, but – oddly for a dragon – he was dressed in a waistcoat. In fact, it was so odd to see a dragon not obviously suffering from Pernicious Dragnemia wearing clothing that the sight of it left Käal boggled. Helltrik and Marrer had their deadly weapons aimed right at his head; he was moments away from death; there was no chance of escape, nowhere to run to and nothing to be done. But all Käal could think of was this strange piece of exterior clothing.

'You're wearing a waistcoat,' he said to the stranger. 'That's odd.'

When the stranger spoke, it was with a deep and resonant authority. 'Oh don't think I haven't tried *washing it off*,' he growled. 'Don't think I haven't tried every cleaning product imaginable, up to and including bleach. But it just won't come off!'

'The waistcoat won't?'

'No!' snapped the stranger. 'Not the waistcoat, you idiot. *This*.' The dragon unbuttoned his covering and slipped it off. On his chest was written: I A FOUL OLD DRAGON WHO ENDULGES IN ORAL SEX PERVERSION.

Käal stared at this. He blinked, and he stared some more. Dust was settling all around. Finally he spoke. 'That's not how you spell "indulges", you know,' he said.

'I KNOW!' exploded the dragon, rage evident in every scale of his body. 'Do you think I *don't know*? Of *course* I know! Why do people always *say that*? It wasn't my bastard spelling! I didn't choose to have this legend inscribed on my bastarding chest! But it means that not only do people think I'm a bastarding sex pervert, they think *I can't even spell correctly*!'

'My,' said Käal, shaking his head to clear the dust from his ears. 'You *are* cross.'

'OF COURSE I AM CROSS!' screamed the dragon, fire spurting in curt, incandescent white-violet gusts from his mouth as he spoke. '*Look at me*! I can't get it off. It won't come off! I don't know what magic paint she used to write it, but nothing I do gets rid of it!'

Lizbreath stirred, pulled herself round and sat up. 'Oh,' she said. 'Hello Burnblast,.'

'There she is!' howled the foul old dragon who once upon a time, but in all likelihood no longer, endulged in oral sex perversion. 'There! The only reason I don't tear you limb from limb, Salamander, right now – the only reason I don't peel your skin scale by blood-soaked scale and *eat you raw*! – is *this writing*! You have one chance, and one chance only. Tell me *how to get it off*, and I shall,' he looked at Helltrik, 'shall make sure your death is painless, at any rate.'

'You can't get it off,' Lizbreath said, mildly. 'It's a tattoo.'

'Arrrrr!' screeched Burnblast. 'I'll chop you into a thousand pieces! Helltrik, I want you to slice her into ten thousand chunks with that magic firestick of yours!'

'Calm down, Burnblast,' said Helltrik. 'Let us not lose our heat.'

'Arrrrr!' Burnblast said again, thrashing his tail and blowing great angry blasts of fire.

'Burnblast? Burnblast!' called Helltrik. 'Calm yourself! Be the Dragon Fonz! You know the Dragon Fonz?'

Burnblast looked at his companion. 'Yes?'

'What is the Dragon Fonz?'

'Hot.'

'There you go!' Burnblast did seem to be calming down. 'You're hot,' said Helltrik. 'We're *all* hot. None of us are going to lose our hotness. Calm, now!'

'All right,' said Burnblast in a steadier voice. 'I have regained my temper. But I still want that Salamander dead.'

'They'll *all* be dead in a moment. But there's no need to make more of a mess. This is still my hoard! We'll get them to move the pieces back, the ones they moved. When they've tidied up a little, we'll take them outside and kill them. The island will cross the Sea of Bothnia in a few days. We'll fill their bellies with concrete and dump them there.'

'Remember the deal, that's all,' said Burnblast. 'I came straight here, with all explosives, to help you. In return, you let *me* kill the Salamander.'

'Sure. Stay hot, Burnblast. Just stay *hot*. It's all going to happen, as we agreed.'

'I tried bleach!' Burnblast burst out. 'Have you ever tried to wash yourself with bleach? I'll tell you what happens! It seeps round the side of your scales, that's what, and works like acid on the flesh beneath!'

'Bleach won't get rid of it,' said Lizbreath. 'It's a tattoo. You seem to have difficulty understanding this. It's not painted on *top* of the scales.'

All through this conversation Käal was having an idea.

Now, Käal was not a coward, exactly; except, per-haps, by the rather exacting standards of dragons. Cer-tainly he did not think of himself as a coward. But he *did* think: 'Wouldn't it be better if I escaped from this situation alive, instead of dying ignominiously?' *And* he was aware that there was a magical portal of some sort buried in the centre of Helltrik's hoard. He hadn't entirely grasped the principle on which this hole was supposed to work, but he comprehended that it was his only hope of survival.

As Burnblast ranted at Lizbreath, a thought germinated inside his dragon brain. I say, thought: it was more like an image, a mental picture of him *diving into the flank of the golden pile*, like a puffin dives into water. He saw himself moving with barely an effort through the granulated heap of gold objects, wriggling with powerful strokes, until his snout touched the apehole and he slid through into safety. This image grew quickly in strength until it assumed a kind of inevitability. His heart began to speed, and the thought fleetingly crossed his consciousness – *what about the others?* – but, although it was clearly a shame that Lizbreath and Asheila would die, it was by any metric better that than Lizbreath, Asheila *and him* dying.

'Dragons!' Helltrik said, in a conciliatory tone, though his weapon was still aimed at Lizbreath. 'Dragons, please! This is a sombre moment; for death always is. Can we not – all of us – agree to meet it with a modicum of dignity?'

'Stuff that,' Käal yelled, suddenly. 'I'm going up the apehole!'

He launched himself at the hoard, pushing off with his muscular hindlegs and thrashing his wings furiously to generate as much velocity as possible. His head hit the heap of gold with considerable momentum. Of course the stacked gold, pressed down by its own weight, was as hard as if it had been a single gigantic piece of granite. There was no way that ramming it at speed was going to penetrate it. Käal bounced off it as from a concrete wall, and landed on his ample draconic backside.

He sat there, half-stunned, looking from dragon to dragon blinking slowly. There was a sudden new great ache inside his skull. 'Owwww,' he drawled, putting both foreclaws to his brow. 'Wwwwww.'

'Enough idiocy! You three – put those pieces of gold back on the main hoard.'

'Why should we labour like firedrakes for you, when you're going to kill us anyway?' asked Lizbreath, reasonably enough.

'Because,' snarled Burnblast stepping forward intimidatingly, to tower over the diminutive she-dragon, '*he* can kill you quickly – a swift chop to the neck – where *I* will kill you very slowly, with icicles in your eyes and cold mud down your throat!'

'It's all *throats* with you, isn't it, Burnblast?' Lizbreath drawled, with just a hint of amused contempt. The old dragon howled with rage, and would have launched himself straight at Lizbreath if Helltrik and Marrer hadn't grabbed hold of his wings to restrain him.

'We will not lose control!' Helltrik gasped. 'We will remain civilized dragons! We are not apes after all! Come! Come!'

For the first time since entering the vault, Burnblast showed something akin to contrition. 'You're right, you're quite right.' He snuffled, coughed out some smoke, and drew back to the door. 'Let's stop this charade. Give them a clean death and be done with it.'

'Owww,' said Käal, rubbing his head. 'Wwww.' He looked up. 'That really hurt. I dinged my skull quite badly, actually.' He stretched his neck and aimed his head in the general direction of his executioners. 'It's like I can see two of you, Helltrik.'

Helltrik looked sorrowfully down at him.

'And now!' said Käal. 'And *now* it's like you're pointing two laser pistols at me! It's quite a . . . thing . . . oh,' he added, realization dawning. 'You're going to shoot me?'

Helltrik nodded.

'Right now?'

'Burnblast is right,' he said. 'A clean death is right.'

'I know where the tongues came from,' said Lizbreath. 'They were cut out of the mouths of your dead ancestors. They're from your own Clawsoleum.'

Helltrik swung his pistol round to point at Lizbreath. 'You're sure of this?' he asked, shortly.

'If you'd searched the room properly yourself, you'd have seen it.'

'I shall enter that sacred space when I am dead,' said Helltrik, in a resonant voice. 'And *not before*.'

'You entered it a few days ago!' said Käal. 'To try and carve Liz and myself into pieces with your crazy pistol!'

'*That*,' said Helltrik, furiously, shifting the aim of his weapon from Lizbreath's head back to Käal's. 'That was to *chase out* two sacrilegious animals, blaspheming the holiest arena in my family! You *forced* me to it! You knocked Bullar off his pedestal! Death is the very least of what you deserve.'

'I didn't know anything about that, Uncle,' said Asheila, hopefully. 'Desecrating the Clawsoleum? This is the first I've heard of it!'

'I know, my dear,' said Helltrik, smoothly, his temper

tucked neatly away again. 'I don't doubt it. Whilst killing these two interlopers will be a pleasure, you can rest assured that killing you will be a painful and unpleasant duty.'

'Oh,' said Asheila.

'I don't think you understand the implications of what I'm telling you,' said Lizbreath. 'All those tongues were taken from your *own* family sepulchre! What does that mean?'

'It means it must have been done by a member of the family,' said Marrer. 'Since the key only works if turned by a somebody with Vagner blood in their veins.'

'Interesting,' agreed Helltrik, dispassionately.

'Wait a minute—' said Lizbreath,

'Since, Granduncle, we can obviously eliminate you and I,' mused Marrer. 'That leaves a limited pool of suspects . . .'

'. . . and once we have disposed of these evil-doers,' said Helltrik, firmly, 'we shall track down the perpetrator.'

'But Granduncle,' said Marrer, lowering his gun. 'It means that it was a *member of our family* that murdered my sister!'

'Come, Marrer – raise your weapon! We always knew that such a thing was possible – likely even. We have business to attend to here.'

'No, seriously, *wait* a minute—' said Lizbreath,

Marrer looked at his uncle, in silence. Käal felt a stir of hope in his dragonheart that the younger Vagner might be about to rebel against the older. But it was not to be. Slowly Marrer raised his weapon, and pointed it at

'Now *wait* a minute,' said Lizbreath for the third time. 'If that lock was a magic lock, and the key could only be turned by somebody with Vagner blood . . .'

At last Käal cottoned on: '. . . then how did we get inside?' he finished.

Helltrik looked at them. 'Do you know what?' he said, wearily. 'I don't care. You got help, obviously, but I don't care how. I don't really even care who.'

'It wasn't me!' squealed Asheila. 'It's true I helped them in here, but not the Clawsoleum!'

'So how *did* we do it?'

'It doesn't matter,' said Helltrik. 'I'm sorry my dear, but it doesn't. This has all been a horrible mess. I allowed my anxiety about Hellfire's death to get the better of me. No, not even anxiety. It was a simple curiosity. Three hundred years is long enough for the natural grief to fade away. But *not knowing* exactly what happened meant that simple curiosity got its claw inside my mind. It compacted down the press of years, the way old trees become coal. After three centuries of not knowing I snapped. But how I wish I had held my nerve! Compared to . . . all this . . . *not knowing* is a simple burden. Compared to the desecration of my ancestral tomb; to all this necessary death and destruction.' He sighed. It had been a long speech. But people had listened to all of it without interruption. That was because he had a gun.

'Nobody *helped* us,' Lizbreath insisted. 'I found the key

in Hellfire's room, put it in the lock and . . . *something happened.*'

'Mis. Salamander,' said Helltrik. 'I appreciate that you wish to postpone the inevitable moment of your own demise by talking. But it will do you no good.'

'I put the key in,' she said, quickly. 'But the lock opened anyway.'

'The lock is a very ancient mechanism,' said Marrer. 'Perhaps it malfunctioned.'

'No!' said Lizbreath. 'No!'

'She's terrified,' said Burnblast, with satisfaction.

But Lizbreath was not terrified. The expression on her face was, on the contrary, one of sudden delight. It said: *I understand!* She had solved the mystery of Hellfire Vagner's disappearance.

'The solution!' she cried. 'Is *Hellfire Vagner*! In *the vault*! With the *candlestick*!'

Helltrik heard this, or he did not, but either way he had reached the moment of his own decision 'Enough,' he said. He aimed his weapon, and fired.

25

Afterwards, Käal could not be sure how much of his memory of events was shaped, retrospectively, by that portion of the brain that arranges the jumble of sense-data into neatly ordered boxes. None of it felt ordered at the time; but afterwards it was possible to distinguish several consecutive stages. There was, for instance, the candlestick. It was a massive golden artefact that was poking out of the main hoard.

As Käal watched, it elevated itself.

It lifted as if by magic, horizontally. Then it righted itself, dipped down, and lifted up again. Käal had never seen a levitating candlestick before. It was a remarkable enough sight for him to be struck by it, even in the teeth of his own impending death.

Then Helltrik fired. Or more precisely, *as* Helltrik fired, the magically levitating candlestick flew suddenly towards him, striking him on the wrist.

The blow, following the principle of conservation of momentum, transferred some motion to the wrist, hand and gun. Helltrik, having intended to shoot Lizbreath in the head, ended up shooting his grandnephew Marrer in the ear.

The thin red line of light passed straight through the

outer scales and inner cartilage and out the other side. Marrer, not expecting this development, screeched – as much in surprise as pain – and dropped his own pistol.

Lizbreath sized up the situation very rapidly indeed. She pounced on the gun, covering the distance between her and the weapon in an instant, plucking it from the floor before it had stopped bouncing.

But Burnblast was just as quick. He saw what was happening, and launched himself straight at her. His aim, evidently, was to disable her before she could bring the pistol round, and he went for it with old-school dragonly ferocity – wings opening, jaw agape, roaring and blasting flame with all his might. He was an old, large dragon. All his might was a lot of might. Fire filled the whole chamber ahead of his thunderous approach: intensely white directly before him, billowing and feathering into incandescent hues of yellow, grey-blue and orange in every direction.

It was so dazzling, in fact, that any but a dragon's eye would have missed the single thead of red running right through the middle of the fire, in the opposite direction to its thrust.

The laser beam struck Burnblast right in the middle of the back of his wide open mouth. If dragons had tonsils the shot would have bisected them perfectly. But of course dragons don't have tonsils. Only a fool would think they did. Instead, the beam broke through the membrane at the back of his mouth, and passed into the brain pan. The difference in respective heights (for Burnblast had reared himself up, and Lizbreath was on the floor) meant that the shot passed through the middle of his brain, and exited through the top of his head.

The dragonfire stopped gushing, leaving only smoke. Burnblast flew up towards the ceiling with several uncoordinated thrashes of his wings, making weird mewing sounds of agony, and then crashed down to land on his side. He clamped his rear claws to his snout, curling himself thereby into a large ball, and began rocking back and forth.

The smoke began to dissipate, to reveal Lizbreath standing there.

Helltrik was holding his laser pistol at an angle, goggling at the sight of his two companions. Marrer was hopping about clutching his ear and yelling 'Ear! Ear! Ear!' over and over. Burnblast was lying on his side, moaning and mumbling.

His astonishment gave Lizbreath the time she needed. She took aim, and fired for a second time. The laser discharged its orderly energy, crossing the space between her and Helltrik almost instantaneously, intersected the casing of his gun, exiting via the flesh of Helltrik's hand, and hitting the stone wall behind. The pistol broke into pieces, and Helltrik hissed with pain, grasping his right with his left hand.

'Ear! Ear! Ear!' said Marrer. He danced, circlingly, through the vault's door and disappeared up the stairs. Helltrik and the supine Burnblast were left alone to face Lizbreath, Käal and the dazed-looking Asheila.

'Hang on a minute,' said Käal, looking wildly around. 'What happened?'

'The tables have turned,' said Lizbreath.

'What?' said Käal, confused. 'Wait a sec. What?'

'So now *you* have the weapon, Mis. Salamander,' said Helltrik, in an ugly tone. 'I suppose you will shoot me now?'

'Why would I do that?'

'And when I am dead,' he went on, 'what will you do? Steal my gold? You are everything I *despise* about modern dragonkind. You have no respect for tradition, or authority, or – fire.'

'What?' said Käal, blinking. 'What?'

'No need to steal the Siegfried gold,' said Lizbreath. 'It's Käal's now, anyway.'

'What?' said Käal

'You made a deal: he solves the mystery of your grandniece's disappearance, and you give him the gold.'

'What are you *talking* about, Salamander?' Helltrik snapped.

'The mystery of Hellfire's disappearance,' said Lizbreath.

'What?' said Käal.

'There's nothing useful you can say to me about her,' said Helltrik, grief entering his voice.

'I'm not saying it to you,' laughed Lizbreath. 'I'm saying it to *her*. Hellfire, it's time, now. Take off the ring.'

The empty air produced a sigh. And then, with a little shiver, like a horizon heat-haze, a good-sized, middle-aged she-dragon of attractive demeanour, pale-blue-and-silver scales and a short snout, suddenly appeared in the middle of the room.

'Hellfire!' gasped Helltrik, hot tears boiling suddenly in his eyes. 'Hellfire! Is it really you?'

'Hello Granduncle,' said the new apparition. 'Yes. It's me.'

'What?' said Käal.

The pain in his claw forgotten, the old dragon stumbled to the newcomer and embraced her, giving way to unconstrained sobs of broken-hearted pleasure.

26

They limped back up to Helltrik's personal suite, where a firedrake with a gloomy expression on his face bandaged up his hurt claw. Burnblast had to be rolled onto a tarpaulin and dragged out of the vault. Though still alive, he was unable to utter articulate sound, and had evidently suffered severe brain damage. When the medical services arrived, Helltrik told them he had had a stroke whilst displaying the fullest stretch of his best flameblast. 'But that doesn't explain this . . . *hole* in the top of his head,' the doctor said, in a puzzled voice. 'It looks like it's gone right through the scales . . .'

'Congenital,' said Lizbreath, easily.

An ambulance Skylligator took the elderly, now-dumb dragon away. Asheila clung to Käal with hysterical gratitude, calling him 'My saviour! My hero!' Marrer was being tended by Red Snapper, and refused to leave his apartment.

As for poor old Ghastly: his death had not been made public, his corpse hidden. 'Nobody will miss him – at least, not for a few weeks,' said Helltrik, his hand wrapped in bandages. He spoke to them all, and Lizbreath in particular, with new respect. 'Let us go out onto my balcony,' he told them, 'and have a drink. It has been a stressful day . . .'

'Only if you promise not to try and kill us,' said Lizbreath, banteringly.

'What?' said Käal.

Helltrik, who had his good arm linked in with his grandniece's, laughed weakly. 'I'm past all that now.'

On the balcony, Helltrik and Hellfire sat together on one side; Käal and Asheila on the other, and Lizbreath stood in the middle, leaning on the balustrade, gazing into the sky. Blue sky. That improbable blue, like the shade of liquid in a pharmacist's yard-tall phial, set in the front window. Cobalt and azure blended.

'How did you know?' Hellfire asked.

'The Siegfried treasure is the stuff of legend,' Lizbreath said, shortly. 'And people take legends for granted. But I did some research on it. On the other side of the wyrmhole – the existence of which Helltrik was prepared to go to such lengths to keep secret – there are many tales, sagas, narratives, operas and books about the Siegfried treasure. Over here, it's just one pile of gold amongst many. But from the research I did, I found out about the ring.'

'The ring!' said Käal, as if reminded of something.

'Brimstön told me that he'd been promised the Siegfried treasure if he could solve the mystery – but also that a piece of the treasure was missing. He said Helltrik acted . . . weird about that fact. As if he didn't really care. Of course he did. But he couldn't bear the shame of admitting that the jewel of his collection was missing. The magic ring – a ring of power, a ring that conferred invisibility.'

'I took it that day,' said Hellfire. She spoke with a pleasantly well-modulated voice, accompanied by little wisps of bright white smoke. 'I just wanted to be alone.'

'Why?'

'I'd stumbled upon Helltrik and my father, Gutfire, discussing the family secret. That we were the hidden guardians of this portal to another world, a place ruled not by noble dragons but by swarming, democratic apes. It was a shock!'

'I can imagine,' said Asheila.

'Oh, it wasn't a complete surprise. But to have it *confirmed*! And to discover that the secret was so close to home! You see, I had a computer; and I had made contact with several groups of young dragons, in Scandragonia and elsewhere, who had suspicions that the Dragonlords were keeping some great secret from us all.'

'Groups of young dragons still gather to discuss those sorts of theory,' said Lizbreath.

'I just wanted to hide. I'd stolen a key to the hoard vault long before – I was something of a tearaway, you know. So that day I crept down there, found the ring and put it on. Amazing! I could spy on everybody, but nobody could see me. I planned wearing it for a day or two, I think, and then on revealing myself. But there's something . . . I don't know. *Addictive*. About it.' She was wearing it, now, on a chain around her neck; and she fiddled with it unconsciously as she spoke. 'I fell into a new mode of life: observer.'

'I was distraught!' said Helltrik. 'I had no idea what happened to you.'

'I'm sorry about that,' said Hellfire. 'But it seemed somehow – appropriate. The whole of Doorbraak, all the senior members of the Vagner clan, it was all dedicated to a monstrous, appalling secret.'

'A *great* secret – entrusted to us by the Dragonlords half a millennium ago,' said Helltrik.

'Well, I made *myself* into a secret,' said Hellfire. 'It meant I could spy on everybody. It meant, for instance, I could satisfy my curiosity about all the family secret. I sat at the back, unseen and unnoticed, at high-level clan meetings, where it was agreed that a fictional affection for "democracy" would be fabricated, and spread about by rumour, as a smokescreen to obscure the *true* secret. I discovered how deep the secrecy went.' She shook her head. 'How far into the family past. It revolted me.'

'Then,' asked Käal, 'why didn't you spill the beans? You could have left the island – told your story.'

'But I was trapped!' said Hellfire. 'Not by any physical barriers, but by the dilemma. These lies, this hypocrisy – it revolted me. What could be less dragonlike? But at the same time, the more I learnt of the situation, the more I understood why the fraud was being perpetrated.' She paused, and then went on. 'Besides: I was a young dragon, barely older than a Salamander. Who would listen to me? I came to the conclusion that what was needed was Helltrik himself to go to the Dragonlords, and for them to come clean, publicly.'

'That,' said Lizbreath, sardonically, 'would be political suicide.'

'Of course! But the more I grew accustomed to my invisible life on the island, the less motivated I became to unveil myself. I had my ring. It had become – precious to me.'

'Why the tongues, though?' asked Käal

Hellfire looked at him. 'The family was turning the place upside down looking for me. I thought to myself: if I can persuade them I am dead, they will stop looking. Better for them, to get over me; better for me, to be able to live unmolested. So I went down into the Clawsoleum, and cut out one of my ancestors' tongues.'

'Hellfire!' Helltrik exclaimed, weakly.

'It was a long time ago, Granduncle,' she replied. 'And I was – desperate. I took it to my room, where I had a secret ice-cream maker . . . another artefact from my reckless youth. I powered it up and burned the tongue in the same place *my* tongue is burned. Then I wrapped it and delivered it to Helltrik, here. But having done that once, I was struck by the appropriateness of it . . . the symbolism. Our family was shamed. Not just guarding the wyrmhole, but *lying* about it to the world. A dragon should speak freely to the wind; truth is in our blood. We have been struck dumb. Every year I would go back down to the vault, and take another tongue. I wanted Granduncle to see that somebody understood what had happened to us.'

'Not a burden,' said Helltrik, sadly shaking his head. 'An honour.'

'A curse!' said Hellfire, urgently. 'I have monitored the ape-world over many years, and they fly higher than we do! Just look at the laser weapons. No dragon could invent such a thing; but the apes did! And not just that: they have houses on the moon, and robot servants and their Sagas are available on ingenious tablet-sized devices as pure data. Why don't *we* have those things? I have given it thought for a long time, and now I know the answer.'

'Which is?' said Lizbreath.

'Our gold is cursed. It's so obvious, it is staring us in the snout. And yet no dragon seems to notice! We all dedicate our lives to accumulating masses of the stuff, and it's perfectly useless!'

'Not all of us . . .' said Lizbreath, mildly.

Hellfire came over and embraced her. 'You, I exempt. I've watched you since you arrived. You're the sign that all is not lost for dragonkind. You, and your friends, have wriggled out from under the curse, and that bodes well for the future – that's why I found myself drawn back into the world, helping you in your investigation. But how do other dragons treat you, now that you've broken the curse? They call you mad, put you under legal sanction. Marginalize and persecute you!'

Lizbreath ducked her head, modestly.

'Where does this curse *come* from?' Käal asked. 'I . . . don't understand.'

'Where from? The gods! Of course, the gods. *They* cursed the gold.'

'But why?'

'Because they hate mortal life. They hate it, because mortality has a focus, intensity and authenticity denied to immortality. To be immortal is to live a life horribly attenuated, *diluted* by eternity. So the gods punish mortals where they can. In our world there used to be many gods – we've managed to reduce that to one. Luckily for us! One god is manageable, even if he is as cranky as Woden. Many gods are dangerous: like wolves, they move in packs. In the ape world, through the wyrmhole, they have done the same thing, although in a more patchy way. Some small pockets of that world still have many gods, but for most of the planet the apes have reduced the number of gods to three – or, best of all, to one. I don't know much about the world of the riverpeople; I haven't been there. But in all three of those worlds – fire, water and earth – the balance of elements has been shifted away from the primacy of the gods. In the world of air it is different. In that world the gods had the edge. The result is a wasteland – lands picked clean by monstrous world-spanning gales, seas churned to muddy whirlpools by the never-ending tempest. Too many gods.' She shook her head.

'So in our world,' Lizbreath said, 'and in the ape world too, the gods cursed Siegfried's treasure.'

'And that curse has worked its way through the millennia.'

'Ordinary dragons deserve to know the truth,' said

Lizbreath, firmly. 'We've no right to keep it from them. If we have not truth, then what do we have?'

Everybody was looking at Helltrik. 'I never thought to see my darling girl again,' he told them. 'I thank you for returning her. For *persuading* her to emerge from her invisibility. I thank you with all my heart. And I apologize for trying to kill you, earlier.'

'Don't mention it,' drawled Lizbreath.

'I suppose you will leave this place and fill the Sagas with tales of the wyrmhole.' He sighed. 'I have worked so hard for so long to stop that from happening – and yet I find myself facing the prospect of exposure with equanimity. Getting my Hellfire back is all the consolation I need. But,' he said, holding up his uninjured claw, 'I will say *one* thing. I will say why the Dragonlords elected to keep the Wyrmhole secret, and why I considered it an honour for the Vagner nest to shoulder this desperate falsehood.'

'They decided to keep it secret because that's what tyrants do,' snapped Lizbreath. 'They don't need another reason!'

'That's not the reason,' said Helltrik, sorrowfully.

'I assumed,' said Hellfire, 'that it was to keep the technological advances derived from apean prototypes to yourselves. Those lucrative technologies!'

'Not that.'

'To stop those horrible hömös apes,' said Asheila, 'from swarming through and re-infesting our world!'

'Especially,' Käal added, 'if they're all armed with those dangerous lazy pistols.'

'No.'

'Why, then?' Lizbreath asked.

'For the sake of the apes, of course! To protect them!'

'Come on,' scoffed Lizbreath.

'I'm perfectly serious. The Dragonlords feel the shame of genocide bitterly. We shared this world with an intelligent species; horrible to look at, of course, and barbaric, but capable of great ingenuity and craft! The technological advances that have come down the wyrmhole prove that. Yet we slew them all. Some we slew nobly, in open battle. Most we burned alive in their towns, or penned them into cages like cattle and ate them, and it was most ignoble of us. The conflict between us was rooted in shame and deceit, and is a stain upon our honour as dragons.'

'So, you want to avoid contamination? Is it something like that?' said Lizbreath.

'It's too late for that. No. The point in not revealing the existence of that portal is *to keep the apes on the other side safe.*'

'I don't understand,' said Hellfire.

'You don't? Yet you say you have monitored that world?' He sighed again. 'What is the most striking feature of that place? It is that there are no dragons in it – none at all. The apes killed them all. If dragonkind discovers that fact, what force will be powerful enough to prevent armies of raging dragons from rushing over there to avenge that terrible fact?'

'You think . . . ?'

'We *know*. And so do you. All you need to do is think about it. Once word gets out, as it must once this wyrmhole becomes public knowledge, what then? You don't think the warrior spirit of dragonkind will be piqued? You don't think the old blood will be roused? And . . . what is more . . .' He seemed to find this next part difficult to say. 'There is . . . over there, I mean, on the other side of the wyrmhole. There is . . . gold.'

Several of the dragons there drew their breath in sharply. 'Gold?' said Asheila. 'Lots of it?'

'As much as in our world. More, perhaps, since the apes are more technologically advanced than we, and have developed ways of extracting it unknown to us: from seawater, for instance. And all of this gold is, according to the legal standing of dragons, *unowned*. The hömöses think they own it, of course; but under dragon law that is a null claim.' Helltrik drew down a great shuddering sigh.

'Look at you all!' cried Hellfire; and she pointed at each of them in turn. 'Even you, Lizbreath! You can't help it! The curse is in your blood. The prospect of a whole planet of unclaimed gold makes you tremble with lust and hunger.'

Everybody on the balcony was silent for a long time.

'So,' said Helltrik eventually. 'You can tell me, Lizbreath Salamander. You too, Käal. Tell me that you think our world should be told the truth. That there is a doorway to a world in which apes swarm over the land, triumphing over the corpses of murdered dragons. A world in which gold lies around just waiting for a brave dragon to claim it Tell me: what will dragons do when they hear this?'

'You may,' said Lizbreath, in a tight voice, 'have a point.'

'You could have tried to explain all this to us before,' said Käal. 'Rather than, you know, trying to kill us.'

Helltrik frowned. 'I have already apologized for that,' he said, in a tight voice. 'You must understand, young dragon, that we have guarded this secret for hundreds of years. The fate of an entire planet of sentient creatures in our hands. We cannot simply explain the state of affairs to every Tomm, ðick and Dragon who comes along. That would, rather, defeat the purpose.'

'But you invited me onto your island,' Käal reminded him.

'To solve the mystery of Hellfire, here,' said Helltrik. 'Nothing more. It was, as perhaps you can understand, a delicate balance – one reason why it took me so long to hire somebody for the job. I needed somebody who might be able to locate my grandniece, but not somebody so clever they would penetrate the true mystery of Doorbraak. I needed somebody with the reputation for finding stuff out, but who was enough of an idiot not to be a threat.'

'Well,' said Käal. 'Thanks for that.'

'Your secret must remain secret, I suppose,' said Lizbreath, heavily.

'Thank you,' said Helltrik, with genuine, unmistakable relief.

'Hey!' said Käal. 'You're deciding on behalf of both of us, are you?'

'I am,' said Lizbreath. 'You'll go back to Starkhelm

with the Siegfried treasure. You'll have nothing to complain about.'

'I suppose that's true,' said Käal.

'But there's something else that occurs to me,' said Lizbreath. She came over and faced Helltrik directly. 'We fought the Scorch Wars against apes who were living at a very basic level, in terms of their technology: spears and swords. Of course we wiped them out, but they inflicted many casualties upon us – dragons drowned, or crushed under rockfalls, or speared in their open mouths. The hömöses on the other side of that wyrmhole are armed with more than spears and swords. We all saw what damage even one of their little hand-pistols can do . . .'

'You think we haven't thought of this too?' said Helltrik. 'The aim has been to keep the wyrmhole thoroughly blocked on both sides: not only physically impassable, but hidden. It is a unique phenomenon of spacetime, a twist in the fabric of the cosmos itself, and it emits a very distinctive radiation signature.'

'Say who-does-the-what, now?' asked Käal.

'The details don't matter,' said Helltrik. 'What matters is that by plugging it with gold, we dampened its signature, and almost completely blocked it. From time to time, we have emptied it out and made exploratory trips over, checking the terrain, snatching examples of technology and so on. But recently we have abandoned even that. The risks are too great. And even stuffed with gold, it is still possible to transmit through the wyrmhole.'

'I know,' said Lizbreath.

'As far as we know, the apes remain unaware of the existence of the wyrmhole. As do the majority of dragonkind. If you help us keep that the state of affairs, then you shall have my gratitude.'

'Gratitude,' said Lizbreath, looking out across the morning skies. 'OK.'

27

They stayed another three days at Doorbraak; long enough to see the island return, more or less, to its normal routines. The story was disseminated that Burnblast had been visiting when a savage stroke had struck him down. In their attempts to help him, both Helltrik and Marrer had been slightly injured; but the life of the eminent old dragon had been saved. Nothing was said of Ghastly. 'We'll leave it a month,' Helltrik confided to Lizbreath. 'Then we'll announce that he died in his sleep.'

As for Hellfire: the story was that she had been in Hostileia after all – that she had suffered a form of dragamnesia, and had not recognized what Käal had said to her when he travelled to bring her back. But that the trauma of the encounter had dislodged the memories, or some such nonsense. It was a lie, of course, and painful to utter. But Hellfire said she had discovered that once one lie is uttered, a second is easier to get out.

The Siegfried treasure was carefully separated from the main hoard by Helltrik himself, and packed into twenty wooden chests. These, in turn, were loaded into the mouth of a fat cargo Skylligator with a complacent expression on its face. Käal and Lizbreath, who were going to travel to Starkhelm along with this booty, made their farewells.

'You're staying?' Lizbreath asked Hellfire, who had come down with her granduncle to see them off.

Hellfire nodded. 'I am – tied to this place,' she said.

'Goodbye,' said Helltrik. 'I appreciate your discretion.'

'Don't mention it,' said Käal.

There was only one moment of awkwardness, and it came as the Skylligator was readying to leave. They had all spoken their formal dragon farewells, when, as a parting shot, Käal said: 'Oh, I almost forgot. The ring?'

He reached out a foreclaw to Hellfire, who was still wearing the ring around her neck on a gold chain.

Her reaction was instant: she flinched back, and wrapped her wings around her chest to hide the precious object. 'No!'

The hard gleam of hunger flickered in Käal's usually placid eye. 'Come on!' he said. To Helltrik he said: 'We had a deal.'

'When we made that deal,' said Helltrik, speaking slowly, 'I made it clear to you that the treasure was incomplete. The deal was for the Siegfried treasure, minus this ring.'

The atmosphere had acquired a malign tingle. Nobody was breathing.

'I don't see it like that,' said Käal. 'The deal was for the Siegfried treasure. That ring is part of the treasure.' He looked to Lizbreath for support, but her eyes were on Hellfire. 'It is true,' Käal went on, 'that when we made the deal you apprised me of the fact that the treasure was, at that point, incomplete. But that is no longer the case. The ring belongs to me.'

'I disagree,' said Helltrik, softly.

For a moment it looked as though the two dragons were going to rush one another, roaring in flame. But then the moment passed. Käal smiled. 'Well, then you and I will *just* have to agree,' he said, ducking his snout, 'to disagree. Goodbye!'

And they departed. On the journey back to Starkhelm, Lizbreath spent most of the time over by the teeth, lifting a portion of lip to watch the land roll by beneath. As Starkhelm came into view below she made her way, slinkily, back over to Käal.

'You did the right thing,' she told him. 'Letting that ring go. There's more than enough treasure for you in all this.'

'I haven't let the ring go,' he said, ominously. 'It's mine, and I want it.'

'Why?' said Lizbreath, surprised. 'It's tiny! You've got a tonne of gold here. What's so desirable about that little O?'

'It's precious,' Käal said. 'The rest of the treasure is all very well, but I can't say it fires my heart. You can have a chest of it, if you like.'

'Thank you,' said Lizbreath.

'I couldn't have done it without you,' he said, condescendingly.

'You're not wrong, there. Boy, I'll take a chest. It'll come in handy. But mostly,' she added, settling herself onto the tongue prior to landing, 'mostly I'm just pleased to be able to come back to Starkhelm without having to worry about Burnblast.'

At the airport they clacked tail-ends together, agreed to meet for lunch the next day, and went their separate ways. Käal supervised the delivery of the Siegfried treasure to his apartment, and then went to the *Köschfa-gold Saga* offices. The receptionist told him that Beargrr had just gone to court, to hear the initial judicial ruling on the Wintermute case.

He flew eagerly to the courthouse, and joined Beargrr at the back of the crowded chamber. The judges had just gone into recess, and were expected out again at any moment.

Beargrr did not seem overly delighted to see Käal. 'You!' she said. 'I thought I'd got you tucked safely out of the way.'

'I've got the treasure, Beargrr,' he told her, his eyes gleaming. 'Well, pretty much all of it, anyhow. You can let the den dragon know.'

She looked at him. 'You're not joking?' she asked him. 'You're not being ironic?'

'No—I solved the mystery, and got the reward.'

Beargrr opened her eyes very wide. 'That,' she said. 'That is fantastic news.'

'It will help?'

'Of course it will! Even if the case goes badly against us, the Siegfried treasure will more than cover any damages. And things don't look as bad as I first thought, legally.'

'You mean, the case might *not* go against us?'

'Maybe not. It's early days, of course,' Beargrr said.

'If I understand the state of play, the main contention of the case so far is that the form of the plaintiff complaint was without substantive provisions with respect of necessary granite-carved specimen testimonial and attestation clauses in conjunction with the drafting notes for the relevant clause contained in the original Saga coverage agreement. Such precedent as was relevant to memorializing generic Saga-relevant provisions was usually, the court ruled, to be found in commercial Saga composition transaction. For example, matters such as the choice of governing alliteration, the mechanism for serving notices and requirements that any amendments be agreed and documented in flame-proof scrolling, to be overlaid by dragonwax. Any provisions to restrict rights of assignment, provide remedy for the plaintiff in the final order of *ab initio* and *sub via* sandwich, contested by either or both parties to the lawsuit, and third-party imposed obligations of confidentiality or define events of *force majeure* when the instituting declaration of judicial litigation may not be capable of enforcement . . .

[*Eleven pages omitted*]

. . . or any implied contract of adhesion, it must be presented in any standard judgement appellant to the declaration of form, and give one party no ability to reapply for regulatory adjudication of the performance of reasonable expectation.'

'Right,' said Käal. 'Well, good. Good!'

'It's an *oblique* suggestion of possible infringement,' said Beargrr.

'Excellent. OK. Well, I just thought I'd touch, eh, base with you. Which I have now done.'

'This is the culmination of a gripping story!' said Beargrr. 'Oh! The judges are returning from recess!'

'See you tomorrow,' said Käal. He slipped from the courtroom, and found himself on the main street of Starkhelm, as dragons and firedrakes and workwyrms bustled to and fro. 'Maybe,' he said to himself. 'Maybe it's time for a sauna.'

ACKNOWLEDGMENTS AND DEDICATION

Thanks to Simon Spandragon, as ever. Darren Gnash, also of Dragollancz Books, supplied one gag to this undertaking, and Malcolm Edragon another (and no, I'm not going to tell you which ones); all other gags in this book are mine. I dedicate it to my wife, Rachel, who is not a dragon. She is the only person I know who could read *The Girl with the Dragon Tattoo* and, when asked afterwards what she considered the most memorable and striking part of it, say: 'Well, they all seem to drink a lot of *coffee* . . .' She wanted me to put coffee into this novel too but, as everybody knows, dragons don't drink coffee.